Ancient Vendetta

Ancients Rising Series

KATIE REUS

D1452402

Cover Art by Sweet 'N Spicy Designs
Editor: Julia Ganis
Author Website: https://katiereus.com

Ancient Vendetta/Katie Reus.—1st ed.

ISBN-13: 9781635561708

eISBN: 9781635561692

For Kaylea Cross, the sister of my heart.

PRAISE FOR THE NOVELS OF KATIE REUS

"Exciting in more ways than one, well-paced and smoothly written, I'd recommend *A Covert Affair* to any romantic suspense reader."
—Harlequin Junkie

"Sexy military romantic suspense." —USA Today

"I could not put this book down. . . . Let me be clear that I am not saying that this was a good book *for* a paranormal genre; it was an excellent romance read, *period.*" —All About Romance

"Reus strikes just the right balance of steamy sexual tension and nail-biting action....This romantic thriller reliably hits every note that fans of the genre will expect." —*Publishers Weekly*

"Prepare yourself for the start of a great new series! . . . I'm excited about reading more about this great group of characters."
—Fresh Fiction

"Wow! This powerful, passionate hero sizzles with sheer deliciousness. I loved every sexy twist of this fun & exhilarating tale. Katie Reus delivers!"
—Carolyn Crane, RITA award winning author

"A sexy, well-crafted paranormal romance that succeeds with smart characters and creative world building."—Kirkus Reviews

"*Mating Instinct*'s romance is taut and passionate . . . Katie Reus's newest installment in her Moon Shifter series will leave readers breathless!"
—Stephanie Tyler, *New York Times* bestselling author

"I just can't get enough of these sexy, growly, dragons and the women who are strong enough to put up with them." —Edgy Reviews

"Katie Reus pulls the reader into a story line of second chances, betrayal, and the truth about forgotten lives and hidden pasts."
—The Reading Café

"Nonstop action, a solid plot, good pacing, and riveting suspense."
—RT Book Reviews

"Enough sexual tension to set the pages on fire."
—*New York Times* bestselling author, Alexandra Ivy

"…a wild hot ride for readers. The story grabs you and doesn't let go."
—*New York Times* bestselling author, Cynthia Eden

"Has all the right ingredients: a hot couple, evil villains, and a killer action-filled plot. . . . [The] Moon Shifter series is what I call Grade-A entertainment!" —Joyfully Reviewed

"*Avenger's Heat* hits the ground running...This is a story of strength, of partnership and healing, and it does it brilliantly."
—Vampire Book Club

"*Mating Instinct* was a great read with complex characters, serious political issues and a world I am looking forward to coming back to."
—All Things Urban Fantasy

CHAPTER ONE

One year ago

Lucius slid onto the barstool and eyed the mostly humans in the dark interior of the one-story bar in a place called Sitka, Alaska. He received a few curious looks, but mostly people ignored him.

Which was how he preferred it. For now.

He'd woken months ago and was still learning much about this new world. The cave he'd crawled out of deep in the wilds had been his resting place for longer than he wanted to think about. Over a hundred years at least; he wasn't sure. He'd learned quite a bit thanks to something called the internet, but knew there was much he still did not know. Like where the bastard who'd killed him was—well, who thought he'd killed Lucius.

"Harry, turn it up," the man with a thick, fur-lined hat a couple stools down from him called out to the bartender.

Without looking up from his book, Harry did just that, grabbing a small piece of technology called a remote control. The man also still hadn't offered to retrieve Lucius a beverage and Lucius knew he was aware of him.

His jaw tightened at the rudeness, but he remained still, studying everyone inside. All men. Ten total. He could feed from all of them, gain the strength he needed—and take anything of monetary value. He had much to do, but feeding was the most important.

As a bastard, hybrid vampire, he did not always feed on blood, though sometimes he chose to. At one time he had fed on blood, almost a hundred and fifty years ago. But he preferred to feed on energy. It sustained him longer. Blood was just when he was angry and needed an outlet.

As he contemplated whether he should feed on everyone in here or wait and take them one at a time, there was a stirring in the room.

"Is that a...wait, a dragon?" Everyone in the place shifted in their seats, a couple men jumping to their feet as they all crowded at the bar, staring up at the television on the wall.

Lucius stared too, surprise flickering through him as dragons and other supernaturals battled in the sky above a city. Fire and death erupted everywhere as various images flashed on-screen. Multiple dragons battling. A...phoenix? *Huh.* A female wielding a flaming sword sliced at a dragon. Screams filled the air as humans ran around like rats. The video started shaking as whoever was taking it started backing up.

Suddenly another dragon swooped down. Then a dark-skinned male with a sword— Lucius sucked in a breath.

King.

"How is this real?" A man likely in his twenties stared, open-mouthed, as he slid up next to Lucius. He smelled of beer and fish.

"Where is this?" Lucius demanded. "On the screen."

"New Orleans," the younger man murmured, but didn't look his way. "That's Jackson Square. Been there once for Mardi Gras. Holy shit."

"New Orleans." He let the name of the place roll off his tongue. That was where he would go. Soon enough. He was far too weak at the moment, but that would change.

He slid off the stool, strode to the door and locked it before turning off the brightly lit *open* sign with a simple click. Then he cast a sealing spell, closing all the exits tight.

No one noticed a thing, everyone transfixed by the images on the screen. Lucius didn't care what was happening. He'd always planned to hunt down King, but had thought it would take decades to find the male. Supernaturals had always lived in secret, and in some cases, in other realms.

Lucius hadn't even been sure if King still lived.

But now? Oh, this was the fates rewarding him. Serving up the mongrel bastard who'd thought to kill him. *Him.*

Lucius sat back at the barstool, reached out and grabbed the young human who stank of beer and fish by the neck. The man stared at him, jerking back, his hands flying up defensively, but Lucius struck fast.

He dug his fingers into the male's neck, injecting a shot of magic from his fingertips. Then he forced the man's mouth open and breathed in his energy.

The man was frozen, his eyes wide with raw terror as a shudder of delight rolled through Lucius. No one noticed him or even turned their way, their attention rapt on the television. Warmth infused him as he began dragging in the energy from the young, robust human. This was prime stuff feeding him.

But it was over too quickly, the male a hollow husk as Lucius dropped him to the floor with a thud.

The bartender turned at the sound, someone finally noticing what he had been doing.

The grizzled old man stepped forward, his wiry eyebrows slanted down. "What the hell—"

Lucius jumped over the bar, lightning fast, and grabbed the man by the front of his shirt, throwing him at the dozens of bottles lining the back of the bar.

Glass shattered under the impact, shards flying everywhere in a blast of sound.

Shouts of alarm rang out, but he ignored them.

"We're going to have some fun," he growled as he lifted the stunned human up by the neck and slammed him against the bar again. This time he didn't let go. Instead he did the same thing to him as he'd done to the young human.

Another human came at him from behind, but he barely felt the bottle that smashed over his head. He just kept drinking in energy.

"Oh shit," someone murmured, fear bleeding from their pores, infusing the air.

"The door won't open!" someone else shouted.

"Here!" Someone threw a stool at the window, but it bounced off it.

He was vaguely aware of the humans trying to escape but the sealing spell held for now. Maybe they could escape with enough time, but likely not by the time he got to them. This had been the right idea, taking them all at one place, one by one.

The energy infused him, making him light-headed and even hungrier.

He now knew where King was. And he was going to hunt him down and kill him. To do that he needed energy, and a lot of it. Starting with every human in this bar. Then he'd move on to the rest of the town.

Once he found King in this place called New Orleans, he would take everything from that upstart male. He was going to make him wish he'd never been born.

CHAPTER TWO

Present day

Aurora stepped up to look at Mia's painting, nodded in approval. It was a black-and-white painting of the bayou, with dark shadows in various shapes creeping out of the water. One almost looked as if it could be a dragon, but with the ripples of water it just teased at it. "Stunning, Mia. Absolutely stunning. And perfect use of shading." Mia was human and one of Aurora's most talented students by far. She was planning to offer to mentor her because the young woman painted with a kind of soul that touched Aurora's own.

"Thank you," Mia murmured, ducking her head slightly so that her long auburn braid fell over one shoulder. She seemed to be unsure of her talent or just unused to praise.

"If you have time, I'd like to talk to you after class?"

Her eyes widened slightly, but she nodded.

"What about *my* painting?" Ingrid, leader of the Cheval vampire coven, asked a few canvases down, her tone indicating she thought it was a masterpiece.

Aurora moved toward her and forced herself to smile. *Oh. My.* "It's very colorful. Wonderful use of all your paints." Her brain fritzed out for a moment as she wondered if that was condescending, but Ingrid beamed at her.

Okay, so that was something at least. This was one of the oddest art classes she'd taught since settling in New Orleans—and with the mix of supernaturals and humans, she'd found that she had to wear kid gloves with the supernaturals more often than not. Ingrid was a powerful vampire, likely over two hundred years old, and couldn't paint to save her life. It looked like a toddler had given their best effort, but Aurora would never say that. Would never even let on that she thought that.

"It looks like a child went wild with fingerpaints," Claudine, leader of the Bonavich vampire coven said with absolutely no inflection. "Really, Ingrid. You can do better." The vampire was old-old, waaaayy older than Aurora wanted to guess. One of her packmates had said that Claudine's eyes reminded them of a shark—and they weren't wrong.

So the fact that two old vampire leaders were taking her art class at all? So weird. Aurora didn't actually understand why they were here. She knew they had a whole lot of important stuff to be doing. Right? They ran two important covens in New Orleans but here they were, taking an art class on Tuesday night among humans, shifters and young vampires.

"Well I like it," Olga, a feline shifter of sorts, said from the row behind them before Ingrid could respond. "It's better than my attempt." She frowned at her own canvas, stepped back and frowned even deeper.

"There will be no insulting anyone's art at all." Aurora shot Claudine a sharp look before she made her way to the sink, gathering paintbrushes as she went. "We're all here to learn, and more than that, have fun. This is about creative expression and finding an outlet for that creativity. The world always needs more art. But we're about done, so start cleaning up your areas now, please."

A low murmur started as everyone did just that. And when she turned around, she found Mia had moved up quietly to stand next to her at the sink. "I can't really stay after class, because I've got another thing, but...is everything okay? You said you needed to talk to me, so..." She cleared her throat.

"Let's set up a time then, whenever is good for you. I really wanted to talk to you about potentially giving you one-on-one classes, and if you're open to it, I'd like to mentor you. You've got so much talent and—"

"Yes!" she shouted, then cleared her throat again. "Ah, I mean, yes, I'd love that." Mia's cheeks flushed bright pink. "I just...wow, thank you. I'll call you about meeting so we can talk more then?"

"Of course. Just let me know what works for you and we'll definitely figure out the details. I want to see what other mediums you might want to try."

"Thank you. I promise I'll call." Then she hurried off, a wide grin on her face.

"Why did you have to ruin my fun?" Claudine murmured as she came to join Aurora at the sink, quickly sliding into Mia's empty spot.

She side-eyed the woman as she washed paintbrushes. Claudine's voice had the slightest lilt to it, was cultured and elegant. Even standing here in simple jeans and a turtleneck sweater—which were both likely from a well-known but expensive designer that had existed before The Fall—she radiated a kind of self-assuredness that Aurora could only aspire to. "Why did you have to poke at her?"

"Because she's so easy to needle and I'm old. I need my fun." She laughed in a rich, throaty way that Aurora felt travel through her.

It was disconcerting, as if the female's power was ricocheting through her, making its presence known. "There are other ways to have fun besides being a dick."

Claudine blinked, then laughed again, her dark curls bouncing slightly. "You are one of the only people to talk to me like that. I find I quite enjoy it. It's so refreshing."

Well that was good, right? "Glad I'm entertaining," she said, laughing lightly. With some of these old supernaturals, you just never knew how they were going to react to something. They might laugh or cut your head off.

"So, why haven't you invited me to your compound?"

Aurora blinked at the blunt, unexpected question. "Invite you?" Like…for what? Tea? Aurora grabbed the nearest clean but paint-stained rag and dried her hands, stepping away from the sink and Claudine as a few others crowded around. "I feel like I'm missing something here."

Claudine stepped with her, her movements fluid and graceful as they moved to the other side of the room by Aurora's desk—which was currently stacked with canvases and supplies.

"For a drink. Or for a meal." She eyed her expectantly, her dark eyes assessing.

"I would love to have you over." Again with the weirdness! It wasn't as if they were friends, though Aurora did really like the female. "Ah…"

"Aurora." Claudine's voice held a hint of…maybe exasperation in it. "You're a power in the city."

"Oh, no—"

Claudine shook her head. "I like you more than I've liked anyone in a very long time so I'm going to give you unsolicited advice. Start inviting—slowly—some of the other leaders from various covens, packs, clans, whoever, over for drinks or dinner. I would tell you to invite humans as well, but they already all adore you as it is. So do the dragons, so you're likely covered there."

"Okay." She so wanted to ask why, but for some reason felt like a child being almost scolded.

"Do you understand why I'm telling you this?" Claudine lifted a dark eyebrow now.

"No." There was no reason to lie.

Claudine looked over her shoulder, saw that there were only a handful of humans left. She dropped her voice as she turned back. "There's a chance that one day you'll be the Alpha's mate—an Alpha yourself—of the territory. You need to get to know the powers in the territory, for your sake and for King's."

Uhhhh. What. The. Hell. "Claudine—"

She held up a hand. "Right now this territory is new and King is a relatively new Alpha. He will take a mate eventually. And if I believed in betting, I would bet on you. Not because you're the strongest, but because you're smart and you're very kind. I can see it, *feel* it in you. You might not want to play politics, but eventually you'll have to if you want to survive. King does not play with others well, so if his mate is in favor with the majority of the territory, they will overlook certain things. Like when he acts like a foolish wolf."

"I..." Many different things warred inside Aurora. Her instinct was to argue with Claudine that she would never be King's mate, that the thought was outrageous. But she craved him with every part of her being. The thought of him mating someone else... If he did, she would move to a new territory. She knew that in her soul. But...she was still dealing with the aftereffects of being held captive for a year and all that entailed. Mating wasn't remotely on her radar. She wasn't sure she could be touched by a male again, not even King. She wanted to be open to it, but...ugh. "Thank you for the advice."

"You're welcome."

She leaned against the side of her desk, narrowed her eyes slightly. There was one thing she knew about supernaturals of Claudine's age— nothing was ever free, not even advice. "Why are you telling me this? What is in it for you?"

Claudine let out a snort at odds with her elegant persona. "That is a fair question." She paused, as if searching for the right words. "I'm going to attempt to explain this in modern terms without sounding condescending."

At Aurora's raised eyebrow, she lifted a shoulder.

"I've been told, by those closest to me, I can be condescending." She sniffed once. "To summarize, I don't plan on moving anytime soon and I like this territory. I lived here a lifetime ago, and now that I'm back, I'm not leaving. It suits me and my people. So while King is a frustrating pup, he's strong, he's fair and he clearly has good enough taste to choose you. A *strong* but kind female. And..." She hesitated, watching Aurora carefully.

"And?"

"And that is all. Talk to your sister. She is now the Alpha female to that strapping Scottish dragon. She will tell you the same thing I have."

"Thank you. But for the record, I have no plans to become an Alpha's mate." Or anyone's mate.

Claudine simply smiled, and it wasn't patronizing exactly, more indulgent. "Have Bella call me and we'll set something up for drinks. That child is so organized."

Bella wasn't a child at forty-plus years old, and King wasn't a pup either as Claudine had stated, but Aurora understood that to this particular vampire, they were young.

"Should I invite Ingrid and some of her coven as well so I'm not playing favorites?" She kept her voice neutral, but couldn't stop the upward curve of her lips. Apparently she liked to poke a little too.

That sharp grin grew sharklike. "Now you're thinking like an Alpha. And please do not invite her at the same time as me." Claudine sniffed imperiously.

"Can I ask you something? How..." Gah, she knew it was rude to ask how old a supernatural was. She faltered. "Ah, how long have you lived in New Orleans?" God, she sounded so pathetic.

Claudine simply smiled. "Long enough. And I know you have more questions—like how old I am. I'll tell you this, I'm old enough to remember when your kind were not almost extinct. And when you invite me for drinks, I might tell you even more." At that, she swept out of the art studio like a queen.

"So that was surreal," Aurora murmured to absolutely no one once she was alone. She was going to have to call Star later and ask for her advice. Normally she would tell one of her packmates about it or even King, since they were close—he was one of her best friends at this point—but...she couldn't tell him about any of this since it involved him. And they were simply friends.

Friends. Nothing more. Never, ever anything more.

After she'd cleaned up, she locked up the studio and found three of her human students standing by the curb outside. Since it was January, they were all bundled up in coats, scarves and gloves, huddled close together as they talked.

The studio was in a residential area, though there was a small elementary school a block away that was finally back in use, as well as a breakfast-only restaurant two blocks in the other direction.

"Hi, ladies. Did you need a ride or want me to walk you somewhere?" Asia, Gianna and Diana were all nineteen and capable, but it was dark and she couldn't help the need to want to take care of them. To protect them. Because humans were the most vulnerable of everyone.

"Oh no, we're fine," Asia said, her breath frosting the air. "We're going to Prima's class—"

Her friend, Diana, nudged her sharply in the ribs. "Ah, we're good, but thanks. The class was awesome today! I thought for sure Claudine and Ingrid were going to come to blows." She shook her head, her eyes wide as she lowered her voice. "They're both scary but my money's on Claudine taking her."

Her other friend, Gianna, shook her head. "No way, Ingrid's got that scrappy look about her."

Aurora pressed a hand to her temple, rubbed once. "Prima's teaching a class?" That was the first she'd heard about it. And Aurora couldn't really think what the ancient dragon would be teaching. Unless it was how to kill a man twenty different ways without breaking a sweat... *Oh God.* She straightened as she watched the women shift on their feet slightly, clearly not wanting to answer. Was...Prima teaching a class like that?

"Oh, our ride's here," Asia said instead of answering. "We'll see you next week though."

Aurora simply nodded and pulled out her phone as the women piled into the back of an antique truck with yellow flames on the side of it.

As they pulled away, Aurora returned a couple texts, then shot off one to Brielle. *Is Prima teaching a class to humans?*

No idea. What would she teach anyway? came the reply. *How to gut someone in two easy steps without getting blood on your clothes? Ohhhh if she is, I'm signing up!*

Aurora laughed at the response and tucked her phone away. Curious now, she glanced around, saw there was no one on the street. That she could see, anyway. She tugged off her sweater so that she was only in her specially cut tank top and let her wings expand.

The pale blue wings of fire grew wide and long, expanding until she arched her back, feeling free in a way she only did like this. In a moment, she lifted into the air, her muscles straining under the sharp flapping motions. She couldn't hide herself, not like dragons could camouflage, but people didn't often look upward so she easily followed the vehicle on the road.

Her students had been far too cagey, and since settling in New Orleans she'd been a sort of liaison for King. A role she'd fallen into so organically, it had just...happened, really. So maybe Claudine was right. Not about the mating thing. That was ridiculous.

But King did depend on her as a liaison, so maybe she should start being equally friendly to all the different types of supernaturals. And not because Claudine had told her to!

It was just so easy to get along with the bears and even the dragons, something that surprised her, considering her dark history with them. But she had been going to a dragon healer for counseling and trusted her.

A cold wind rolled over Aurora and she released more of her fire, letting it engulf her and keep her warm as she sailed over treetops and buildings. She followed the car across the Lake Pontchartrain Causeway, her curiosity growing even more.

As she flew, a darkness seemed to fall over the water, a thick fog starting to roll in, blurring everything below her, but it was easy enough to keep an eye on the direction of the headlights since there weren't many vehicles on the road. Not anymore, not like it had once been. With so much of the world now destroyed and still rebuilding, most people lived and worked within their neighborhoods now and mostly walked. Though witches had spelled the majority of vehicles in the territory so driving wasn't an issue—people had just cut back on doing it. There was so much unknown now, though the functioning territories around the world did communicate as much as possible. She was lucky because her sister was Alpha of a territory in northern Scotland so she heard more than most.

The headlights flickered off in the parking lot of what looked to be a warehouse so she swooped in the opposite direction, deciding to do a wide circle to see what this place was. As she circled lower, she clearly saw light glowing from the building's windows, many of which were broken. Along this area, there were no homes, just abandoned buildings she knew King had plans for. As of yet, they were still unoccupied. Or they were supposed to be.

She spotted a dozen vehicles lined up near a door and finally landed. After pulling her wings in, but leaving her sweater off, she tugged open the door and...blinked in surprise.

CHAPTER THREE

King stepped onto the back patio of his pack's compound—one of them. This was the one he lived at.

Claudine was waiting at the long outdoor table, a glass of wine or blood one of his packmates must have gotten for her in front of her. She gave him what she probably thought passed for a smile as he approached and nodded respectfully.

"Thank you for meeting me here. I know you're busy." Hell, they were all busy, but he'd been learning that niceties went a long way.

"It is no problem. I enjoyed the walk tonight. The weather is perfect." She took a sip of her drink, her gaze drifting to Hunter, a dragonling the size of a small elephant, who had somehow become King's pet.

He currently had the lower half of his body in the pool, and his wings and front legs draped over the side, his eyes closed in bliss. His wings and body were a sparkly gray, but since he had a natural camouflage he could shift colors to blend with his surroundings. Right now his colors shimmered, mostly gray, but on occasion shimmered to reflect the pool water.

"Is something wrong with your pet?" she murmured in clear fascination.

"Yes, he's broken." His tone was dry.

Hunter opened his bright purple eyes then and chirped at King, as if scolding him. And there it was—King swore Hunter understood him. But the lazy dragonling still didn't move, just flapped his wings once, flipping water everywhere before settling back.

"I very much doubt that." Claudine eyed the little beast speculatively, then turned back to King. In dark jeans, a dark turtleneck and flat shoes, she should have appeared casual, but the woman was still a predator in human clothing.

"How did the testing go?" He sat across from her, resisting the urge to collapse into the chair. He hadn't slept in…three days, maybe. Running on fumes, he was beyond the point of exhaustion. And he hadn't seen Aurora in two days. Two days too many.

His wolf was getting cranky at not seeing her. If he had her in his bed at night, this wouldn't be an issue.

Claudine sniffed slightly, but instead of taking him to task for not making small talk, as she was wont to do, she said, "Well, I believe. We approached the schools from various angles, and attempted to infiltrate covertly from any angle possible. The only angle we have not tried is teleportation and that's such a rare ability, it's something to worry about at a future date."

He nodded as she continued.

"All the spells held. Even I could not infiltrate." She paused. "I could have, if I'd used enough brute force, but the spells are done well. I'm impressed with the witch."

"I am too." And King wasn't impressed lightly. But the witch, Dallas Kinley, was a force of nature. She'd recently created spells to protect all of the newly formed schools in New Orleans and the surrounding territory.

The last six months he and everyone in the city had been working at a brutal pace to get some semblance of normalcy, to set up an infrastructure that wasn't quite the same as before but had some similar bones. Schools and education were a priority. While their territory was relatively safe, King knew there would come a time when they might be attacked. Someone would think they could move in and take over, destroy what they'd all built.

And though he hated to think of anyone targeting children, he knew that evil would target the weakest, the most fragile. That included kids.

So one of his priorities was ensuring that all schools or places that kids, pups and cubs frequented were the safest. Right now they'd set up a system that ensured only kids, their parents, their teachers and administrators, and he and some of his pack had access to schools. No one else. The protective wards created by Dallas and a local coven of witches were like invisible titanium cages, keeping out anyone not welcome. It wasn't a foolproof system, but if rogue dragons decided to go scorched earth again, at least the schools would be protected.

Eventually he wanted to set up something that would at least protect buildings from dragon fire, but that was on his long-ass and never-ending to-do list.

"You're wise to prepare for war. Though the peace now is quite pleasant, if bizarre."

He lifted a shoulder. Peace was always temporary, unfortunately. He'd lived long enough to understand that nothing remained static. Claudine would know that more than him. "Thank you for testing the wards. You've been a big help in getting the city to where it is."

"It's my home too." She looked into her wineglass, swirled it once. "But you are welcome. If you can hold the territory, I think you'll make a fair Alpha. I'm pleased to be one of your allies."

Her words stunned him. Hell, she could have turned into a kitten and it wouldn't have surprised him more. He understood that her comment about him holding the territory wasn't an insult. Because his hold on it was new. And while he wasn't untried, he was young compared to some of the ancients living in the city. But her telling him she was pleased to be one of his allies? High praise indeed. "Thank you."

"You need to take a mate, however. I suggest sooner than later."

From the water, Hunter chirped animatedly at that. King narrowed his gaze at the dragonling, who quickly shut his eyes and did a poor job of pretending to sleep. Then he looked back at Claudine, who was watching him carefully.

Oh. He blinked. He had not expected this. Was she...suggesting herself as his potential mate? He tried to think of something polite to say. Though he knew she was at least over five hundred years old, she appeared forty by human standards. The female was stunning with dark brown skin, sharp, dark eyes, long, perfectly curled dark brown hair, a toned body that would make angels weep, and a kind of confidence that was rare, but...no. Just, no.

She laughed at his expression, her eyes crinkling at the corners. "Child, you are not remotely my type. You need a mate to find balance. Peace."

He snorted, annoyed for reasons he didn't want to examine too closely. One of those reasons being that she reminded him of his mother in that moment—the way she was doling out unsolicited advice, her tone, everything. "There are plenty of successful unmated Alphas."

"Maybe."

"You're a powerhouse, Claudine. You rule your coven with an iron fist, but your people stay with you out of loyalty, not fear. I would say you're doing fine without a mate."

She set her now empty glass on the table and stood. "I never said I wasn't mated."

He couldn't hide his reaction, a quick blink of surprise. There was much about Claudine that he did not know, but if she was mated, he needed to know to whom. Something like that mattered.

"Alphas need a solid partner, one person who will always have their back above all else. Someone who can see the bigger picture, tell you when you're being...a dick."

He blinked again, but stood as well. "A dick?" That seemed bizarre coming from Claudine.

"Aurora called me one today. In a roundabout way. She was correct, of course." Now the predator was in her eyes, watching him, and he knew she'd mentioned Aurora on purpose. Especially since she'd done it during a conversation about mating. Oh, she was very good. If annoying.

"I'll keep your advice in mind. Thank you again for your help. My pack and I appreciate it."

She nodded at him, then made her exit across the lawn, blending into the shadows as well as any of his wolves before suddenly she was gone. He knew that some vampires could fly and wondered if she was one of them. He'd never seen her do it but...he wouldn't be surprised if she could.

Hunter suddenly flew up from the pool, shaking his wings wildly, scattering water in all directions before arrowing for King.

"Oh, now you come to life?"

Hunter chirped in agreement and kept chattering away to himself.

King scratched behind the dragonling's ear. He'd never imagined himself owning a pet—he was a *wolf shifter*. But Hunter had wiggled his way into King's heart. His wolf side had accepted the dragonling even before King had. "Were you scared of the big, bad vampire?"

Hunter nodded, chirping even louder.

Yeah, Hunter understood more than King wanted to even think

about. Shaking his head, King grabbed a short metal pole he'd been using to play fetch with Hunter, hauled back and threw it.

The little dragon who was less than two years old zipped after it, his flying having improved immensely in a few short months. He caught it high above one of the oak trees and brought it back moments later. Indents from his teeth marred the well-used toy, but it had stood up to Hunter's handling much better than anything else so far.

As they played fetch, Ace strode outside to stand next to King, a half-smile on his face as he took the outstretched pole from Hunter and tossed it high into the air.

"Have you ever heard rumors of Claudine being mated?" King asked.

Ace blinked, his hard expression going blank for a moment. "Claudine Bonavich? Uh, no. Never. *Damn.* She's mated?"

King lifted an eyebrow at his childhood friend, a wolf he'd known since he was roughly ten. They'd run wild with each other for years and he'd never known Ace to be interested in a vampire. "You care?"

"Just surprised is all. That's a big secret to keep locked down."

"She might not be. She just hinted at it, though she could have been screwing with me."

"Nah. She seems pretty straightforward. The kind of vampire that would stab you right in the heart from the front, not the back."

"You sound impressed by her."

"I've seen her fight. I *am* impressed by her."

King's mouth curved up slightly as he took the stick from Hunter, who was now starting to wind down. He flopped in front of them, looked up at Ace with big eyes, clearly begging for—

Ace pulled a handful of cherries out of his pocket and fed them to Hunter, who gobbled them up like a starving thing.

"He's been getting treats all day," King murmured. "You guys are spoiling him."

Ace tossed another cherry to Hunter. "No more than the pups in the pack."

"True enough."

"I saw Aurora fly off earlier," Ace said suddenly. "She disappeared above the clouds, but she was headed out of the city, toward the

Causeway."

King simply nodded, not bothering to respond. He certainly didn't keep tabs on Aurora, had never asked any of his packmates to. He would never do that to her. They were simply friends and it wasn't as if she was a threat to the city. No, just a threat to his heart. All his packmates insisted on telling him where she was, however. All. The. Time.

Just friends? Pathetic, his wolf growled.

He ignored the asshole. "The testing at the schools went well," he said to Ace, needing to shift the subject off the badass phoenix shifter with a big heart and bright violet eyes. Lately his wolf had been edgy, hungry, the need to mate growing. For a while he'd been able to lock it down, to simply focus on rebuilding his territory.

"I figured as much. And you need some sleep."

He turned to look at his friend. "What?"

"You're burning yourself out. I'm saying this as a friend, not as your lieutenant."

"I've got one more meeting, then I'll sleep." He surrounded himself with smart, capable people, and if Ace was telling him to sleep, he knew he should. Hell, he knew it, regardless. It was simply finding the time when there was so much to be done.

Hunter made a happy sound at the word sleep—probably because King had been sleeping out in the yard in wolf form with Hunter most nights. Though the last three, he'd only gotten a couple hours max. Hunter might be a tiny beast the size of a small elephant and capable of defending himself, but he didn't like to be alone. So King or a cluster of wolves stayed with him. It was easy to forget that he was like a toddler in some ways.

Ace nodded, but they both turned as Delphine strode out, annoyance in every line of her face. "There's an annoying vamp at the gates demanding to speak to you. And I do mean demanding." Her jaw clenched, her wolf flashing in her eyes for a moment. "If you give the order, I'll throw him out on his ass right now." She looked way too gleeful at the prospect.

King smothered a smile, kept his expression neutral. "I'll be out front in a few minutes. Don't invite him in, just leave him at the gates."

Delphine nodded, gave a quick wave to Hunter, and disappeared back into the mansion.

"You know who it is?" Ace asked, having noticed that King hadn't even asked Delphine the identity of the vampire.

"I have a feeling I do." A relatively young vampire who was nothing but a troublemaker. Something King was going to have to squash sooner than later.

CHAPTER FOUR

Aurora stared at the twenty women in the middle of a warehouse that had been turned into a gym of sorts. Racks of sparring weapons lined the walls and a huge mat was spread out in the middle of the space.

The women were all facing off with each other with long batons in each hand. They all wore tiny shorts and sports bras or T-shirts and looked ready to rip each other's heads off. She couldn't be sure, but she thought they mostly looked human. Unlike other shifters, Aurora didn't have the same sense of acute smell and simply couldn't tell.

Prima, wearing a tight tank top and tight black shorts that showed off ridiculously long, muscled legs, held up a hand at Aurora's presence. "Aurora! What a delight." She then turned to a brunette with a long braid against her back. "Candy, you lead this round." Then she hurried around the massive rectangular mat and strode toward Aurora.

Prima's jet-black hair was also pulled back in a braid, but unlike the female she'd told to lead what had turned out to be a full-on sparring session that made Aurora think of Amazon warriors, wisps frayed out everywhere, the braid a mess. Which was on-brand for the tall dragon shifter. Nothing was ever neat or tidy with her. She was walking chaos.

"What is all this?" Aurora dropped her small pack with her sweater and other things by the door, letting it shut behind her with a clang as she pulled her wings completely in.

"I'm teaching these humans and shifters to fight. Some of them have no survival skills and I've decided to help them learn to protect themselves."

Oh. "That's very cool, Prima." *Damn. Very cool.*

She grinned. "I know. I'm so glad you're here... Why *are* you here anyway?"

"I followed some of my students after art class. They were acting cagey and I wanted to know what they were up to." Aurora didn't bother lying because Prima would scent it anyway.

Prima's grin grew. "I'll have to teach them skills to evade trackers."

Aurora simply snorted and glanced over at the women. Asia had a long pole in her hand, was slamming it down on Gianna, who defended herself skillfully, using all her weight to shove back and jump to her feet. "It wasn't hard to track them."

"Hmm. I'll have to work on something, then. Since you're here, spar with me. We can show them some new moves I've been working on."

"And let you kill me? No thanks." Prima was very likely older than *actual* dirt and was terrifying on a good day. *Nope.* Aurora did not have a death wish.

Prima rolled her eyes and turned away. "Come on. You'd come back anyway." Her tone was slightly dry, which made Aurora blink at the dark, unexpected joke.

Phoenixes weren't immortal, but yes, she would likely survive dragon fire. Maybe. "So is this a thing where I talk and you don't listen?" Aurora grumbled even as she followed after her.

"I know you've been sparring with Axel and Harlow," Prima said over her shoulder as she strode toward one of the walls. Hands on hips, she stared at the array of carved weapons.

"How do you know that?"

"Axel told me over tea."

"You had tea with Axel?" Since when? And why was the lion talking about her?

"At least once a week." She turned to Aurora. "Hmm. Let's skip the weapons so I can go over something else instead."

"Are you asking me, or…?"

"Please?"

Aurora blinked at the use of the P-word. "Okay."

She strode with Prima to one end of the class and stood next to the dragon, who simply said, "Ladies."

Everyone stopped, some breathing hard, and Prima nodded once. "Luckily for all of you, Aurora has decided to join us today. We're going to show you some defensive moves that are meant to stun so you can escape. In life there will always be predators bigger than you. Always. And sometimes it is much smarter to incapacitate and run so you live to fight another day."

It was pretty damn hard to imagine a predator being bigger or scarier than Prima, but Aurora kept that to herself as Prima continued.

"We'll start with simple moves. And there are things I want you to remember—anything can be a weapon. For example, if someone were to attack Aurora in her art studio, she could defend herself with any number of her art tools. If she was human of course," Prima added as she looked at Aurora. "What would you use to defend yourself if you didn't have your fire and ability to fly?"

"Ah..." She turned back to the women. "A palette knife, craft knife, any number of scissors, a utility knife—basically all knives." She wasn't sure why she was listing them all out, other than feeling put on the spot. "Anything sharp, and I'd go for their eyes or a major artery to incapacitate. That goes for if it's a supernatural or human attacking you. If it's a supernatural, you're going to want to get away fast and that means putting them down hard enough that they can't get up." She just wished she'd been able to do that when she'd been attacked and kidnapped almost two years ago. A whole year of her life had been stolen because of a greedy dragon who'd wanted the power of her phoenix blood. At least the bastard was dead now—by her hand.

But she still had nightmares.

Prima nodded in approval. "That's right. There's a human from my nephew's clan who killed multiple wolves because she was smart and prepared." Prima went on to tell a story about a human female who'd slowed down a wolf shifter with silver spray, a nail gun, and then ran away long enough to be able to kill him with silver bullets. As she wound down, she turned to Aurora. "Would you mind showing where the major arteries are on me for the class?"

The way Prima spoke was so polite and...normal. It was odd to see Prima in this teacher mode, but Aurora liked it. And it was a reminder that all beings had layers upon layers, that they weren't defined by one thing.

"Sure."

Prima shifted her feet slightly, spreading them and her arms out so Aurora could point to weak spots on the body. As an artist, she knew much about human anatomy, and thanks to Axel and Harlow she'd been learning where to attack to incapacitate. She'd learned the hard way that she couldn't depend on just her fire, powerful as it was.

As she finished, Prima nodded in approval and clapped once. "Any questions?"

There were a few, so as Prima answered, Aurora scanned the class, realized that in addition to her art students she recognized a couple other shifters from around the city. Maybe deer shifters? She wasn't sure.

"How does that sound?"

Aurora turned at Prima's question. She hadn't been listening. "Um. Good."

"Excellent." Her grin was…mischievous wasn't the right word, but it was close. "I'll attack you and you'll defend yourself. For the purposes of this, we'll stay in our human forms and we won't use our fire."

Ooohh. She turned to the others, then back to Prima. "Really?" she muttered. It had been a long day and she really didn't want to get her ass kicked in front of a bunch of her students.

"Come on. Use the moves Axel and Harlow taught you."

She nodded once, and after Prima flicked her hand all the women moved to the sides of the mat, clearing the way. In jeans and her tank top, Aurora braced herself, preparing.

But nothing could have prepared her for the sheer force and quickness of Prima, who moved like lightning as she barreled at her like one of those human football players.

She dodged to the side, not able to defend herself. Heart racing, she swiveled, turned and…Prima wasn't there.

Arms attacked her from behind, wrapping around her tight, and Aurora fought her inner fire, reminding herself this was sparring, all in the span of a millisecond. She reacted as her packmates had taught her, slamming her head back into Prima's face as she stomped on Prima's instep. There were other various ways to get out of this hold, but this was one of her favorites. In reality, if someone ever attacked her with the intent to kill, she'd go supernova on them. She'd paused years ago when she'd been attacked, hadn't given in to her instinct to turn to pure fire, and she wouldn't make that mistake ever again.

When Prima simply grunted, Aurora shifted her body weight in a faux escape move, then flipped the dragon.

As Prima slammed onto the mat, then rolled up to her feet in one graceful move, she grinned. "Perfect." Then she turned to the class. "Not everyone will withstand a headbutt but if you manage to flip an attacker, immediately stab, punch or kick them in one of the weak spots we showed you. Or the heart or head are also perfect targets." She went on to reiterate various punching moves. Then she ordered them to start practicing.

"Would you like to spar for real? We can use whichever weapon you choose." Prima nodded to the wall of weapons as they stepped all the way off the mat.

"Maybe another day?" Like when Hell froze over.

"I *will* get you to spar with me. It would be fun."

"I think we have different definitions of fun."

Prima laughed lightly as they turned to watch the women. "Perhaps. So, I have a favor to ask you."

"Okay."

"King has asked me and some others to go on a scouting mission to look for humans who might be stuck in different settlements, to see if they want to join our territory."

Aurora knew he'd sent various shifters off on intermittent missions, searching for lost humans who'd been displaced during The Fall. "You want me to join you?" She hadn't been on any of those missions, but she could ask someone to take over her classes, given enough time.

"Oh, no. I mean, I *would* be pleased to have you with me, but I wanted to ask if you could teach this class while I'm gone. Ask some of your packmates to help if you don't want to teach it alone. It feels fitting you showed up tonight when I'd planned to ask you already."

She blinked in surprise, glanced at the warrior female. "You had?"

A short nod. "Everyone raves about your art classes and what a good teacher you are. And everyone in the city who knows you enjoys your company, says you're 'delightful.' You would be perfect for this while I'm gone. You're good at what you do and they will feel safe with you."

"Why are you teaching these particular women? How did you even start this class?" This all seemed so random and Aurora was surprised she hadn't heard about it—was surprised Axel hadn't told her, if he knew about this. Since he and Prima were now apparently having weekly tea, she figured he might.

"It came about organically. Greer mentioned some humans who had been…abused." She lowered her voice so that there was no chance of anyone overhearing them, not that Aurora thought they could over the melee of voices and grunts. "I offered to teach self-defense and…" She cleared her throat. "It turned into an official thing and here we are."

Aurora was silent, watching the women, impressed with some of their moves. "Does King know about this?"

"Does he need to know?"

"I…" That was a good question. She doubted King knew of every single thing in his territory, let alone a self-defense class. "I don't know."

"He has a lot on his plate," Prima said. "I don't know why he would care one way or the other about this class."

"He might want to suggest other people to take it."

"Hmm. So will you teach it?"

"I might have to shift the time to later, but yes. And I'm likely going to tell King about it."

Prima lifted a shoulder.

All right, then. That was that. She would tell King about it…in a text. She'd been sort of avoiding him the last week. Not quite intentionally at first, but lately she'd been keeping her distance.

He made her feel far too many things she wasn't sure she was ready to explore yet. Maybe ever.

CHAPTER FIVE

Six months ago

"*S*uck it!" *Gracie shouted to Scout as she sank the air hockey puck into place for the fifth time in a row. "I'm undefeatable!"*

"*It's air hockey," Scout grumbled, even as she half-smiled. "You're a sore winner. And kind of a psycho."*

"*True. But I'm a sore loser too, so it evens out." Gracie fist-pumped the air and did a little dance.*

"*How is that logical?" Scout lifted an eyebrow.*

"*It's not," Aurora murmured, staring at the two teenage wolf shifters. They'd asked her over to King's pack's mansion after one of her art classes and she'd agreed.*

Partially because she'd wanted a glimpse of King.

Okay, mainly.

Then she'd gotten dragged into one of the game rooms and was currently lying on her back on one of the oversized beanbags as three baby wolf shifters—in wolf form—pounced all over her. They had absolutely no concept of personal space and were treating her like their personal gym. She groaned slightly when one of them dove onto her stomach and used it as a springboard to jump off.

The playroom was filled with noisy teens and pups playing video games and board games. Some were climbing up a rock wall while others were eating and engaging in other random activities. A couple of the older packmates were supervising. Probably just to make sure stuff didn't get set on fire, she figured.

"*It's definitely logical. Come on, Zuri, you're gonna kill Aurora." Gracie scooped the little gray and white wolf up and tossed the pup into the air with ease.*

Aurora was used to roughhousing—she'd grown up in an artist's compound with Harlow and Brielle as her aunts/extra big sisters, after all.

Zuri yelped in delight before growling low in her throat as Gracie caught her.

Then Gracie did a whole staring thing at the pup that Aurora was also used to. It was a sort of dominance thing all shifters did. Or most of them. Especially cubs and pups who were still figuring out their place in their pack. Zuri played dead, going completely limp in Gracie's arms, and when Gracie went to put her down, Zuri pounced at her. If she'd been in human form, Aurora had no doubt the four-year-old would be cackling maniacally.

She eased the two wolves who were still crawling all over her onto the nearby mat and stood. She tried to adjust her ponytail as King strode in. Of course he looked like a sexy god—cheekbones carved from stone, and sleek, hard lines of muscles that clothing couldn't hide. The male was an artist's dream. And her fantasy come to life. His dark hair was in a sharp buzz cut, which just served to show off that gorgeous face. And his ice-blue eyes were bright, seeming more so against his dark brown skin.

"Hey, didn't expect to see you tonight." Was that pleasure in his voice?

She thought so but tried not to read into it. They were friends, something she'd been repeating to herself a lot lately. "The kids asked me to come by after class." She shrugged.

"She flew a bunch of us around the yard," Scout said excitedly before turning to Gracie with a smug look. "And I got to go twice."

Aurora had planned to fly all of them around twice, at least, but it had started raining so they'd all hurried inside. The pups and teens hadn't seemed to care about getting wet, but one of the older wolves had come out and herded them all in, muttering something about not planning to clean up a bunch of muddy pawprints later.

The two girls started bickering slightly so King nodded once at Aurora. Covertly, she followed him out of the playroom and up the stairs.

"We're just sneaking out?" she asked. Not that she was complaining.

"Figured you could use a break if you've been in there for any amount of time. There's a reason we call that room the madhouse."

She laughed. "That's totally accurate. But really, being around them is like being around the twins. And Axel." The rest of her pack was mostly well-behaved, but those three? They liked to brawl for fun. It didn't matter that they were in their forties—they had the mentality of six-year-olds half the time.

King shook his head as they reached the third floor.

"Where are we going?" She'd never been this far into the wolf pack's mansion. The place was sprawling and only one of the many locations his pack lived. But she knew that his room was in this place. He couldn't be leading her there, could he?

"My room."

She nearly stumbled at his words. Oh, he really was taking her to his room.

"It's the only place I get any privacy. Usually," he tacked on with a laugh.

This was...unexpected. But not unwelcome. She'd been fighting her feelings for him, fighting the raw fear deep inside as she battled whether she should do anything about her attraction or not.

She'd gotten peeks that he was interested in her but he'd never made a move or anything. And she didn't think that was what this was either. King wouldn't just lead her to his room and then expect something. No way.

He opened and shut the door behind them, leaned against it with a sigh.

That was when she noticed how exhausted he looked. She stared at him for a moment, seeing the faint circles under his ice-blue eyes. "When's the last time you slept?"

He paused, blinked.

"If you have to think about it, it's been too long."

He stared down at her, his blue eyes flaring slightly.

She turned away, unable to hold his gaze right now. And not because he was an Alpha, but because he made her feel things. She looked around his space, taking everything in. It was big, but not as huge as she'd expected. He had a sleeping area and a sort of sitting/work area as well as an extra fridge and small bar. His bed was bigger than a king size, if she had to guess, and everything was minimal in style. Dark furniture, sleek lines and... She smiled at the wall of bookshelves. She knew he liked to read. The insulation must be incredible because she couldn't hear anyone else either. And his rich, masculine scent filled the room. Even with her limited olfactory senses, his scent surrounded her.

"You want anything to drink?" He moved over to a small bar area by a huge window. The thing took up almost a whole wall and she imagined that during the day the natural light made it feel like he was outdoors. Which was probably the point.

"I'm okay," she said as she strode to the window that overlooked part of the backyard. She could see the pool and beyond. "Where's Hunter?"

"On patrol." His tone was dry.

She turned to see he'd poured himself a glass of bourbon, his favorite, before he collapsed on a Scandinavian-style leather couch in the nook by the window.

She sat on the other end of the couch. "He's patrolling?"

King shook his head, a small smile playing at his full lips. Goddess, he was sexy when he smiled. "Sort of. I swear that dragon understands everything. I jokingly said something about him going on patrol and now he's off with Delphine, who's already texted me that he's a natural at finding and terrorizing rabbits. And that he's adopted another cat."

She grinned. "How many is that now?"

"Four. And I think one's knocked up."

She snickered, stretching her legs out as she leaned back. The leather was butter smooth. "Those cats are fearless." Aurora often found them climbing all over Hunter, using his thick scales as scratching posts—and Hunter didn't mind.

He closed his eyes, leaned his head back against the couch. "Felines have no sense."

He looked so tired. She had the urge to go over and stroke her fingers through his short hair, just to soothe him. The mantle of responsibility he carried had to be exhausting. "As I live with almost all felines...that's mostly true." Bella was the exception.

He grinned but didn't open his eyes.

"Want to talk about your day?"

Groaning, he raised his head. "It's just more of the same. For three days straight. I'm just tired." He lifted a shoulder.

"I'm sorry. Is there anything I can do?" She wished...a lot of things. Like she had the right to comfort him, to hold him, to take care of him.

"You're already doing it." He gave her a real smile then and it erased years off his handsome face. "I've already heard from Claudine and Santiago how perfect you are today. Santiago was a little too effusive," he grumbled, a frown replacing his smile.

She rolled her eyes, brushing off the compliment. "They're easy to keep happy."

King snorted. "Claudine is not easy."

Before he could respond further, his phone started buzzing and she could see the exhaustion creep back into his face as he looked at the screen. She saw Ace's name pop up and plucked it from King's hand. Aurora knew that if he hadn't wanted to give it to her, he wouldn't have.

"What are you doing?" Amusement laced his words.

She held up a finger and answered. "King's phone. He's unavailable for the next six hours. But you may leave a message with me." She knew he needed more sleep than that but figured it was all she could talk him into. Maybe.

Ace let out a startled laugh. "Everything okay?"

"Yes. But your Alpha is exhausted. Tell the pack to leave him alone for a little bit."

"Will do." He disconnected without arguing or anything. She tucked King's phone into her pocket then pointed to his bed. "Sleep."

His look was a mix of amusement and something else she couldn't quite define. Heat, maybe. But she wasn't sure that made sense, given the situation.

"No one but you ever bosses me around." His voice was deep, rumbly—tired.

"I've seen Hunter try."

Groaning, he set his empty glass on the table next to him. "Fair enough. Goddess, I'm tired."

She pointed at the bed again, eyebrows raised.

He lifted a shoulder. "I'm good."

"You're just being obnoxious now. Come on." She stood and held out her hands. "If this was any of your packmates, you'd be ordering them to sleep. Otherwise they'd be a danger to the rest of the pack without proper rest."

He grumbled slightly, but put his hands in hers as he stood. A jolt of heat arched through her at the contact. "I'll sleep but...will you stay?" There was a hint of vulnerability in his voice she'd never heard before. "I've missed you the last couple days."

Her heart skipped a beat at the admission, at the rawness from him. They hadn't seen each other in four days and she'd been missing him too. Texting wasn't enough. Secretly she wished he was asking her to stay in his bed, but...he couldn't mean that. Or she didn't think so. "Of course. I'm going to raid your library. I'll read until you wake up." And she would be the gatekeeper of his phone—no one was going to bother him unless something was on fire. Maybe not even then.

He yawned, then his gaze fell to her mouth before he quickly looked away.

She blinked, not sure how to read it.

Lies. She knew exactly how to read that look, however brief. But she ignored it as he stripped off his shirt and stumbled to the bed, tossing it onto the ground before he basically face-planted onto one of his pillows.

She stared at his muscular back, calmed the increase of her heart rate as she pulled her own phone out and texted Ace, telling him that King was resting for seven hours instead of six. Shifters didn't need as much sleep as humans, but if King kept pushing himself like this, burning the candle at both ends, he was going to spectacularly burn out.

And that could be bad on an epic scale.

Not that she was even thinking about that, not really. She simply wanted him to take care of himself because she cared about him. Far deeper than she wanted to admit. She snagged a fluffy blanket from the end of the bed and draped it over him.

When he didn't stir, she realized how badly he needed this.

Turning down the volume on his phone so he wouldn't hear it even if someone called, she then went to his bookshelves and grabbed a book. His taste seemed to be across the board, some of his books ancient.

She wouldn't leave until he woke up. She knew he wasn't hers to take care of, not in the mate sense, but he was her friend. And screw it, she wanted to take care of him. Wanted to dream about a future where maybe they were more than friends.

Sighing, she flipped the paperback open and stretched out on the couch by the window. First she needed to work through her own baggage before she could even contemplate a relationship. Or...anything.

CHAPTER SIX

Present day

King strode to the front gate of his pack's compound alone. Some of his packmates waited in the shadows, and Hunter had flown atop one of the oak trees, but was camouflaged enough that King had a feeling most of the vamps would miss the dragonling if they looked up. As he approached, Myles, the leader of the relatively new Hill coven, stepped forward.

He'd brought five of his vampires and they all had a similar look—young, beefed up, with muscle and hard expressions.

King ignored them and lifted a hand when Myles went to speak. "Showing up without contacting one of my lieutenants first is against protocol. And it's rude." In that moment, he wondered if this was what Claudine felt like when scolding him—beyond ancient and tired of dealing with young supernaturals. He had an open-door policy for the most part for issues around the city, but he'd designated very capable people from all supernatural walks of life as liaisons. He had far too many big-picture things to deal with right now to be bothered with micromanaging anything.

Myles, a male with dark brown hair and matching brown eyes, nodded but there was no contriteness to him. "I apologize. I'm concerned about one of the dragons in the city and thought I should come directly to you."

King kept his expression neutral. He knew that Delphine had attempted to handle this, but Myles had made it clear he wouldn't talk to her. And something told King it had nothing to do with her being a wolf, and everything to do with her gender. "What's the issue?"

"The dragon female, Prima, the old one, she's been infecting humans, has stolen a few of my vampires away."

"You're accusing Prima of kidnapping your vampires? As in, she's holding them against their will?" He didn't bother keeping the skepticism out of his voice. This was not likely. He didn't know Prima as well as he wanted to, had a feeling that most people didn't truly know the ancient female who had been born so long ago that she didn't even know her true age. But he trusted the powerful ancient. Mostly.

Myles let out an exasperated growl, his fangs gleaming under the lamplights of the two brick columns on either side of the gate. "Not physically! But she's done something to them. *Infected* them," he stressed, as if that made any sense. "They've left our coven and aren't coming back. They're all leaving because of that dragon!"

This was the male's emergency? King shouldn't be surprised, but he actually was shocked by this level of "asshattery," as one of his young packmates liked to say. "This is clearly an internal problem. You don't own your coven members any more than I own my packmates. They are free to leave any time they wish. Unless you have a real issue, we're done." He turned his back, beyond exhausted and now truly on his way to being pissed off at this asinine interruption.

King never should have given the coven shelter in New Orleans, but they'd had a handful of young, recently turned females and something about them had pulled at his protective instincts. Ace always told him he couldn't save the world, but apparently he liked to try.

He'd taken one step when he felt fingers brush over his leather jacket.

Moving lightning fast, he whipped around, had Myles by the throat, the male's feet dangling off the ground as he held him up.

The vampires behind him took a step forward, but he growled low in his throat. Myles held his hands up, choking as King squeezed, but he didn't fight back. Just stared at him with fear and rage in his eyes.

Yeah, King was going to have to do something about this male soon. He dropped him and stared down at the male who was now attempting to save face as he straightened.

King let his wolf flare in his eyes as he stared at the vampire.

In milliseconds, the vampire looked down, averting his gaze. "I'm sorry, I meant no offense," he rasped out. "We're just losing too many coven members. The woman I love left and…" He swallowed hard. "I thought you could talk to the dragon, that you should at least know what she's up to."

"Don't come by here again unannounced." King didn't bother responding to anything else, simply turned and walked away, giving them his back again. He knew the insult would piss this male off even more.

As he reached the midpoint of the long, winding driveway, Ace dropped down from one of the trees. "To state the obvious, that one's trouble."

"Follow them," he said as he pulled his cell phone out. He knew Prima wasn't infecting anyone, but he needed to talk to her about whatever this was, regardless. "Once they get to their residence, do a sweep with them and let any vampires living there know they can leave with you if they choose. I have a feeling Claudine or Ingrid will take them in. Take Ari and Cat with you." Ari was huge and intimidating and Cat had a soothing presence. He had a feeling both would do well with whatever awaited them.

Ace nodded and disappeared down the driveway.

King whistled once for Hunter, who swooped down fairly silently compared to the noise he used to make when flying. After texting Prima, he tucked his phone away and motioned toward the back of the mansion. There was a huge area there for all his wolves to run or sleep, and now was time to sleep.

As he continued across the grass his phone buzzed, and when he glanced at the screen his heart skipped a beat.

It wasn't Prima, but Aurora. *We still on for tomorrow morning?*

He'd thought she'd forgotten since he hadn't heard from her in days, but texted back immediately. *Yes.*

See you then! Her response was just as immediate and she included a couple emojis. Which he shouldn't care about. But he did.

Feeling lighter than he had all day, he'd stripped off his shirt as he and Hunter reached a heavily wooded section by one of the walls, getting ready to shift, when he got a return text from Prima, telling him she was free now.

He groaned, but texted back that she could come to the compound. Sleep was starting to look less and less likely at this point.

* * *

In his pack's massive kitchen, King looked up when Prima strode in with Darius escorting her. The big male nodded at King and disappeared back into the bustle of the mansion.

King had already ordered everyone to steer clear of the kitchen for the next ten minutes—about the longest he could keep his wolves from the main source of food.

Prima smiled at him as she sat at the island and the faintest hint of Aurora rolled toward him, as if Prima had been with the female recently. He had to force his wolf not to inhale deeply—and force himself not to ask about Aurora.

"You didn't want to meet out back?" Prima asked.

It was normally where they met, but he knew what would happen if they did. She would get distracted by Hunter, shift to her dragon form and then roll around with him as if she was a dragonling as well for a solid hour before King and Prima got to actually talk. "Next time. Hunter is resting."

"Ah, of course. Growing dragonlings need their rest. How is that sweet angel doing?" Prima's earned reputation was one of a savage fighter—he'd seen firsthand how vicious she could be—but when she was with the dragonling she showed a different side. A softer one.

"Spoiled."

"Good. It's as it should be, then. So what is it you need?" she asked, getting right to the point.

Something he appreciated about her. "A vampire named Myles came to visit me today."

The shift in her was subtle, a single twitch of one of her fingers as she sat across from him. "And?"

"He says that you have stolen some vampires from his coven."

She lifted a dark eyebrow. "He is accusing me of kidnapping?" Her question mirrored his earlier one. "That is a bold, unsubstantiated thing to say."

"Look, I know you didn't kidnap anyone. And to be blunt, I don't think he's going to be in my territory much longer." King would be kicking him out sooner than later, he was certain. "But I need to know what's going on. Why is he accusing you of this?"

"Because he is a fool?"

"Prima." He growled more out of frustration than anger. He simply didn't have time for bullshit tonight. He was tired. Edgy. His wolf restless and craving Aurora.

"Fine. I heard from someone that some human females who had been abused or assaulted were looking to take self-defense classes. So I started a class, as I am an excellent fighter and instructor. At first it was just humans, but now I have a few shifters and vampires in my class as well. The vampires are young, were turned when they were emotionally vulnerable and...I did encourage some of his vampires to look for a new coven when I heard about the state of his. I certainly did not force them."

King's hackles rose. "What's he doing to them?"

She sighed. "I don't know. Not specifically. They approached me, asked if they could take classes and hinted that they were unhappy. But there was nothing they said that would have allowed me to burn his home to the ground with him in it. Unfortunately."

He didn't think she was joking, and ignored that as he said, "So you simply encouraged them to move?"

She nodded.

"I figured as much." He paused, weighing his words. He didn't give any credence to what Myles had said about her infecting them, but he still wanted to make sure he had all bases covered. "He also said that you were infecting them."

She snorted, but a hint of something flashed in her eyes. So quickly he might have missed it if he hadn't been paying close attention. "That's an odd thing to say."

"Do you know what he meant by it?"

"Who knows what anyone means by anything?"

He held his growl in check. "Prima."

"Fine." Her gray eyes flickered with annoyance and he knew that someone of her age didn't like to be questioned. But it was happening. "I'm not infecting anyone. But I have given a very small part of myself to some of the humans."

"Explain further," he ordered when she just sat there, as if her explanation made complete sense.

"I've given them the smallest bit of…essence, I think you would call it. It does not make them immortal, but it does make them stronger, able to protect themselves better. And I'm following that up with fighting instructions. The world is changing, as it often does. I'm simply helping evolution along."

He blinked once, unable to hide his surprise. "Dragons can share their strength?" There was so much about dragons he didn't know, but this truly surprised him.

"No. But I can. And it is all consensual. I don't give them this gift without their consent. And for the record, the two vampires who left his coven—I didn't need to give them anything but encouragement. They left because he scares them, and they're training under me to learn how to protect themselves. That's it."

"Thank you. I've got someone watching his coven now. I think he'll be gone within a month." As an Alpha, he couldn't simply rule with an iron fist and toss people out of his territory without a reason. Technically he could, but in the long run it made for bad precedence.

"Good. It will save me the trouble of killing him." He started to respond, but she continued. "Aurora will be teaching my class while I'm on that mission for you."

He hadn't even known about the class and was annoyed on a few levels that Prima hadn't told him. But the fact that Aurora had known about it and hadn't said anything bothered him for different reasons. He kept his expression neutral as he said, "Good. She's an excellent teacher."

"I think so too. I think one of the tigers will likely help out as well." She stood, pushing the stool back. "And Arthur and I are ready. We'll be heading out in the morning. We might be out of contact for a while."

He stood as well and nodded. "Safe travels… Hunter would love to see you if you'd like to say hi before you leave."

Her expression lightened and she grinned before she hurried out another entrance than the one she'd arrived through with Darius, heading toward the back of the house.

At least he knew that Hunter would sleep well tonight after playing with the ancient dragon. The moment after Prima had gone, a handful of teens from the pack rushed in toward one of the refrigerators, acting as if they were starving as they tore into it.

Laughing, he stood just as Ace entered the kitchen, his lieutenant's expression grim. Now he was glad Prima had stopped by, because at least he knew Hunter would be entertained while he dealt with whatever this was.

CHAPTER SEVEN

"Thank you again for stopping by," Jo said to Casimir, her cheeks flushed the faintest shade of pink as he slid out from under the sink. The human female he was in love with—but who had no idea—was leaning against one of the countertops, a coffee cup in hand as she watched him with big green eyes.

Cas shrugged and shoved up from the floor, trying not to stare too hard at her. His dragon half snarled at him, annoyed, but after a year, things weren't changing. "It's no big deal. And this was an easy fix."

She glanced over her shoulder toward the doorway, then turned back to him as he tested the water at the sink. No leaks. "Next time if my grandmother calls you, just check in with me first," she whispered. "I feel bad that she asked you, and I could have told you this could wait."

He frowned slightly, unsure of the mix of scents coming off Jo. She was…difficult to read sometimes, though her scent was always pleasant. Sweet, delicate, enticing. "She's an elder," he said simply. "I would never tell her no."

Jo blinked, her red, wavy hair shifting against her silky robe. A robe he was delighted to have found her wearing when she'd answered the door—because it showed off her full breasts and shapely legs. She'd clearly been surprised to see him so early in the morning, otherwise she would have been dressed. He should surprise her more often. "Of course, I just… I feel bad that you showed up so early like this when I know you have a full day of work."

She did too. Everyone did. But he'd wanted to see her, so when her older namesake—Josephine—had called and asked for help fixing their kitchen sink, he'd jumped at the chance. And he wasn't ashamed to admit it. Getting to see Jo in the morning with mussed hair and a soft smile was a good way to start off the day. Even if she had no idea how he felt.

Before he could respond, her sisters, Luna and Grace, stumbled in and basically growled at him before they shoved each other to get to the coffee maker first.

He snort-laughed at them, shaking his head even as Jo did the same. "So it was an easy fix?" she asked him.

"What was an easy fix?" Luna stood to the side of Grace, who had won in the quest to get to the coffee maker first.

"Something was wrong with the plumbing." Jo nodded to the sink.

Cas nodded in agreement. It had been simple, almost as if someone had just loosened the brackets.

"Thanks for stopping by," Luna said, rubbing at her eyes.

"Yeah," Grace said, yawning. "It's freaking early." She handed her cup to Luna, a caring gesture he'd seen more than once from the sisters. They all took care of each other.

It was seven o'clock, which wasn't early for a dragon who liked to get up and fly before sunrise, but he simply nodded again. He did that a lot with the sisters. They talked, he listened. It had been that way for about a year. Ever since he'd found them struggling to cut up an oak tree that had fallen across their driveway. He'd been going around the city with other shifters and helping people after The Fall. Though the tree hadn't toppled because of rogue dragons, just a freak of nature. He hadn't been the same since meeting the little family.

"I'm hungry," Luna whined. "Please tell me we have something other than fruit and cereal."

"Your hands are not broken," Josephine elder said as she stepped into the room.

Cas wasn't great at gauging the age of humans, but he thought she might be seventy or eighty. Her hair was a faded auburn, with streaks of gray filtered throughout, but she had the same delicate bone structure as her granddaughters. And she had a lilting accent he knew was because she was originally from Ireland. He knew of the place, had been there thousands of years ago more than once, though it hadn't been called that then. He...couldn't even remember what it had been called before his Hibernation.

"But I'll cook for you anyway, my sweet girls. Hurry, go shower or you'll be late." She shooed Luna and Grace out before giving Jo a kiss on the cheek and then doing the same to him. Then she patted his stomach, something he was used to. "Have you eaten yet?"

"Ah, no, but—"

"Then you'll stay." She motioned for him to sit and then did the same to Jo, who obeyed, though she frowned slightly in annoyance.

Cas had noticed that Jo rarely disagreed with her grandmother. He noticed everything about her. Especially the fact that she didn't have a bra on this morning. He forced himself not to stare. They were friends; he had no claim on her and should not be ogling her.

"How's your job going?" Jo asked as her grandmother started humming to herself and pulling things out of the refrigerator.

He knew that Jo would help if needed, had seen her offer so many times to do just that, but Josephine always shooed her away and either ordered her out of the kitchen or to sit and just talk. Though sometimes she let Jo make salads or hot tea in the evenings. "Good. Busy." He worked construction with various crews around the city as they rebuilt everything and added more housing. Though King had asked him multiple times if he'd like to work the patrols around the city instead. He found he liked working with his hands. Strange for a warrior who'd only known wars so long ago. "But we've just received a big delivery from a clan up in Montana and should meet our deadline."

"Grace says The Grove building is spectacular." She let out a little sigh. "I'm so jealous she's getting to help with it."

"Why don't you stop by? I can give you a tour." The construction crew he worked with were currently building a ten-story residential building with huge terraces that would have over eight hundred trees and hundreds of plants implemented into the actual building itself. For the first year after The Fall they'd been focused on simply getting people in housing. Now, in addition to the microfarms in the territory, King had decided to implement "vertical forests" around the city proper and beyond.

"Oh, no—"

"She'd love to," her grandmother said from the stove without turning around. "And so would I."

But Jo shook her head. "Grace said it's too busy right now."

Her sister was a plant geneticist and was helping with the plant and tree side of things. "I live with the foreman of the project and she's mated to my brother," he said dryly because Jo already knew that. His older brother Mikael was mated with a human, Avery, who ran the construction crew for many projects around the city, including this one. "Trust me, it's fine. Just let me know when you two would like to visit."

"We will," her grandmother answered before Jo could say no.

And he could read her body language clearly—she'd planned to say no. Though he wasn't sure why. "What do you have going on today? A full load?"

She nodded, took a sip of her coffee. "Yeah. A couple surgeries and then just routine stuff. But we're booked up the whole day."

Jo was a vet, and from what he'd heard, a great one. He loved that she took care of animals, loved everything about her. He just wished he was better with females. With human females. Okay, with *one* human female in particular. They had been friends for almost a year and he wanted so much more, but she'd never given any indication that she might. Or if she had, he couldn't tell.

And the truth was, she didn't know what he was. That he was a dragon shifter. Part of the same species that had killed her parents. He'd started to respond when his phone rang. Assuming it was one of his brothers, he pulled his phone out to silence it—since awakening, he'd found that humans had made some incredible technology—but frowned when he saw the name on the screen.

"Ah, excuse me." Standing, he answered and headed for the back door. "Aurora, is everything okay?" The phoenix shifter never called him and he couldn't imagine why she was now.

"Oh, yes, sorry to bother you so early. I called Avery this morning about something and she directed me to you. We're hoping to add another greenhouse and she said that might be a project you would want to help out with—only if you have time. No pressure. This isn't a necessity or anything and I figured you probably couldn't start until spring anyway. She just said that you had a friend who was really good with plants and...have I lost you?"

He laughed lightly as he stepped onto the back porch. "No, it's no problem. I can work something out. Do you need dates right now?"

"No, I just wanted to get on your radar so you could figuratively pencil me in, and thought a call was easier than a text. And Avery said you were awake."

He smiled at that. His whole house woke up early whether they wanted to or not. Maybe it was dragon biology. "Okay, give me a week or so and I'll eye our schedule, but yeah, I'm thinking March sounds good. We've probably got enough leftover supplies as it is. I should be able to reuse some stuff." It was January now and that would give him enough time to add it to his schedule. And...maybe he would ask Grace if she wanted to help with all the plant stuff—but he'd done a good job of keeping his family and work stuff separated from Jo and her family so far.

Because he was afraid that if she learned he was a dragon, she'd want nothing to do with him. It was rude to ask a supernatural what they were, so thankfully she'd never asked him. Though she had once made an offhand comment about him being a bear and he...hadn't denied it.

A lie of omission is still a lie. Goddess, he could actually hear his mother in his head right now. Or his brother Mikael. Growling at absolutely no one but himself, he stepped back inside.

As he inhaled, his stomach growled. Immediately he sought out Jo, his gaze drawn to her without thought. He found her watching him...curiously. He wished she would look at him with lust instead. Obsession, maybe? He sighed.

He didn't know how to read that look and found himself tongue-tied. He hated talking sometimes, wished he could just show her how he felt— with his tongue between her legs. He internally sighed again.

"Who is Aurora?" Josephine asked as she slid a pan off the stovetop to reveal cheesy scrambled eggs.

"Nana," Jo admonished.

He blinked at the two of them, unsure what was going on. "She's a friend of my brother's mate. Me too, I suppose." Or they were friendly. He liked the phoenix shifter, had a feeling she would one day be Alpha female of the territory.

"When are we going to meet your brothers?" Josephine continued with a sweet smile as she slid a pot with something called grits onto a trivet. "I've heard so much about them and I have two single granddaughters—"

"Nana." Jo's voice was a little louder now.

And what did she mean by *two*? Weren't...all three of them single? He frowned. "Ah, they would love to meet you. We could have you over—"

"No, no, we'll have you over here so I can cook."

He looked at Jo, whose expression was tight and...he couldn't help but wonder why. He hadn't invited her to his place because he'd been afraid she would figure out that he was a dragon shifter before he could tell her—they certainly didn't hide it among themselves.

The obvious answer was to just *tell her*, but he was afraid. Thousands of years ago he'd gone into a long Hibernation after fighting in too many battles to count. He'd never experienced real fear before. He was a dragon after all; very little scared him. But if she rejected him... He couldn't even fathom that. She was so ingrained into his life now, this small human female who stole his breath and made him ache inside. "Okay, thank you."

"How does Saturday sound?" Josephine continued.

"Good." He looked at Jo, whose expression had gone carefully neutral, but she stood and started getting plates out as her sisters hurried into the kitchen in various states of dress, their wet hair wrapped up in small towels as they gossiped about one of their neighbors. They more or less treated him like a big brother, the same way Avery treated him, and he liked it. Human females were a lot different than dragon females. Softer, but just as scary. In different ways though, and he found them fascinating.

To his surprise, Jo didn't join them at the table, but instead murmured something about grabbing a quick shower before work. And she barely met his gaze before she hurried out.

What had just happened?

* * *

Aurora tucked her cell phone away, glad that was taken care of. Her list of "things to do" was a never-ending one, but she really wanted another greenhouse on the property and was glad they might be getting one soon.

"Coffee really is the breakfast of champions." Brielle leaned back in her chair, a smile on her face.

"That's not how the saying goes." Marley shook her head slightly as she took a sip of her own drink. Her long, dark braids were pulled back into a ponytail and she'd already changed out of her pajamas and into her standard beat-up jeans and a sweater for the day.

"What saying?" Harlow strode up to the table, already geared up and ready to go. She was on patrol for King today, working with some wolves to monitor part of the perimeter of the city. The redheaded tiger shifter was a skilled tracker and great at scenting things that were out of place.

Aurora took a sip of her doctored coffee, watching everyone but not participating in what she knew was going to devolve into a ridiculous argument. Like most mornings. They often ate their meals out on the patio behind the mansion that housed all of them. Their crew had grown up together, her own sister Star acting as the Alpha from the time they were toddlers. Then Aurora had come later, and she was more or less a little sister to all of them.

But...things had shifted lately. They'd been coming to her for things in the same way they had Star before she'd moved to Scotland. Aurora was starting to take on the role of leader in the house and she wasn't sure how she felt about it.

Axel strode out the back door then, his expression...surly. She glanced at Bella, who simply lifted a sleek eyebrow.

Whoa. She'd never seen the happy-go-lucky lion look like...well, like he was sucking on a lemon.

"You barbarians save any coffee?" he growled as he stalked toward the clearly half-full carafe.

"Oooh, what's wrong with you? Got a thorn in your paw?" Brielle cackled.

"Oh my God, don't poke him! It's too early for your shit," Harlow muttered.

"Leave him alone," Aurora said. "Though I would like to know about you and Prima having weekly tea."

Everyone quieted and stared at Axel. Shirtless, in lounge pants, the male really did have a killer body honed from running and climbing. His long hair was pulled up into a bun and he stared at them all now, shrugged. "What?"

"You're having tea with the crazy one?" Bella asked, her mouth falling open.

"Yeah, we talk shit about you," he growled, back to being surly. The scent of his lie rolled off him because he clearly didn't talk about any of them. Not meanly anyway. But he was in a *mood*.

"Ooh, I don't like angry Axel!" Marley stared in horror, her amber eyes wide. "Make it stop." She looked at Aurora as if she could do anything.

The steam went out of Axel and he sighed, flopping down onto the nearest chair. Then he threw an arm over his face. "I hate everything right now."

"Oh, no," Aurora breathed, understanding setting in. "You met someone. You're…in love." It was just a guess, but…he had that look.

He lifted his arm, his expression mournful. Then he threw his arm back over his eyes and just groaned in pure Axel fashion—dramatically.

Marley winced, and everyone went from messing with him to tackle-hugging him. Finally they all stepped back and he plucked up his coffee cup, frowning into it.

"So?" Brielle pushed, unable to give the lion space. "Who is he or she? Have we met this person?"

Axel loved males and females of all species, and had dated so much over the years that before they'd settled in New Orleans it had been hard to keep track of his love interests. Since moving here, however, he'd just flirted a lot with everyone. Much to the annoyance of a whole lot of supernaturals.

"Maybe. I don't know." He groaned again, acting like a child basically. "He's such a jackass." Axel straightened in his chair, his jaw tightening as he seemed to latch onto anger instead of the sullenness. "Stupid, handsome vampire thinks he's hot shit, that he's better than me. He's so obnoxious, and flirty and…" He growled low in his throat. "He thinks he knows everything about everything. I mean, he *is* smart, but I just want to punch his smug face. And then make out with him."

"You're in love with a vampire?" Harlow blurted, her look of astonishment mirroring everyone else's. "One who is apparently your twin?"

"Hey!" He swiveled on her, glaring. "Did you not hear what I said? I'm nothing like him!"

"Hmm, handsome, obnoxious, flirty, thinks he knows everything. I definitely heard what you said." Harlow's tone was dry.

"I also said he was stupid."

"Hey, if the shoe fits."

Axel threw his coffee mug at her, but she swiftly ducked. With lightning-quick reflexes, Brielle jumped from her chair and snagged it out of the air before it could smash on anything, then dumped out the remnants on the grass.

"So what did this supposed jackass do?" Bella asked, leaning back casually in her chair as if nothing had happened.

"He *exists*," Axel growled out, then turned as Prima and Arthur walked up from the side of the yard.

Aurora was sure the others had already scented them, but she could only scent them now as they got closer. And she certainly hadn't heard them, they were too quiet for that. Stealth dragons.

"Lion, we need to talk." Prima jerked her chin at Axel, and to Aurora's surprise he jumped out of his seat and hurried after her into the house.

Something that Arthur did not seem to like, if his scowl was anything to go on. Since she actually liked the big Scottish dragon with the flaming red beard and hearty laugh, she patted his arm. "Don't worry, they're probably just going to talk about tea flavors."

The dragon shifter just blinked at her in surprise.

She was curious about what Prima and Axel were talking about, but she had too much to worry about this morning anyway. Like her meetup with King.

She had to steel herself to see him, to not go all weak-kneed over the Alpha wolf. Right about now she contemplated throwing her arm over her face too and just blocking out the world.

Too bad life didn't work like that.

CHAPTER EIGHT

Three months ago

King hung back a couple paces as Aurora and River walked in front of him, the teens and pups running wild in the outdoor market ahead of them.

"You're so good with her," River murmured to Aurora, eyeing Zuri, who'd decided to ride on Aurora's shoulders. "She's not like this with everyone."

King snorted softly, which earned him an arch look from River—Zuri's mom. "I'm simply agreeing with you," he said.

River chuckled as she turned back to Aurora. "Zuri challenged him when she was two."

"Seriously?" Aurora turned to look at him, her expression of shock almost comical. "This sweet girl?"

Zuri patted Aurora's head and bared her teeth at King before giggling and turning around again. Her spiral curls bounced with the movement, the angelic chubby cheeks of hers making her look far too innocent. At four, she was stealthier and faster than any human child would ever be. He had a feeling she'd be an Alpha herself one day. There was no fear in that one.

Aurora was a shifter, but not like a wolf. And her pack of mostly felines operated in a way he'd never seen with cats. There weren't any challenges to each other that he knew of—they worked as a cohesive unit and everyone acted as a team. Much like his wolves. And Aurora was in a class by herself as a phoenix—he didn't know much about how they operated. "Yep, that sweet girl," he said, glancing around at the various vendors, always on alert for a threat.

Not that he expected one. Today was an unplanned visit on his part. There'd recently been a summer harvest so everyone was out getting fresh vegetables, trees to plant, and a whole host of other things. Some nonessential. So far his territory was operating with a barter system and it seemed to be effective. Some things his pack provided outright, like housing and healthcare, but the other stuff...supernaturals and humans alike had started working together for the good of everyone. At least here—he knew it wasn't the same everywhere unfortunately.

"It happens with the super Alpha pups sometimes," River explained as they passed a vendor stand where witches were offering various potions.

"You challenged me when you were five," King added as he nodded at one *of the fruit vendors.*

Krishna nodded back and held up the small cloth bag.

He'd contacted Krishna a week ago and asked about procuring dried mango since it was Aurora's favorite. He quickly took it from him with a thanks, having already traded some baby fruit trees days ago.

"Ugh," River groaned to Aurora. "He's never going to let me live that down. I was a tiny terror, trying to take on all the lieutenants until I was ten." She shook her head and started explaining more pack dynamics to Aurora.

Over the last year his pack had basically adopted her as part of them. Aurora had her own small pack, but she'd found a place in everyone's hearts, his wolves specifically. He didn't know if it was because they knew how much she meant to him, or simply because of who she was.

Probably a bit of both.

She was easy to love.

"What did you just get?" River asked without turning around, her eyes firmly on the teens in front of them getting too rowdy.

"None of your nosy business," he said to the grown lieutenant who would always be more of a little sister to him than anything.

"I'll find out," she said before she picked up her pace and grabbed the back of some of the teens' necks and growled at them to behave.

King was glad she'd intervened, not that he'd expected anything less. He held his wolves to a higher standard than anyone else. His people had to be the standard.

Aurora looked at the little bag, eyebrows raised. "Is that chocolate?"

He grinned, held it out to her. She didn't have a heightened scent ability like wolves did. "It's for you. Save it for later or my pack will steal it."

She peeked inside and her violet eyes lit up. "You got this for me?"

He wasn't sure why she sounded shocked—he brought her little things all the time. "Of course."

Grinning, she nudged him with her hip even as Zuri dove off her shoulders at him, knowing he'd catch her.

King caught her midair even as she shifted to wolf, her clothes shredding before she hit the hard ground and ran after her mom, yipping away.

Aurora laughed as she bent down with King to pick up the discarded clothes. "It's wild how freely the pups shift."

He knew she'd had to hide what she was for most of her life. "I know. I like it." Hell, he loved it even if he didn't love the reason the world had changed so drastically. He would take the silver linings where he could get them.

"Are you going to the movie night tonight?" she asked, eyeing one of the

stalls filled with small lemon trees.

"Movie night?" There weren't any actual new movies out anymore, but there were plenty of DVDs that had survived The Fall.

"Yeah, Ari told me about it. Said it's going to be at the place in the Irish Channel. They're setting up a big screen or something. It's a kids' movie."

"You going?"

She shrugged. "I was thinking about it. Some of the teens from class asked if I'd be there."

"I'll be there." Especially if she was. He didn't often get downtime, but he needed to spend time with his pack, to remind them that he wasn't just the Alpha who ran the territory, but their Alpha. The wolf who loved them.

"I'll go too, then." She snuck out a piece of the dried mango, popped it into her mouth and groaned before she held out the bag to him. When he shook his head, she shoved it into her shorts' pocket.

The groan that came from her went straight to his core. And his dick. Goddess help him. He wondered if that was what she sounded like when she came and... He shut that down right now.

He couldn't start fantasizing about her in an open market surrounded by his pack and other supernaturals. What the hell was wrong with him?

He slid a gaze over to her again, stole a glance at her bare, tanned legs. She'd gone with shorts because of the heat and he'd been in a state of distraction all day. Clearing his throat, he looked away, needing to stay focused on their surroundings. "Have you thought about offering your art here, as a vendor?" Her art was...incredible didn't do it justice. Her sculptures in particular were so realistic and detailed, they stole his breath.

"Yeah, I've been thinking about it but I can't decide if I should go with paintings or sculptures. Most of my sculptures are kind of big and I don't know that there's really a need for it." She shrugged.

The vampires, especially the ancient ones, coveted any kind of art. Anything unique. "Your work would get snapped up—ask some of the vampires for a trade. You'd be able to trade for anything you wanted. Guaranteed."

"Even dried mango?" Her grin was teasing, making her look young and carefree.

Goddess, that smile. His throat tightened once. When she looked at him like that, he fought to breathe. "Definitely dried mango."

CHAPTER NINE

Present day

"What?" Aurora shot King a look as they walked up the pathway to one of the city's healing centers. "You keep giving me weird looks." This was the third place they'd been to that morning, and they still had a couple more stops left. Some of this was just checking in with people, but they had dealt with a few issues. And even if she wanted to deny the Alpha tendencies she could feel growing inside her, she liked helping, *liked* being a liaison in the city. Before she'd been kidnapped, she'd been a social butterfly, as her sister had always called her. Being in the thick of things? Yes, please.

"I...it's your sweater. What the hell is up with it?" Confusion and something a little darker crossed his way-too-handsome face, his blue eyes going wolf for a moment.

She let out a surprised snort and glanced down. She'd snagged this off one of the kitchen stools before King had shown up. "Don't judge me, but I had no clean laundry so I grabbed this."

The sweater said *King of the Jungle*, had a picture of a cartoon lion on it, and Lola had bejeweled the mane.

"The lion wears that?"

"With pride." Her tone was dry. Axel loved the sparkly additions.

King gave the sweater another hard look and...oh. She wondered if he didn't like her wearing it because it belonged to Axel. *Oooohhhh.* She liked that, if it was true, but then wondered if she was just projecting. She'd be pissed if King was wearing some female's clothing. Which would be kind of weird. But still. King had never made a move on her. At all. And if he did...she wasn't even sure she could handle it. Not after what she'd been through. *Ugh.* She was a mess.

"Axel's in love with someone. Or so he says," she blurted. Then she inwardly winced. Normally she didn't like to gossip about her crew, but she had this weird urge to soothe whatever was going on with King. He'd been tense all morning.

Nothing overt, but it was like this energy buzzed around him. His shoulders were tense and they hadn't been joking around like they normally did. That could be on her though—she was all up in her head over him. Twisted up and annoyed at herself.

Some of the tension eased from his shoulders as they reached the front door. "Seriously?"

Huh. Maybe it *had* been the Axel thing. "Oh yeah. Don't say anything though. He's really sensitive right now. I've never seen him like this. He's been...whiny."

King just grunted as if he didn't believe it, but his mouth curved up ever so slightly in amusement. Then he opened the front door—they didn't need to knock at the healing center, even though it was in a residential location in the Irish Channel District. They had daylight and evening hours.

"Aurora, King! What a delight." She turned at the sound of Greer's voice. The tall dragon shifter with copper-colored hair and bright green eyes smiled at them as she stepped out of a sitting room off to the left that was more or less an intake room now.

Aurora let herself be enveloped by the tall female, closing her eyes for a moment. Greer reminded her of her own sister in a way, and damn, she missed Star right now. She desperately needed sisterly advice. "It's so good to see you." It had only been a week since she'd visited with the healer but it felt longer.

"You too." She gave King a welcoming smile and motioned for both of them to join her in the darkened sitting room.

Aurora was surprised all the curtains were drawn but then saw the male sitting by the fireplace. A vampire. She didn't know him, though he looked vaguely familiar.

"King." The blond male rose, nodding politely. When he stood, she realized he was just as tall as Greer. But he was lean and had a sort of boyish charm to that smile, though something about the way he moved and his subtle scent told her that he wasn't a newly turned vampire. He was dressed like he'd stepped out of the nineteen forties—and he pulled it off.

King nodded back, his expression neutral. "Christian. You've been injured?"

The vampire blinked. "What...no. I was visiting Greer last night, and before I knew it, it was daylight. So. Here I stay." He gave an elegant shrug, then glanced at Aurora with curiosity. Then...he frowned at her sweater.

Okay, it wasn't *that* weird.

"I'm glad to see you here, Christian," King continued. "Speak with me in another room privately?" It came out as a question but there was a subtle pulse of power in King's tone. One even Greer noticed because she straightened slightly.

"Ah," Greer cleared her throat and looked at the male. Then at King. "Right down the hallway through there." She pointed toward the foyer area to the left. "The first room on the right has the curtains drawn and the exterior panels closed. It's safe." She looked back at Christian, her expression softening into something almost maternal.

When they were alone, Greer pulled Aurora into another hug and squeezed.

"What was that for?" Aurora asked laughingly as Greer then motioned for her to sit in one of the comfy chairs by the fire.

"You look like you need a hug. And honestly, I do too. Reaper's only been gone for a day but I miss him."

"Oh, that's right. He's on one of the patrols looking for displaced humans and supernaturals, right?"

She nodded, pushing her long hair back over her shoulder. "It's shocking to me how many people they find each trip." Sympathy filled her eyes. "I'm a dragon so I wouldn't have been trapped anywhere. I just can't imagine how awful it's been for humans trapped without any real communication."

"I know. It's...I feel lucky." She knew she was, that everyone in the cities or territories run by solid Alphas were. "At least the people they find will have housing and some comforts. Have you seen the 'vertical forest' they've been working on?" Her friend Avery was the lead on the construction of The Grove and the place was incredible. Each balcony had a small fruit tree of some kind and there were natural plants positioned all over to help keep away mosquitos and other nuisances. She knew that they had witches and plant geneticists working on "top secret" ideas to implement as well.

"I saw it when I was out flying the other night. It's beautiful. So much color already. I heard they were going to add some waterfalls too?"

"Yes, and it's brilliant. They're going to be including a rainwater recycling system—and they've included that in all new builds over the last year. I'm fascinated to see how the city is changing, how things are becoming more sustainable. It gives me hope for the future." King gave her hope because he cared so damn much. He hadn't just rebuilt the city the way it had always been. No, he was planning for the future in a way humans simply hadn't. It was impossible not to have feelings for the man. Feelings she really, really didn't want to examine too closely.

"Me too."

"Is it extra quiet today or is it just me?"

Greer sighed and stretched her legs out. "It's quiet. I've only got two supernaturals upstairs, both here from work-related injuries. And they're going to be fine. Fewer patients is a good thing, but I hate not being busy when Reaper is gone. Gives me time to worry."

She reached out and squeezed her friend's hand. "Can you leave for a few hours tonight? With Marley back in town we'd planned to go out tonight to celebrate. We'd love to have you." Marley had moved back from Scotland, the original move with Star not suiting her. The weather was too cold, she'd said.

"Maybe?" She sighed. "The healers I would normally have cover for me are out of town on one of the recovery missions, so I'd hate to leave and have people show up hurt and not be here to help."

"I get it. Well, we need to get together sooner than later, regardless."

"Agreed. For just a minute I'm going to put on my healer hat—how are you? You haven't contacted me to talk officially in over a month so I just want to make sure you're good."

She glanced at the open doorway. She couldn't hear King, but that didn't mean King or others couldn't hear her. "I'm..." Her instinct was to say she was fine, but she bit her bottom lip. Greer had been her official therapist for the last year and Aurora trusted her. "I could use a talk. But not now. Later?"

"I'm wide-open today, so if you want to stop by before you head out tonight, we'll have privacy. Christian would never eavesdrop and he'll be gone anyway. I imagine my two patients will be gone in a couple hours too."

"Okay, I will. Thank you. I'll text before I come over though, just to confirm."

"Good." She smiled such a serene smile, it eased something inside Aurora. There really was something special about healers. "So…king of the jungle?" Greer snickered slightly.

"I think I'm going to turn this thing inside out," she murmured, laughing too.

* * *

King watched Christian lean against the whitewashed brick fireplace not currently in use. He was dressed elegantly in a style reminiscent of the nineteen forties, though King knew the vampire was much older than that era. He was older than King. But not as powerful. Right about now he was regretting asking to speak to Christian alone.

He'd never had an issue with the male. But the way the vampire had looked at Aurora had set off an alarm bell inside him.

Aurora was unique, had been kidnapped for the phoenix blood in her veins. She would always be a target because of that, and while he liked Christian on a superficial level, he didn't truly know or trust the male.

What he knew would fit in a matchbox, but the vampire had never caused trouble, didn't belong to an official coven—never had—and had once been mated. And he was friends with Greer, someone King respected. Which gave Christian points. He watched the vampire, his wolf in his eyes as he contemplated him.

"Have I done something to annoy the Alpha of New Orleans?" The question was asked mildly enough, but there was a hint of maybe not fear, but concern in his tone.

"How well do you know Aurora?"

Christian blinked, clearly taken off guard. "The female with you? Not at all."

"The look you gave her says otherwise." King knew he was likely overreacting, but he didn't take Aurora's safety lightly. She was his to protect, so if that meant he got possessive and extra protective, so be it. He was okay with that side of himself. And this wasn't just an Alpha thing—it was a mate thing. He knew she was his, even if she didn't seem to recognize it.

Christian pushed off the fireplace, no longer lounging casually. "It's the sweater that surprised me. I've seen it before. On someone else."

Now it was King's turn to blink. "The lion?"

The vampire's expression went neutral, but he nodded.

"They're roommates." Though King hated when Aurora wore that damn lion's clothes. He knew the male was a brotherly figure to her, but his wolf didn't care. His wolf wanted to rip the lion's head off on occasion. More often than not.

"I realized who she was a second after I saw the sweater. I was simply startled to see it on her, that's all." He sniffed haughtily. "It looks better on her anyway."

"True." The word was out before he could stop himself.

Christian lifted an eyebrow, but didn't respond.

"Is Claudine Bonavich mated?" King asked with no segue, wanting to take Christian off guard. Because Christian might not belong to a coven, but he knew the two were friendly.

Something flickered in Christian's dark eyes, there one instant and then gone the next. So he did know. He cleared his throat, and to King's relief the male nodded. "She is."

King would have hated it if the vampire had lied straight to his face. That would have meant he couldn't trust the male. "Okay."

Christian narrowed his gaze when King didn't continue. "You're not going to ask to whom?"

"No. I won't put you in the position to tell me something you don't want to. I know she's your friend." He actually did want to ask, and maybe he would later, if necessary. But he didn't want to force the male to give up information he wasn't comfortable with. That wouldn't create loyalty among his people. And Christian lived in his territory.

His expression thawed. "Thank you. I will say…you'll like her mate."

King simply nodded and motioned that the conversation was over. His wolf had been separated from Aurora for too long as it was.

As they stepped back into the sitting room, he had eyes only for Aurora. Today she'd allowed some of her phoenix to shine through, wasn't hiding her natural glow. He loved when she didn't hide that part of herself, though he understood that she'd had to for a very long time. Her long, dark hair was down in soft waves around her shoulders, and her dark violet eyes filled with warmth when she smiled at him. He wished he got all her smiles.

"Things are great here," she said, standing.

"Yes," Greer added. "I can take spillover from one of the human hospitals if necessary."

"I'll check, but I think things are quiet now." And something about that bothered him. As if this was the calm before the storm. After they'd said goodbyes and they were alone on the sidewalk, he said, "Do you know that male?"

"The vampire? No." She shot him a surprised look. "Why? Is he…bad news?" She lowered her voice, glancing around as if worried they'd be overheard.

Sometimes he forgot she didn't have the same senses he did. There was no one close enough to hear them. There were humans across the street walking, and shifters in nearby homes, but no one within earshot. "No. But I think he's the one the lion is involved with."

She blinked. "Ohhhhh. Oh, Axel," she said, shaking her head more to herself than anything. "Poor, sweet Axel."

"Sweet?" King snorted now. The lion was a troublemaker.

Aurora nudged him in the side, and just like that the ball of tension in his core eased a fraction. Things had been off between them today. She was one of the few beings who treated him like King. The male. Not the Alpha. From the moment they'd met she'd been honest with him about what she was. And it had humbled him.

"Come on, haven't you ever been in love?" she asked.

Well, that was a loaded question. One he wasn't touching. He deflected instead. "The lion—"

"His name is Axel," she said pointedly.

"I know, but it humanizes him to say it," he deadpanned. "And if I ever have to kill him—"

"King!" She nudged him again, this time harder.

Damn, he loved it when she said his name. He rolled his shoulders once. "He likes to push my buttons."

She snickered. "True. Speaking of button pushers, Prima asked me to teach a self-defense class she apparently started."

And there went the rest of the tension. Most of it. "I was wondering why you hadn't told me."

She frowned, stopping on the sidewalk. "What?"

"She told me about the class last night, said you'd be taking over while she was gone."

Aurora watched him for a long moment. "She told me about it *last night* too. Literally. Probably an hour or so before she apparently told you. Did you think I was keeping it from you?"

"No. Maybe." And it had bothered him right to his marrow. He always wanted her to share what was going on with her. Wanted to be involved in her life.

She took a step closer, her violet eyes bright. "I wouldn't do that. I..." She cleared her throat, glanced away, though her jaw ticked once. "You're the Alpha, yes," she said as she looked back at him, "but you're also my friend. I'll always have your back."

Claudine's words about needing a mate to support him echoed back to him, but he simply nodded, the knot completely unraveled at this point. "I know." No matter what, he trusted Aurora on a level that defied logic. But he simply couldn't push her. The power imbalance was too great. He was Alpha of the territory and he had an idea of what she'd been through when she'd been kidnapped. He could never, ever make her feel pressured, feel like she owed him or...hell. Holding back went against his nature, but that was too damn bad.

"Good." She started walking again and the weird energy that had hung suspended between them dissipated. "The class is fairly hardcore. I think I'll have to bring the tigers with me. And maybe Marley. Prima's got them doing drills and all sorts of badass stuff."

Absently rubbing at the middle of his chest, he half-smiled. "It sounds like the class is needed." He paused, then told her what Prima had said about the vampire females, about the vampire Myles who'd stopped by and how he figured he'd end up handling the male.

By the time he was done, they were close to a construction site where he was meeting up with Logan, one of the bear Alphas.

"Since Marley's back in town, Bella set up a night out tonight," Aurora said as they reached the crosswalk across the street from one of the schools. The playground was currently occupied by dozens of screaming, laughing kids, both supernatural and human. "If you feel like stopping by, we'll be at Cynara's club most likely the whole time."

He didn't frequent clubs or bars, not with his schedule. Hell, he never had. But if Aurora was going... "I'll be there. Have you heard anything regarding the new curfew?" He waved at one of the teachers he knew who was standing by the fence.

She snorted. "A few complaints, but most people understand. It's a smart move."

He'd made the decision to implement a "two nights a week only" thing where clubs were open all night. The rest of the week, places had to close at nine. Months ago, things had gotten out of control to the point where the nightlife was affecting the rebuilding of the city. The territory.

Once the territory was strong enough to withstand an attack and everyone had enough housing and other necessities, then life could gain more normalcy. Until then, he had to keep a measure of control. To his surprise, the pushback had been minimal, but he still liked to keep a pulse on things.

"From the sound of it, Lola and Bella are ready to let loose tonight." Aurora shook her head slightly. "And Lola's gotten it into her head to try to set me up on a date. How crazy is that? Do people even date anymore?" She snorted as if the very idea was insane.

His heart skipped a beat at her words, but he kept his expression neutral as they crossed the next street, even closer to their destination. *Date?* His wolf swiped at him. *Date?* The thought of her seeing another male made him want to kill something. Someone—this fictional male.

"How do you think Hunter would do at a club? I'm guessing not well," she said as the sounds of banging and voices grew louder. The construction site was fenced off, but as they turned onto another street, they got a view of The Grove sprouting up before them.

"It'd be too much sensory overload." Part of the reason he'd left the dragonling at home this morning. He was stopping at too many places, talking to too many people. Even as he answered her, the word *date* ricocheted around in his head.

It was one of the last things he'd ever expected her to say to him. She'd laughed it off, but her words were a reminder that she wasn't his. And he sure didn't need the reminder.

If the day came that she chose another male, that she mated with someone... King tightened his jaw. A red haze tinged the edge of his vision for a moment, but he shook it off.

He didn't want to think about how he'd react—how his wolf would.

CHAPTER TEN

"Thank you for taking the time to talk to me." Aurora looked at her sister's gorgeous face through her laptop screen—and was so damn grateful they still had some technology. Though even as she had the thought, the screen flickered once, Star's face fading out before it came back on-screen.

Star lifted a dark eyebrow. "I better never hear you thanking me for talking to *you*, my baby *sister*. Now what's going on? Your text was weird."

Aurora glanced at her closed bedroom door on instinct, but she knew everyone was down two floors and out of earshot. "I just miss you," she sighed, taking in her very happy-looking sister. Her chestnut-colored hair was pulled up into a bun, she wore a thick turtleneck sweater with a cowl-neck, and Aurora could see and hear a fire crackling in the background. A real one, in a huge stone fireplace of the castle Star lived in.

"I miss you too, but I know that's not it. Come on. Have you talked to Greer lately?"

"I saw her today and I'd planned to talk to her before we go out tonight, but I just canceled," she admitted.

"Why?"

"Because I'm feeling moody and only my big sister can help." A sister who'd been more like a mother since their own parents had been killed when Aurora was young. They'd always been close. Her sister had done everything to rescue her from captivity, would have outed all supernaturals to the world to save her.

Star watched her, the fire crackling in the background. Her violet eyes brightened slightly but she didn't say anything, just waited. She really had that whole patience thing down.

"I...I'm worried I'll never be able to have a normal relationship. To have sex again. To...have good sex." Saying the words aloud terrified her, but a weight also lifted. Talking to Star was just as good as therapy.

"That's a normal fear. But life is long. I think you'll get there. You're obviously thinking about sex if you're bringing this up. Right?"

"No. Maybe. Probably… Yes. I'm just scared. And feel pathetic admitting it. Especially after everything so many people have lost."

Temper flared in Star's eyes. "Please don't compare yourself to others. People have lost a lot. So have *you*. You lost a year of your life. No, it was *stolen* from you. You were held captive and had to make hard decisions to survive. There is no shame in that. None at all. You're a survivor."

"That's the problem," she blurted. "I do feel shame. That I let that bastard touch me at all." Nausea swelled up inside her when she thought of him. Time was helping her heal, but the visceral reaction still sometimes shocked her.

"You did what you had to, and you weren't letting him. Captives can't consent." Star's words were whiplash sharp. "You should never feel any shame," she repeated. "The only one who should is dead."

Yeah, by her. Killing him had helped her move on faster than she'd thought possible, but healing was a process. "I know that on an intellectual level, but…it's hard to get everything to line up in my heart, I guess." She blinked back a sudden rush of tears, not wanting to cry right now. She'd cried enough. "Claudine said something odd to me," she said, changing the subject.

Star didn't miss a beat. "What?"

"She said I needed to start inviting various powers around the territory over, to get to know them better. That I have the potential to be an Alpha's mate one day and should understand who's who more. I mean, that's essentially what she said. She basically chided me for not inviting her over before now. Is she…right?"

Her sister let out a soft sigh. "I hate to agree, but yes. I've learned as the Alpha female here that things are different when you're in charge, when people look to you for guidance. If…you think there's a chance that you and King will ever mate, then you need to prepare for that. And your territory is different than mine. Lachlan is from here, is established. King is a relatively new power, and claiming a territory previously considered neutral. You'll have different obstacles. But none of that matters if you decide you don't want to be mated."

"It's not like he's asked or anything." And she didn't want to be mated anyway. Right? Ugh, she was such a liar.

"Aurora."

"We've never even kissed."

"Aurora."

"Or held hands. Or cuddled. Or talked about the future. Or…anything."

Her sister simply watched her, her expression knowing. Far too knowing!

"What happens if we kiss and he wants more and I'm not ready?"

"Then you're not ready."

"What if I freak out and he can't handle it?"

"Then he's not the male for you."

Her phoenix pushed against her, not liking that sentiment at all. For so long she'd felt nothing but fear or loathing at the thought of physical touch from anyone, but lately with King…it was as if he was helping her come out of a fog. "You make it sound so simple."

"No, not simple. But you can toss out all the reasons you want and it won't change the fact that you want him. And I've seen the way he looks at you."

Yeah, she'd seen it too. A lot lately. At this point it was impossible to deny. Six months ago there had been a subtle shift between them, right after he'd slept in his room with her keeping watch, keeping everyone away so he could simply rest.

"What if I tell him about…everything and he judges me? Doesn't want me?"

Purple fire flared in Star's eyes, a brief flash of anger. "If he did—and I truly can't imagine that—then he would not deserve you. And I would likely burn him to ash."

"Star!"

"I'm joking." She shrugged. "Mostly. Why don't you take things one step at a time with him? Maybe let him know you're open to…something more than friendship?"

"You make it sound so easy." And she had no clue how to make the first move anyway. Or at least let him know she wanted more. She couldn't just come out and say it—mainly because she didn't know what she wanted. She shuddered at trying to have that kind of conversation. Too much awkward.

Star snort-laughed and shook her head. "I don't think it'll be easy. But I think it'll be worth it."

Aurora looked away, unable to hold her sister's gaze in that moment. She didn't want to be a coward, but actually opening herself up to more with King... What if he rejected her? Deep down, she knew he wanted her. He was always respectful, but there had been a shift in him lately when he looked at her. A shift that was echoed inside her as well. But wanting someone didn't really mean anything other than that.

Shaking those thoughts away and needing something lighter to talk about, she looked back at Star. "Axel is in love."

Her sister's eyes widened in true shock so clearly no one else had told her yet. "Tell me *everything*."

* * *

Cas did not care for the thumping music of the nightclub. Or the overwhelming scents and sounds surrounding them. But Jo and her sisters had wanted to go out.

And Jo...was stunning, in a wraparound dress the same color as her emerald eyes. He'd had far too many fantasies of slowly unpeeling the dress from her. Then devouring her, inch by inch.

She returned to the high-top table with her sisters, all laughing with each other. She was a few years older than her sisters and often took on a role of responsibility that he'd seen his own brother Mikael take on. But tonight she'd let her hair down literally and figuratively. And he loved the way her auburn hair fell around her shoulders and down her back in big, soft waves.

"Are you sure you don't want to come dance with us?" Luna said as she slid onto one of the barstools at the high-top table.

Jo simply snickered as she sat next to him. "Pretty sure he'd rather sit on hot coals."

He grinned at her because it was true. The only reason he was here at all was because she'd asked him to come. And he would never say no to her. Not even to sitting on hot coals.

Suddenly her eyes widened as her gaze trailed past him. A pop of delight rolled off her, sharp and wild, the scent sweet and heady.

Jealousy surged through him and he turned to see what had brought out this reaction. Then he frowned to see a table of females he knew. *Ugh.* And that stupid lion. Did…she find that annoying cat handsome? He looked back at Jo, found her still watching the other table, wide-eyed.

Without looking at him or her sisters, she blindly reached across the table and patted Luna's arm. "Guys," she hissed. "Oh my God, I think that's Marley. From Star's band. Right? That has to be her?"

Some of his tension eased as he realized she wasn't looking at the lion.

"Oh my God, that *is* her," Luna breathed.

"She's even more gorgeous in person," Grace continued. "I can't believe she's here."

"I can introduce you," he found himself saying against his will. The more he intertwined parts of his life, the more likely it would be that Jo found out he was a dragon. Which…he knew he should tell her. Kept trying to find the right way to. He tucked that thought away, tired of going around in circles in his head.

All three women stared at him with eyes of varying shades of green. He focused on Jo, who blinked. "Are you serious?" she whispered.

"Yeah. I don't know her well, but that's Aurora, one of her roommates."

"That's the Aurora you were talking to this morning? She's related to *the* Star?"

He nodded.

"Oh my God, please introduce us," Luna said.

He looked at Jo, eyebrow raised, basically asking if that was what she wanted.

Her mouth parted slightly and, oh goddess, he had thoughts. So. Many. Thoughts. Then she nodded, looking a little starstruck.

"Give me a couple minutes." He threaded his way through the mass of tables, ignoring the growing throb at the base of his skull from all the scents. Luckily he was a dragon and people tended to move out of the way.

"Cas!" Bella gave him a light hug as he reached the table.

"Ladies. Lion."

The females snickered at that, but instead of smirking, Axel just gave him a sullen look. That was odd. He ignored the lion and cleared his throat. "Ah, the human females I'm with are fans of yours, Marley." He felt odd being here at all, when he barely knew the snow leopard shifter. Her long braids were pulled back into a ponytail and she wore ripped jeans and an oversized sweater with a big rainbow on it.

Her amber eyes widened in surprise and she looked past him and half waved, a smile on her face. "Do they want to meet me?" she asked, looking up at him.

"Yes."

She jumped off the stool and gave her friends a smug look—but there was a hint of sadness in her expression she quickly masked. "Don't be jealous, y'all."

The others laughed as she and Cas headed back, and for once Jo's sisters were silent as they stared at Marley in awe.

He quickly made introductions, and within seconds Luna and Grace lost their shyness. Which was good, because it was unnerving.

He slid onto the stool next to Jo as Grace said, "I saw you live at Howlin' Wolf, and that solo you did… Amazing!"

Jo squeezed his knee once and gave him a wide-eyed look as she mouthed *Thank you*. And he felt twenty feet tall in that moment.

"Thank you." Marley's pale brown skin flushed under the compliment and her scent was pleased. "It's been a while since I played for fun."

"Seriously? If you ever want to jam, I'm free. Always," Luna blurted, then covered her face with her hands. "Sorry, I'm not even remotely cool enough to pretend it's not awesome meeting you."

Marley laughed, relaxing even more.

But all Cas could focus on was the fact that Jo had left her hand splayed lightly on his knee. Just…kept it there, almost as if she wasn't aware of it.

Conversation continued, with all four women talking about music and then science and…other stuff. And Jo's hand remained where it was, the imprint of it burning into his skin and making his entire body come alive. Was she aware of how she was touching him? Or was this an unconscious thing?

When Marley finally left the table with promises of calling Luna, who apparently played guitar, all three females stared at him.

Then Jo and her sisters tackle-hugged him. He froze for a moment as they all wrapped their arms around him, focusing more on Jo's hold than the others.

"You've been keeping secrets," Jo said as they all sat back.

Music still thumped around him, and though he tried to keep on smiling, the word *secret* had his throat seizing. He *was* keeping a big secret. One that could mean the end of their friendship.

"I'm kidding!" She must have misread his guilty expression because she squeezed his forearm.

"Well I'm not." Luna stared at him. "Any other wildly famous drummers you know?"

"She's the only one."

"Nana is going to flip when she hears about this," Grace said.

"Your grandmother likes her?"

"Well, she likes the band, but she's not a fangirl like Luna," Grace said, tossing back the last of her drink. "And I'm about done for the night. I don't think it can get any better so I say we leave now while we're riding this high."

Cas slid off his chair before she'd finished, making Jo and Luna cackle.

"Well I think we know where Cas stands," Jo said, linking her arm through his.

He had no clue what was happening, what had shifted between them—if it even had—but he liked how much she was touching him tonight.

It had to mean something. Right? Human females were so different from dragon females. Maybe she was just steadying herself—she'd had a couple drinks. He would always be there to steady her if she allowed it.

Instead of heading down the stairs and into the club, he motioned that they should all follow him to the back of the VIP room. There was an exit this way and it would be much easier to get out.

"Ooh, this is cool." Grace's eyes were wide as they stepped into a long hallway with purple walls and odd-looking wall hangings.

"Are we supposed to be back here?" Jo whispered, glancing up at him.

He grinned. "What if we're not? What happens if we break the rules?"

She blinked, then nudged him. "Oh, you're messing with me."

As they moved down the hallway, he breathed in deeply, drinking in Jo's sweet scent, thankful that the place had such good insulation. He could barely hear the music from before.

One of the side doors opened and Cynara—owner of the place—stepped out wearing a shocking purple dress that matched her hair. She blinked to see them, then smiled. "Hey, Cas. Surprised to see you here. Are your brothers here?"

"Not tonight. Mikael and Avery are out of town, but should be back soon." Mikael had surprised all of them, Avery included, and planned a trip to Scotland, a place Avery had always wanted to go.

"Oh right! Bo told me they asked Nyx for a favor. How long are they gone for?"

"They left this morning so…a week." Sort of a belated honeymoon. "And I have no idea where my other brothers are." Normally they told each other everything about their schedules, but Zephyr was on some sort of mission for King, and Ivyn was off helping a friend with something.

Cynara nodded and eyed the females curiously. "I'm Cynara. I own this place," she said warmly, her fangs flashing slightly.

"Apologies." He quickly introduced the three sisters, keeping his arm firmly linked with Jo's. He was glad she was still holding on to him.

"Oh my God, I saw you on TV after…everything." Luna stared, then punched Cas in the arm. "Seriously, how do you know all these famous people?"

Cynara snickered. "I wouldn't go that far. Not even close. But it's nice to meet all of you. I hope to see you around more." She gave Cas a curious look, but then frowned when one of her employees stepped into the hall with an emergency. "Duty calls," she murmured, hurrying away.

"How are your brother and his mate in Scotland?" Jo asked as they reached the top of a set of stairs that led to the back exit. "Did they…fly or something? I didn't really think many flights were happening right now. Not with the world…" Pain flashed in her eyes for a brief moment.

"Ah, it's going to sound bizarre."

"Nothing surprises us anymore," Grace said as she hurried down the steps in front of them.

"The female you just met, her brother is mated to a demigod. And she can transport people to places within moments."

As they reached the bottom of the stairs, Jo stared up at him. "I think my sister's wrong. That is…fascinating."

"Right?" Luna shoved open the exit door and he breathed in the cool, fresh air.

"That's like…sci-fi cool. Hey, Cynara is the one who pulled out that flaming purple sword, like out of thin air, right? From that video we saw?" Grace said.

The door shut behind them with a clang and he guided them down the quiet cobblestone street toward one bustling with people out to have a good time.

"Uh, *yeah*, that's why I said she was famous." Luna glanced back at him and Jo. "Can you tell us what she is?"

"Guys," Jo admonished. "It's not polite to ask."

"I thought you just couldn't ask someone to their face. Besides, I've had supernaturals straight up sniff me and tell me I smell awesome for a human," Grace said before stumbling once in her heels.

Luna cackled—and then stumbled next to Grace. Which just sent them into a bout of laughter.

"Oh boy, I think they've had too much to drink." Jo shook her head slightly, amusement clear in her scent and expression.

"We can hear you," one of them said above their laughter.

"Cynara is half-vampire, half-demon," Cas said for Jo's ears only as they hung back a couple paces.

She shot him a surprised look, her lips parting a fraction. "That's a lot to process. But so is the whole 'immediate transportation by a demigod' thing. I have so many questions about that."

Cas's gaze fell to her mouth. "Maybe I have answers."

She sucked in a breath and glanced away suddenly. In that moment he knew what he scented. *Raw lust.*

Oh fuck.

It nearly knocked him over, and his dragon suddenly blasted to the surface. Cas looked away quickly, knowing his dragon was in his eyes. Forcing the beast back, barely, he cleared his throat and hurried to catch up with the sisters as they turned onto St. Peter Street. There wasn't much crime since everything had happened, but he still wanted to keep them close. Because they were humans in a supernatural-run world and were vulnerable. And hell, he was protective of all of them.

The walk back to their place took a solid half hour—he wished he could have just flown them. Jo's sisters disappeared inside, still giggling and loudly shushing each other at the same time.

"You're correct about how much alcohol they imbibed. I believe it was too much."

Jo snort-laughed and tugged him over to the swinging bench seat on the wide front veranda instead of heading inside. "Can I ask you something?"

"Anything." *How about to get naked?* his dragon purred.

"Are you dating anyone?" she blurted. Her eyes widened, presumably at herself, but then she just watched him, waiting for his answer.

"No." He understood the human concept of dating, but dragons didn't do that. He frowned. Wait, why was she asking? "Are you?" he demanded, far too harshly.

But she just laughed lightly. "Uh, no." Her gaze fell to his mouth and he scented that wild lust again. It punched through to his core, intertwining with his last shred of sanity.

Fuuuck. It was so overpowering, his dragon clawed at the surface, demanding that he finally claim his female. But if they kissed...

He jolted to his feet and she let out a little yelp as the bench swung back under the force. "I have to go," he said as he steadied the chain. "It's late." It was like midnight.

"Oh." She stared at him with a mix of emotions and looked as if she wanted to protest, but she stood too. "Okay," she said as she pulled him into a quick hug.

He held on to her, inhaled against the top of her head, the mix of her shampoo and natural scent making him feel out of control. So he acted like a coward and turned and left. All he had to do was just admit what he was, and if she rejected him, then he would know where he stood.

He didn't run as he left, but he was running.

From himself. Her. Everything.

Fuck him.

CHAPTER ELEVEN

King stepped into the PT room of a local physical therapy place to find it bustling despite being after midnight. After spending most of the day with Aurora, he was still going strong. And not obsessing about the fact that she'd brought up dating.

Nope. Not one bit.

She hadn't said she was looking to date other males—not that they were dating. But she'd brought up the subject all the same.

He scanned the room, saw that two of the stationary bikes, one rowing machine and three treadmills were in use, and a human recovering from something was using resistance bands.

A few of his wolves were sitting on the edge of some of the physical therapy beds, each talking to a physical therapist.

The only person not talking to anyone was Ezekiel, who was slowly making his way across the room on his new prosthetic leg. King didn't have much knowledge in this area, but he'd never seen anything like this prosthetic before.

"Hey, King." Ezekiel grinned at him as he approached, moving a little faster, strutting like a feline instead of the wolf he was. "Check me out." He jumped straight up, nearly touched the ten-foot ceiling and landed with only a wobble. His prosthetic attached right below the knee and was a sleek silver rod.

"Damn. Is this the new one I've been hearing the witches talk about?"

"Witches and humans," Ezekiel said pointedly. "And yes." He stretched his left leg out slightly, his blue gym shorts shifting with the movement.

King looked it over, amazed by how the top part molded to his skin with pure seamlessness. "How do you like it?"

"So far it's incredible. I never imagined I'd be here, but..." He shrugged.

King simply nodded. Ezekiel had been on a rescue mission of humans that had turned into an ambush by two rogue dragons who'd been living out in the wild, preying on anyone they could. One of the dragons had managed to clip his left leg, and with the heat of its fire had destroyed Ezekiel's leg. Some shifters could eventually grow back body parts, but the damage had been too severe.

"Any phantom pains?" King asked.

"Some, but not like I used to have. One of the human scientists who works at the lab stopped by earlier in the week and explained some of it to me...though most of it's over my head. I don't care, as long as this works." He shifted from foot to foot, clearly enjoying the freedom of movement.

"Are you planning on making it permanent if it's offered?" Right now humans and witches were working on a prototype that would essentially become part of a patient's body, not something that could be removed. At least not easily. The only issue with a shifter was, figuring out how to integrate that after shifts.

"Maybe. I'll see what Luna thinks." He shrugged, in a much better mood than the last time King had seen him.

"Luna?"

Ezekiel cleared his throat, his bronze cheeks flushing slightly. "Ah, Dr. O'Connor. She's the scientist I told you about."

King knew who she was—she came from a talented family. "I'm glad to see you well." He clasped Ezekiel's upper arm once, squeezed.

Ezekiel smiled. "Me too. I...I've been talking to Greer. She's helped me put things into perspective a lot. She's also made it clear that it's okay to have setbacks, just that I have to admit to myself if I'm feeling depressed. She says acknowledging emotions is a good thing."

King blinked in surprise at Ezekiel's openness, but nodded. "She's correct."

"So what are you doing here tonight anyway?"

"Just checking on you."

"Seriously?"

"You're one of my people," he said simply. Ezekiel had been injured on a mission King had sent him on. He knew he shouldn't feel guilt over what had happened, but heavy was the head that wore the figurative crown.

"Oh…thank you." Ezekiel's cheeks flushed again.

"I also wanted to talk to you in person about getting back on patrols. I know you'll need to think about—"

"I'm ready!" His shout caused a few heads to turn.

"I want you to think about it."

"I don't need to. I miss working, miss being around my pack on the regular."

King nodded, trusting Ezekiel to know what he was capable of. "All right, then. Ari will contact you about getting back on the rotation."

"Thanks. I'll let you get back to it, then. Hey, if you see Aurora, will you thank her for the class? I had to leave before I could talk to her, but it was really cool what she did."

"Class?"

"Yeah, she brought a bunch of canvases and supplies down here a week ago and taught a class for those who aren't mobile enough to make it to her place. I could've, but not everyone can. It was dope."

King wouldn't use the word "dope," but he would pass along Ezekiel's thanks. "I'll let her know."

Damn, there she went again, getting under his skin. In his bones. She was always taking care of people, even in small ways. She went out of her way to help others and never made a big deal about it. Speaking of…

When he heard her ringtone, he murmured goodbye to Ezekiel and pulled his cell out, already heading for the door. He'd planned to talk to one of the physical therapists about something, but if Aurora was calling him after midnight, there was an issue.

"Hey," he said.

"We have a problem." Her voice was pitched low, and he could hear others faintly in the background.

He straightened as he stepped out into the cold night air, a full moon illuminating the quiet street. Other than the physical therapy center, all the other industrial buildings in the area were closed. "Are you okay?" The one thing that mattered most.

"I'm fine. But," she dropped her voice again, "Harlow called me. Said she found something really strange. A bunch of humans in a sort of coma-like state. They're not dead, but something's wrong with them." Her voice got even lower and it sounded as if she was covering her phone. "Harlow doesn't get freaked out by anything and she's worried. No one else knows. She wanted me to call you. Where are you? I'll meet you and we can go to her together."

Harlow should have called him first, but... He quickly gave her his location.

"I'll be there in five. I'll be flying." She hung up without waiting for a response.

King quickly messaged Ace to tell him what he knew, then called Harlow. When she didn't answer, he stripped and rolled his clothes into a bundle he could carry. As he stood, Aurora descended from the sky, a gorgeous phoenix with flames of pale blue covering her entire body. She didn't fully shift to her phoenix form, however. She kept her human form, only extending her wings and releasing her brilliant fire. Even her wings were made of pure fire. He stared at her, bathed in the beauty of her light.

"King," she breathed out as she touched down, her gaze sweeping his mostly naked form with a trace of shock.

He kept his bundle of clothes held directly in front of his dick, but he wasn't ashamed of his nudity. Shifters didn't care much about it. Though she lived with shifters like him, she was different, didn't need to strip to release her wings. "Does this bother you?"

"No, of course not," she rasped out too quickly, clearly not daring to look anywhere but his face. And the scents rolling off her were...very interesting.

Right in that moment, he hated being Alpha. Because they had shit to take care of. He didn't have time to analyze those scents. "Do you have an exact location on Harlow?" He'd texted Ace before because he was patrolling in the same vicinity as Harlow. Hell, she should have contacted Ace about this before Aurora too. He'd deal with that later.

"Sort of." She held out her cell phone and the GPS screen was...flickering in and out.

"I know exactly where this is. It's in the vicinity of her patrol area. I'll get there faster in my wolf form than if we drive. You good to follow from the air?" So far she'd been his liaison for all the assholes in the territory he didn't want to deal with. And even the people he liked but still didn't want to deal with. This was different. This could be dangerous.

"Yeah."

He nodded and dropped his bundle of clothes, heard her gasp as he shifted to his wolf form. His wolf practically purred at that sound, but he bottled everything up, scooped up his clothes and started running. In his wolf form he was faster than regular wolves, faster than most shifters and even vampires.

Buildings, then houses, then more buildings rolled by him in a blur as he ran through the city. He raced down I-10—which currently had no vehicles on it—winding his way slightly north toward a wildlife management area in Ponchatoula. Before everything, it would have taken forty minutes with traffic. It took them fifteen minutes.

As they reached the swamplands, he glanced upward and Aurora started to descend, a bright beacon who'd been guiding his entire run.

She landed when he stopped by the start of a wood-planked walking trail. The gravel parking lot was empty, save for a couple backpacks of food supplies and clothes left by those patrolling tonight. "You want me to stay in the air and follow?"

"Maybe." He tugged on his clothes and glanced out at the open freshwater marsh, inhaled the scents of wild vegetation. He could also scent a couple of his people, including Harlow. He'd been here many times over the years, and the trails wrapped around for miles, in and out of the marsh. Kayakers paddled here in droves during the day—or they had before The Fall. Now it was more sporadic. "I need to check in with Ace. Did you see anything from the air?"

"Nothing out of the ordinary."

Ace and Harlow jogged out of the shadows, both in human form as they hurried down the planked walkway. As they reached them, Harlow nodded once at Aurora then looked at King with a sort of wince. "I'm sorry for not calling you first. It's not an excuse but Star was my Alpha for a long damn time and that's transferred to Aurora. I should have followed the chain of command."

He blinked at how quickly she owned up to it. Well damn, it was hard to be too annoyed with her for the exact reasons she'd just spelled out. And...his wolf was sometimes crafty, liked to play the long game. *Use this to make a point*, his wolf growled. "It's okay. You can always contact Aurora about anything, even on missions."

Ace's eyes widened at the clear implication. Hell, not implication—King was spelling it out clearly in a way he never had before. He couldn't push Aurora but he could be clearer. With his people and her people.

Surprise flickered in the tall redhead's eyes for a moment, but then she nodded, quickly taking that in stride.

Aurora...didn't seem to even understand what he'd just done. *You need to be more blunt*, his wolf growled even louder.

Harlow nudged Ace. "Don't be all sulky. I said I was sorry about not contacting you either."

"I don't sulk." His tone was dry.

She rolled her eyes and looked back at King and Aurora, all business. "The humans I found look as if they'd been out kayaking, then decided to explore on foot. There weren't any drag marks near the bodies or indications of a struggle. We found kayaks about half a mile from their location on the water and we've both scent-tracked all the humans back to the kayaks so it's ninety-nine percent certain the boats are theirs. They're...all sort of peaceful looking. But they're not able to wake up, nothing. It's truly like they're in a coma."

"Cat's guarding them," Ace added. "No one else knows about this."

Coldness spread through him as he digested Harlow's words. When Aurora gently touched his forearm, the band of tension inside him loosened. He knew he hadn't given anything away with his expression but she seemed to read him.

"You know what this is?" she asked him.

Damn, she did read him. "Maybe."

Ace looked surprised and Harlow was just scanning the area at high alert, her tiger in her eyes.

"Let's go. Stick with us," he said to Aurora. He didn't want her flying ahead of them. He knew she could protect herself, but...this had echoes of his past.

A bloody past he'd long since buried, and he wanted her safe.

She nodded and they fell in step together, following Harlow's lead.

"It's about two miles from here," Harlow said before breaking into a jog.

Moving at their supernatural pace it didn't take long to reach their destination. And King scented it—him—before they'd stopped. Traces of the male he'd killed long ago.

Lucius.

The vampire hybrid wasn't here anymore, but for a moment images flashed in his mind.

Blood-soaked grass.

Screaming.

Flames licking into the twilight sky, bathing the blues and purples in red.

He blinked the images away as he neared the four humans. They were propped up against an oak tree, one after the other, surrounding it. Their eyes were closed, hands limp beside them, but their chests rose and fell.

"Are they glowing?" Aurora murmured as she knelt down in front of a woman possibly in her thirties.

The woman's dark hair was pulled up into a ponytail, and she wore a puffy vest over a long-sleeved T-shirt and yoga-style pants. She looked exactly as if she'd been out kayaking. They all wore similar gear. And Harlow was right, there were no drag marks.

"It'll fade." He'd seen this before, seen Lucius steal life force from humans but leave them alive. They went through stages and should awaken eventually. It was anyone's guess if they would wake up with their memories. It just depended on how much the bastard had taken. The only reason Lucius would have left them alive, however, would be if he'd been interrupted. Hadn't wanted to be caught.

"You're very sure of that," Ace said.

Nodding, he looked up at his lieutenant, his friend. "I am. I've seen this before. I...this smells like a vampire hybrid I thought I killed over a hundred years ago. He shouldn't be alive, shouldn't be here at all. But if he is, he's in my territory for one reason. To kill me. We need to transport the bodies back to Greer's center," he said as he stood, scanning the wooded area. Because Lucius was a powerful hybrid with unknown, vast powers.

"Kill you?" Aurora frowned, her eyes glowing.

"He'll try."

"He'll fail," she snapped out, whiplash sharp.

King simply nodded, watching her. Moonlight filtered through the trees, but Aurora's natural glow gave off enough light that everything was highlighted clearly around them.

"What's the plan after we get the humans to the healer?" Ace asked, drawing his attention away.

"Then..." King sighed. "I'm going to call a meeting with all the powers in the city. I want to keep this quiet for now, only tell those who need to know. I'm going to reach out to some researchers I trust too."

"How powerful is this hybrid?" Aurora asked. Her tone was neutral enough, but her glowing eyes gave away her emotions.

"If he survived what I did to him...he's more powerful than I realized. His bloodline is ancient and dark. He drinks the life force of beings to sustain himself. He's evil. To his marrow."

Aurora's expression was tense. "If you want to transport the humans covertly, I saw Casimir, ah Cas, out earlier. He could carry all of them."

King nodded then looked at Ace, nodded again for him to make the call to Cas.

Things had just gotten a lot more complicated.

CHAPTER TWELVE

"You want to talk about this ancient evil that's decided to come to New Orleans?" Aurora asked as she and King walked down the deserted two-lane highway.

He'd already assured her that no one was close enough to overhear their conversation so she felt free to talk. She'd asked him if they could just walk, the two of them, after Cas had transported the humans back to the city proper. Something told her that he needed just a couple minutes to process what was going on, before he returned to all his Alpha duties.

They'd both reached out to the powers in the city and would be meeting with everyone in less than an hour.

"Not really." His tone was as dry as his expression when he glanced at her.

She glanced up at the moonlit sky as they strode down the quiet highway. It was almost eerie out here like this, but for the moment she liked it. Liked being alone with just King. "I've been struggling, emotionally, the last couple weeks," she said into the quiet. If she wanted King to open up, she figured she should go first. And she wanted him to know this part of her. She might be a mess inside, but she understood that if she wanted to take any sort of "relationship" step with him, she had to open up.

"How so?"

"Having dreams—nightmares—about my time in captivity. He took a lot of my blood at a time, to keep me weak. Whenever I started to feel stronger, he'd drain more again. Round and round. And he kept me trapped in..." She cleared her throat. As a phoenix, she tended to keep information about her kind private. All phoenixes did. But she trusted King. It was just years of habit—born out of a sense of survival—that had her stumbling. "A room laced with iron. It was a very effective prison for my kind."

King's jaw tightened once. "I'm glad you killed him." His tone was savage, lethal.

"Me too." She wasn't remotely violent by nature, but killing the dragon who'd imprisoned her had set something free inside her. "I've been doing so well. Or I thought I was."

"Has anything changed for you lately?" His deep voice was soothing, a comfort right down to her soul.

"I don't know." She did know, but she didn't want to come out and say that she'd been thinking about sex—with him—on an industrial level. Her thoughts had been consumed with it. But not just sex. Her mind was a jumbled mess where King was concerned. "Like what?"

He looked up at the sky for a moment as they walked, a sudden breeze rolling over them.

She let her wings extend farther, though she wasn't flying, enjoying the way her muscles stretched and flexed.

"Any important dates coming up?"

She looked up at the sky too, saw the shadows of large dragons swooping through the clouds. And that was when it registered. "The anniversary of my parents' murder. It's a week away." Was that why she was all twisted up? No. Maybe. Huh. It was probably at least part of what was going on with her.

"It could be affecting you. And I'm sorry about your parents."

"Thank you. I was five when we were attacked. Star ran away with me, to get me to safety. She was barely grown herself, but our parents screamed at her to run. Ordered her to. So she flew faster than I'd ever seen and then the screams were over."

He cursed softly. "Dragons have not been kind to your family."

She lifted a shoulder. "It still stuns me that my sister mated with one—but he would die for her. And he loves her." And her sister's mate had definitely killed for her. Aurora adored Lachlan, and his family. She was friends with other dragons now as well—something that would have been an odd concept years ago. "She killed the dragons who killed our parents. I didn't fully understand what she was doing at the time. I was still five and she left me with Kartini's parents. You remember her?" Kartini had moved to Scotland with Star.

He nodded. "Of course."

"Star told me that she had to take care of things, to make sure I would be safe. Then she and the others just left. I overheard Kartini's parents talking, and it finally registered what she'd meant. I was still scarred by their deaths, by losing half of my whole world in an instant. But when I realized she'd gone off to kill their murderers…I was glad for it."

"Nothing wrong with that."

"Maybe, maybe not."

"No maybe about it. They went after your family simply for the blood that runs in your veins, for *greed*. You were five. A child. They would have stolen your blood, killed you too. Beings like that don't deserve to draw breath, to walk on the same planet as us." He said it so matter-of-fact.

"You don't struggle with…killing?"

"No." His answer was short, simple. Then he looked at her, his wolf in his eyes. "I've only ever killed to protect my own. I don't hunt down others for the thrill of it. If anyone ever threatens my family, my people, I will kill them with no guilt, no compunction. My wolf knows who he is."

A shiver ran down her spine, not from fear of him, but from the Alpha she could feel rolling off him. It was sharp, potent waves pulsing in the air, the faintest shimmer of energy coming off him. And a reminder that he wasn't human—*they* weren't. "Glad you're on my side."

His lips curved up slightly, his wolf fading away as they neared the on-ramp for I-10. "You want to keep walking?"

"I'm enjoying this uninterrupted time with you," she said bluntly. She'd heard his phone buzz with a few texts, but he'd ignored them.

He blinked, surprised by her words, but nodded and they headed up the ramp once used only for vehicles. Right now it wasn't seeing much use, but that might change in the future. He had people working on the roads, improving them so things weren't just crumbling.

"Lucius is the male I scented in the woods," King said. "He left his scent on the humans. The fact that he left them alive and out in the open…" He paused. "Relatively in the open. It's an odd choice."

"You think it's a message?"

"Possibly. But it would have been smarter to simply come after me without giving me warning. Not leave the humans for me to find."

"Maybe he didn't mean to leave them. Maybe he was interrupted."

King nodded. "That's my thought too."

"Why is he coming after you at all?"

King was silent as they trekked up the ramp, the moment stretching so long between them she'd given up on him answering when he said, "When I was five years old, he kidnapped my mother and me when we were out in the woods. I...don't even know where we were. I just remember it was green everywhere and the sun was warm on my face. We were set upon by this monster. I don't know why, but I know he hated my father. That's why he took us."

"Who is your father?"

He glanced at her, his expression opaque. "I don't know. But Lucius took us to hurt him. And he loved to hurt my mother—to hurt me to hurt her. He was this being made of rage and anger. He'd broken all of my bones more than once before I turned six. He found it fascinating how fast I healed. And he loved to hear me cry. So I stopped giving him what he wanted." His jaw tightened.

Aurora sucked in a breath, a haze of pain and rage descending on her vision. He'd been only five years old, the same age as her when her parents had been killed. But she'd been protected by her sister, her pack. And he'd been... She couldn't even imagine.

King gave her a startled look. "Your eyes are glowing."

She blinked once, got her emotions under control. Mostly. "You were a baby, to be protected." If that monster came after King, she would be by his side, ready to fight, to blast that bastard into the afterlife.

His expression darkened as he nodded, and he looked ahead instead of at her. "When I was seven, I escaped my prison because one of his people had been careless. I killed that vampire—a regular one, not a hybrid—then managed to unlock my mother's prison. He kept us separated—a special hell for my mother, keeping her from her child. He wasn't there that day. It's the only reason we escaped. He'd have hunted us down, but as it was we had a head start. I hid the body of the vampire I killed and we escaped using daylight to get as far away from our prison as possible."

"Where did you go?"

"A lot of places at first. Our prison was in Alaska—what's now Alaska. It was a Russian colony then. My mother was smart and resourceful and she convinced a boat captain to take us all the way down the coast to Mexico. The trip was long and uncomfortable but traveling by water is what kept anyone from tracking us. At least that's what I think. From there we just kept running and hiding. We spent a lot of time in South America, various Caribbean islands, then we came back to La Nouvelle-Orléans. The place of my birth." There was a sort of wistful note in his voice. "We didn't stay long though. We joined a pack living in the wilds of Wyoming, built up allies, and Lucius eventually came for me. But I was older then, not a child—and I killed him."

"Did he..." She cleared her throat. "Kill your mother?" He'd never said what happened to her.

"No. She died of a sort of blood sickness. It's rare, only affects shifters. The healers of our pack tried everything they could, but..." He shook his head, his jaw clenching tight.

"I'm sorry. Maybe...it's not Lucius you scented in the woods?"

King shook his head. "It's him. Though I don't know how, if I'm being honest. I ripped his heart out then set him on fire."

Yep, that should have done it. And was better than what that monster deserved. "Can I ask you something personal?"

"More personal than all this?" He lifted an eyebrow, amusement in his ice-blue eyes despite the heavy topics.

"A different kind of personal. I'm just curious why you want to run a territory? Humans seem to crave being in power for all the wrong reasons. Selfish ones. But you..." She blew out a breath. "It's different. And it's different with some of the other Alphas I know. I'm just being curious, I guess. Running the whole territory of New Orleans and beyond is a lot of responsibility. One you don't *have* to take on."

He didn't even pause. "When I was young I couldn't protect my mom. I don't know if that plays into it, but I've got this burning, innate need to protect. Ace always says it's part of my DNA. Says I was like that when I was a teenager. A pup, really."

"Were you?"

He snorted softly. "Yeah. I loathe bullies and never backed down from protecting anyone who couldn't defend themselves. I think if the dragons hadn't gone rogue, destroyed so much, humans would have destroyed the planet anyway. At least now we've got a chance to do things differently. Better. I'm probably not answering your question right, but I want to give people the chance to live the lives they deserve."

Damn. Aurora digested his words, rolled them around in her head. He really was a good male. Just...good right down to his core.

At that thought, his earlier words replayed in her head about the monster who'd broken a little boy's bones just for fun. Her fire pulsed around her, and on impulse she reached for King's hand. She couldn't protect that little boy, but she was damn sure going to be by the man's side if the vamp hybrid came for him.

To her relief, he took her hand. And he kept holding it.

CHAPTER THIRTEEN

King stood in front of the room full of shifters, vampires, witches and a handful of humans. He'd asked everyone who was in charge of a sector of the territory to speak with him in a relatively empty warehouse. He had a few of his wolves outside keeping guard, but there was no one around for at least half a mile so no one should be able to overhear.

"We need to make sure we protect the humans," Logan said. It wasn't much of a secret the bear shifter was obsessed with a human female—who was currently out of the city working on a construction project for King.

"What kind of powers does this hybrid have?" Ingrid asked, ignoring Logan completely.

"Should we call in all the dragons and others who are out on rescue missions?" This was from Dallas, a powerful witch, concern in her voice. Her mate was a dragon, but not out on a mission. He was right next to her, his expression unreadable as usual.

King dug deep for patience. He'd known calling this meeting would create a lot of questions. Understandable ones. "Lucius is powerful. He likes to target those weaker than him—humans specifically. But he loathes shifters of all kinds. And if you're alone and he thinks he can take you, he'll come after you and suck out your life force, regardless of species. I don't know enough about him, just that he's dangerous to everyone, especially humans. If he was at full power right now, we wouldn't be having this conversation because he would have already attacked the city. I think us finding those humans was a mistake on his part. He must have been interrupted and ran."

Logan started to say something else, but Aurora stepped up next to King.

"Logan, we're going to protect all humans. King's going to implement a curfew starting tomorrow—ah, tonight. Any work in the city will be limited to daylight hours right now." She looked up at King, but he just nodded. He wanted her to grow into this role, and whether she realized it or not, she was made for it. Made for him. He just wished she realized it. "And everyone, human and supernatural alike, will be asked to take a partner everywhere they go."

"I expect every leader to have check-ins with your people. Keep track of everyone," King said, looking out at all of them. "He is one being, but if I were in his shoes, I know what I'd do. I'd go after loners, people on the outskirts of the territory." He looked at Dallas and Rhys. "Which is why I'm bringing in most of our people now to shore up all outer areas of the territory."

Dallas and Rhys both nodded, satisfied. Rhys lived with Dallas in a farming community on the outskirts and was a big help in protecting that area.

"What are his specific powers?" Claudine asked, her tone neutral.

"He can control earth elements. And he can call forth reapers." Creatures from a Hell realm with no soul who loved nothing more than to kill.

Silence descended on the warehouse for a long moment as they digested this information. Reapers were the stuff of nightmares for supernaturals. Forget about the humans' boogeyman. The only reason King had been able to kill Lucius was because he'd been prepared—had been preparing for the day Lucius came after him for decades. So when it happened, he'd been ready and had separated him from his precious reapers.

King fielded more questions as Aurora spoke quietly to Claudine, then Logan—who gave her a big hug when they were done talking. King wasn't sure what they'd talked about, but he'd heard her say "Zia" once so she must have been assuring him Zia was fine.

King tried to keep his focus on Thurman—a human seer—but his gaze kept straying back to Aurora. To his surprise, Thurman clapped him once on the upper arm, his face crinkling as he smiled. "You've got a lot to handle right now so I'm going to go. But I'll keep my neighborhood safe. Always have."

Not many people were allowed to touch him physically—no one outside his pack anyway—but Thurman was different. The man was part of New Orleans itself, woven into its fabric. And even though King was older than the male, Thurman had earned his respect in more ways than one. Plus King's mother had adored the man's now deceased father—and had made King promise to look out for him and his bloodline.

King knew multiple vampires over the years had offered to turn Thurman, but he'd said no to every one of them. He didn't want a longer life, he said. He was happy with the one he had. At seventy or eighty, he'd already lived a full one, though King hoped he had more years to come.

King cleared his throat. "I apologize for my distraction." He also didn't apologize to many, but he realized he was being rude and not paying attention. At all.

Thurman simply looked over at Aurora, then back to King. "I remember how it was when I was young and in love. Let me know if you need anything." Then he was gone, heading over to speak to Dallas, who Thurman had a soft spot for.

Half an hour later, everyone was gone except Aurora and Ace, who only now stepped back into the warehouse. Ace nodded once, letting King know all was fine outside.

"How are you going to make sure everyone checks in?" Aurora asked, looking exhausted. She'd pulled her wings completely in so they weren't visible at all. He wasn't exactly sure how that worked, but only a soft blue glow lit her skin. No flames, just a subtle hue that literally lit up the space around her.

King tempered the urge to reach out and cup her cheek, stroke her skin. He didn't have that privilege. She'd held his hand earlier, but he'd taken that for what it was. A stolen moment. She was still holding back from him and he was still trying to respect the pace she was setting. A difficult feat when his wolf was clawing away at him, demanding action.

"I'm trusting everyone to do what they're supposed to do." His territory was vast and there was no actual way to know everything. It was why he had strong people he trusted in charge of different areas.

She nodded, stifling a yawn.

"We need to handle the Hill coven," Ace said without emotion, but his wolf flared in his eyes as he spoke.

"I know." He hadn't included Myles in this meeting because he wasn't a power in the territory—he was nothing. "Claudine will be keeping an eye on his coven, but I'm not letting him know about this. I'll handle him once Lucius is dealt with." Or sooner if the situation warranted. But Hill was a gnat compared to the real threat.

Aurora yawned again and this time he didn't temper the need to touch her. He pulled her up against him, wrapping his arm around her shoulders and tugging her close as he guided them out of the warehouse. Her rich scent wrapped around him, settled into him.

"You need sleep," he murmured.

"I'm fine. Could go for another couple hours," she said around a yawn, even as she leaned into him.

She molded right up against him, exactly where she should be.

"Clearly," Ace murmured, amusement in his gaze as he looked at the two of them. "Come on, I'll escort you home."

King's instinct was to protest and his wolf must have shown in his gaze because Ace froze, looking surprised. He'd already asked Ace to take Aurora home after this meeting—he still had things to deal with before dawn. But his mating instinct swelled up, wanting to keep her by his side, to claw anyone who tried to get between the two of them.

His wolf really was an asshole.

Luckily Aurora didn't seem to notice as they stepped out into the cool night air. She leaned her head against King for a moment, then pulled away as she said, "I'm going to crash so hard. Please tell me you're going to go home and get some sleep too?"

"I could tell you that." His tone was dry. The truth was, he never wanted to lie to her, not even about something small. He wouldn't be resting for a long while.

"I'll make sure he gets some sleep," Ace said as he tugged her toward a waiting Jeep.

Aurora grumbled but didn't argue and he was glad they were driving. She didn't look awake enough to fly home. The look she gave him as Ace pulled out of the parking lot was... He wasn't sure what it was.

But he knew he liked it.

Things had shifted between them on the walk back tonight. He just wasn't sure what that meant. And the lack of control, the not knowing, was making his wolf edgy. Pushing him to distraction at a time he couldn't afford it.

* * *

Aurora stepped out of her bathroom, fresh from a shower, hair wrapped in a towel. Last night, or this morning really, had been emotionally exhausting but she also felt a hundred times better after opening up to King. Almost charged up.

Her cell phone buzzed on her nightstand and she recognized the ring, hurried to grab it. "Hey!"

"Hey yourself. Just checking in on you," Star said, and Aurora could practically hear the smile in her voice. "How are you feeling this morning?"

"A hundred times better."

"Good."

"So what's up with you this morning?" She glanced out her window, could just see ribbons of color on the horizon. The sun would be up in less than an hour. Which meant she'd gotten all of three hours of sleep.

"Eh, it's afternoon here," Star said, laughing. "And Lachlan and I have a trip planned to visit an ally in a couple days. I'll be harder to reach so I wanted to let you know I'd be mostly dark for a while."

"Fun Alpha stuff?"

Star snorted. "It's never-ending, I swear."

"Is it weird not being able to tell your friends—Kartini and the others—stuff? Like, to keep things from them when necessary?"

"Oof. Yeah, sometimes. But that's just the mantle of responsibility. Are you asking for a specific reason?"

"Eh." She wasn't supposed to say anything to anyone about what they'd found last night. King wanted to keep the circle small. "Sort of."

"But you can't talk about it?"

"Not really."

"I get it. But I've got your back no matter what."

"I know. And in case I don't say it enough, I love you more than anything. You took on the role of raising me and made everything look so easy. You protected me my whole life and then saved me from a greedy dragon. You're the walking definition of what it is to be selfless. You're the best sister I could have ever asked for, Star." When she didn't respond, Aurora looked at her phone screen to see if it had disconnected. "Star?"

"Yeah, sorry, tearing up a little." Her voice was watery. "Wasn't expecting that."

"Well it's true." At a loud shout from outside, she peeked her head out the window. The solar Edison-style lights were still throwing off a glow. "Crap. Axel's in a brawl with that vampire," she hurried out. "I've gotta go, but I'll call you back."

"You better."

Aurora tossed her phone onto her bed, threw on a sports bra and lounge pants and jumped out the third-story window, letting her wings extend in a flash. Cupping them, she glided down to the back patio area, receiving surprised looks from Brielle and Lola, but everyone else was staring at the two males rolling around like lunatics under the oak tree twenty feet away.

"What's going on?" She stared as Axel punched the handsome blond vampire right in the jaw.

She winced, the sound of the impact far too loud.

"Pretty sure this is foreplay," Bella murmured, moving up next to her, coffee mug in hand. Her hair was wrapped up in a towel and she had on a robe with a wild hydrangea print covering it tied loosely around her petite frame.

Aurora looked at the males again. Winced *again* as the vampire punched Axel in the stomach. "Something is seriously wrong with these two."

"Nah, they need to let this out and then get naked," Harlow said. She must have just arrived back because she was still dressed in her same gear from hours ago.

When Axel tackled the vampire into the tree, making it tremble under the impact, Aurora hurried forward. Enough was enough.

Letting loose a stream of controlled fire, she shot Axel in the butt. It wouldn't hurt him much, but it would give him a jolt.

"Hey!" He yelped and jumped off the other male, whipping around to stare at her.

They both stared now, breathing hard. The vampire had on a button-down shirt, torn open to reveal half his chest.

"You're acting worse than children. And we have neighbors. Talk this out or you leave now," she ordered Christian.

He tightened his jaw, turned to glare at Axel, then looked back at Aurora. "I apologize for my behavior. I did not mean to disrespect anyone here." It was pretty clear he was excluding Axel in that. He didn't bother looking back at Axel, just stalked away, rounding the side of the house. If he wasn't a day walker, he'd have to get back home soon. She just hoped it was close to here.

"You're not going after him?" Harlow asked, frowning.

Axel glared at her, then looked at Aurora, his expression shifting slightly. "I'm sorry. I didn't mean for that to get so out of hand. I just wanted to wipe that smug look off his face."

Aurora sighed. "Go inside. Make a fresh pot of coffee. I'll be inside in a sec."

She scrubbed a hand over her face as he did just that. She still didn't turn around to face the others because for this one moment she was wondering if this was what it was like to be Alpha. Did you have to deal with this insanity all the time—on a much bigger scale?

"Where'd you get off to last night anyway?" Lola asked as Aurora turned around. Her hair was her natural dark brown with the faintest tinge of pink highlights throughout.

"Ah…" She glanced at Harlow, whose expression was neutral. Okay, so she wasn't saying anything either. *Good.* She'd started to give a vague answer when Brielle stalked around the side of the house from the direction Christian had come, a teenage girl with her.

The girl had copper-colored hair, a golden skin tone and green eyes.

"I caught this one lurking by the front gate." Brielle's tone was neutral.

The young teenager frowned up at Brielle, her body language tense. "I wasn't lurking like some creeper. I was trying to make sure this was the right place. The roads here are really confusing."

"For what?" Aurora asked.

Brielle shrugged. "She said she'd only talk to you."

She blinked. "Me?"

"Yes. I just arrived in the territory today."

"Are you alone?"

"My parents are dead," she said bluntly, but even Aurora could feel the pain rippling off her in waves. It also wasn't an answer as to whether she was alone.

"I'm really sorry to hear that. Are you here to stay with relatives?"

The girl shook her head.

"What's your name?"

"Phoebe." She wrapped her arms around her middle, looking too thin even with her naturally slender frame.

Aurora nodded at the others and Bella hurried off, hopefully to grab food for the kid. She motioned toward the table, which was littered with coffee cups. "You want to sit and talk?"

"Yes." But Phoebe was rooted to the spot, just staring at Aurora.

"Look, there's more than one intake center in the city. If you don't have family, we've set up a system to place kids—supernatural and humans alike—with packs or families. It's one of the first things King, our Alpha, did. And it's not like the former crappy human foster system. We take care of our kids. You're not human, are you?" Aurora's ability to scent wasn't as strong as the others so she wasn't one hundred percent sure.

The girl shook her head.

Brielle was just watching her curiously, her head tilted in that very feline way of hers as she studied the girl. "Definitely not human," she murmured.

Phoebe stepped away from her, her arms still wrapped around her middle. "I'm not going to go live with a bunch of weirdos."

Aurora snorted softly. "Why are you here specifically? How do you even know who I am?"

"I saw a video of you. It was taken like a year ago, I think. So we headed toward New Orleans. It's taken us a while to get here because not all of the roads are working."

"What video?" Aurora kept her tone neutral, but had a feeling she knew which one it had been.

"Of you and the famous singer. Ah, your sister. Killing a dragon."

"And it's the video that made you want to come see me?" she asked, trying to siphon out exactly why that video mattered. She also noticed that the girl had said *we*, not *I* when mentioning she'd made her way to New Orleans. So she definitely wasn't alone. "Why?"

Aurora tensed slightly, on alert if this was some sort of trap because she was a phoenix. She hated to think that someone would use a teenager to attempt to trap her, but—

Suddenly flaming green wings shot out from the girl's back and a pale glowing fire covered her entire body.

Aurora blinked, shock rippling through her. *Okay. Not a trap.* This girl was a phoenix. Aurora had never met another of her kind, other than family.

"You lost your parents in The Fall?" she asked, slowly stepping forward.

Phoebe let her arms fall from around her middle as she nodded, looking even younger and more scared in that moment.

Aurora rubbed both hands over her face. She definitely couldn't put this girl in a different home. Not when she was a phoenix. "How exactly did you get here? Has anyone seen what you are?"

"I drove some, flew a little bit, then I found an abandoned RV. You know, the kind you can drive. I ran into a couple wolves patrolling on the way here and told them where I was going. They didn't seem overly concerned, said I needed to talk to someone named Greer and gave me her location and yours. I did lie and tell them I was sixteen."

Aurora didn't think they cared whether she was old enough to drive. "How old are you?"

"Fourteen."

Jeez, so damn young. "Where's your RV?"

"It's parked down the block," Brielle said.

The girl shot her a surprised look.

Brielle shrugged. "I saw you park it."

"We've got some stuff to figure out, and I've got questions," Aurora continued. "Like who is this 'we' you're referring to?"

The girl paused, clearly weighing whether she was going to answer or not.

Aurora released her own wings again, flaring them out behind her in a showy display of blue fire. "You came to see me for a reason. Let me help you. We've got a couple extra rooms here. If you have more people with you, some of us can bunk up together."

"It's me and my little brothers. Enzo and Legend. They're seven."

Oh hell, this sweet kid. "Are they like us?"

She nodded.

"They're in the RV right now?" she asked.

"Yes. They're hiding in a compartment in case..." She cleared her throat and pulled her own wings back in, the fire covering her body disappearing.

"Go with Brielle to get them. Just park the RV in the driveway." It was certainly long and winding enough. "I'm going to get breakfast spread out for you guys. I take it you're all hungry?"

The girl's eyes widened when Bella strode outside with a tray full of fruit, and she nodded.

As soon as they were out of sight, she turned back to the others. "We can't put them somewhere else. There aren't any other phoenixes in the city." Well, other than her aunt, who was off on some covert mission again.

"Of course not!" Lola looked horrified at the thought.

The others all murmured in agreement, even Axel who strode out, coffee in hand, looking a bit less surly than before. "Poor kids," he murmured. "I can only imagine how tough it was for them making a trip here all alone. They can have my room for tonight if they want and I'll move my stuff to the study or something."

"Nah," Lola said. "Mine's bigger. They're not going to want to be separated. I'll just move into Kartini's old room."

Aurora didn't think it was possible to love her crew more, but in that moment she did. "We have a lot to figure out." And she definitely needed to call King about this.

CHAPTER FOURTEEN

A rthur's wings burned as he flew after his female. Prima. They'd been searching for humans stranded out in unclaimed territories and had camped for the night along a bluff, both in dragon form.

Prima had woken up suddenly as dawn broke and started flying northeast without a word.

So he'd followed.

As he always did. She was a complex female, an ancient dragon shifter like him. Yet nothing like him at the same time.

She was a bright, burning meteor who'd always drawn him to her. Thousands upon thousands of years and she'd always been it for him. And this time, this awakening, he would convince her to mate with him. He'd let her go before and then she'd gone into a long Hibernation.

More in touch with her dragon side than her human one, she called to his most primal nature. He knew she felt the tug too, the mating instinct. Yet she continued to resist it. Resist him—or at least pretend she didn't feel it.

Icy wind rolled over him, though he barely felt it against his scales as she dipped toward a still lake surrounded by a mass of thick, green trees. He wasn't sure where they were, maybe an area formerly known as northern Mississippi? Or it could be northern Louisiana. They'd already helped a handful of humans get to where they needed to be.

They'd passed various dragons in the skies, seen completely burned-down cities and towns now being retaken by nature. As it always happened.

Humans had been so sure they'd been at the top of the food chain. They could be such a petty race, more and more lacking in empathy as the years passed. Eager to strike out at others, to hurt, to cause pain for the pleasure of it. Their small-mindedness when it came to inconsequential things was something he could simply not comprehend. So he did not try to understand them.

He lived in the world with them, but would never be one of them, something he was very aware of even as he helped an Alpha wolf to rebuild it.

Prima suddenly banked upward, the span of her gorgeous jade wings glittering under the breaking sunlight enough to stop his heart for a moment. She slowed, turned, her wings still outspread as she looked at him.

Then she threw her head back and breathed a wild purple fire he'd never seen from any other dragon. It lit up the sky, fireworks erupting in a fountain of pure light he could only stare at.

Just as suddenly she turned, dipping low, arrowing for a flat plane of a snow-covered riverbank. By the time he landed, shifted, she'd shifted as well and had stretched out on a patch of snow.

He stared at her gloriously naked body, drank in every sleek line of her toned, muscled form. She was a pure, raw weapon. The heat rolling from her melted the snow around her and as she looked at him, eyes narrowed, she sniffed in a haughty way she'd perfected over the centuries. It was no wonder that at one point humans had worshiped her. "I scented something in the air."

Her explanation for leaving the way she had, he assumed as he stretched out next to her. The snow felt good against his back, cooling. "What?"

"An ancient scent... I don't know what it was. I tried to follow it, but it disappeared." She frowned, staring up at the sky and trees.

He hadn't scented it, but then he wasn't as good of a tracker as her. "There are humans about a mile from here." Now *that*, he could scent. Or he assumed it was humans. There were a couple campfires going nearby.

"I know. I was hoping if we stayed here for a moment, I'd catch the scent again." Frustration made her words a growl. "The scent is bothersome."

"A foe?"

"I don't know!" Snarling, she shoved up, the snow now water rolling down her back.

"At the risk of getting my head bitten off, can you attempt to describe the scent?" He kept his tone neutral.

She turned back to glare at him as he remained on the packed snow where he was. It was only a light covering, barely blanketing the area, and would likely melt completely off by midday.

Instead of responding, she turned suddenly and straddled him, taking his cock in her hand.

He was instantly hard at her touch, even as he was surprised by it. She flipped from cold to hot in an instant and he didn't mind one bit.

His female kept him on his toes, just the way he liked it.

CHAPTER FIFTEEN

"Thank you again for talking to me." King stepped a little farther into the bedroom at Greer's healing center.

This room was on the larger side, with three beds used for spillover. Right now the place wasn't full, but she'd put the human kayakers together anyway, pulling in another twin bed and setting it by the window so they could all be together. They'd woken up and had been scared, wanted to be with their family. Many humans were like shifters in that regard.

The dark-haired woman, who'd been wearing the puffer vest, nodded. He'd learned her name was Samantha—aka Sam. And she'd been the spokesperson for the others over the last ten minutes.

"We're grateful we were found…even if we are still confused." She looked over at her sister, brother and cousin and they all nodded.

"Greer thinks you're going to make a full recovery. She says you're just going to need extra sleep for a couple days. We've had someone contact your neighbors and where you work. Everyone knows you're okay. I've instructed them to give you space for now, but if you're up to seeing people, just let Greer know."

"Maybe…" She looked over at the others, who were more drawn-looking than she was. "Ah, maybe tomorrow."

The others let out a sort of collective sigh of relief.

"This is a dumb question," the redhead, Aubrey, said. "But what happened to our kayaks?"

He bit back a smile at the mundane question. "One of my wolves brought them back. They're in your garage on the wall racks. They even rinsed them off for you."

"That was really nice." The redhead teared up as she spoke. "Sorry, not sure why I'm crying."

"You've been through a lot. Your reaction is normal. I know you don't remember anything now, but if you start having dreams that seem weird. Or…anything else out of the ordinary happens, I don't care how small, I want to know. I don't care if it's three in the morning. Call me or my lieutenant, Ace. Greer has all my information and she'll be passing it on to you before you leave. Or you can just tell her and she'll let me know."

"Thank you," Sam murmured. "It's scary not remembering what happened to us, having black holes in our memories."

There were ways to retrieve memories, but they involved magic and King wasn't going to ask them to attempt it now. Maybe not at all. That kind of magic didn't always work as planned and these humans had been through a lot. He just nodded and stepped back toward the door. "Did you need anything before I leave?"

They all shook their heads and Sam spoke again. "We're good. Going to get some more sleep, but thanks."

Downstairs he found Greer in the kitchen fixing a pot of soup. "Do you want me to call Reaper back in from the field?" he asked.

She looked up in surprise from the stove. "No. I can handle four humans. I'm going to inject some healing power into them before they sleep. I think they'll bounce back even quicker."

"I know you can handle four humans. I just want to make sure you're not missing your mate too much."

She blinked, then smiled. "I'll always miss him, but this is good for him. He likes to help, to be busy doing things. No idle hands on my dragon."

King understood that. "Okay, then. You know I'm always a call away."

"I know, thank you."

Once he was outside in the cool morning air he pulled his phone out. He'd received multiple texts when he'd been upstairs but hadn't wanted to check them in front of the humans. They'd deserved his full attention.

He'd started to pull up a text from Ace when Aurora's name flashed on his screen.

He answered immediately, his heart rate kicking up at simply seeing her name. "Hey."

"Are you free for a couple minutes?"

"Yeah." He'd make time for Aurora. Always.

"We need to talk. In person." There was a sense of urgency in her tone.

"What's wrong?" He was already heading in the direction of her place, would be able to run in wolf form there faster than drive. "Are you home?"

"Yeah, and nothing's wrong. It's just…I need to talk in person. I need to show you something. If you're busy, this can wait a little bit."

Even as he started to respond, he received a text from Ace with the word emergency in all caps. He inwardly cursed. "Are you sure it can wait?"

"Of course. Is everything okay with you?"

"Maybe," he said on a sigh. "I'll contact you as soon as I can." After they disconnected, he called Ace. "What's up?"

"Two of the female vampires from the Hill coven have accused Myles of rape. Officially. They've come forward and want to press charges. They told Claudine and she reached out."

King's jaw clenched. "Where is he?" He had one of his people watching Myles Hill's place.

"I'm headed to their coven house now. Scott said they haven't left since last night."

And none of them were day walkers so they'd be holed up until dusk. "Call Everleigh, have her on standby." She was the witch who worked her truthsense magic on anyone accused of a crime. "I'm on my way there now." He didn't always partake in captures of criminals, but he was making an exception for this. King had allowed the male into his territory. He needed to be part of this.

In wolf form, he raced through the streets, avoiding people walking, bicycling, and the very few driving vehicles before he neared the residential neighborhood.

He scented Zaid, Corbyn and Della.

King shifted to his human form, whistled softly as he dressed. When he heard returning whistles, he withdrew his sword. Normally they prepped more for a takedown but sometimes they had to act quickly.

He had the brief thought that Prima would be disappointed that she wouldn't be able to burn this vampire to a crisp but it was probably better that she wasn't in town.

He would take care of this vampire today one way or another.

He and his wolves converged on the two-story house, looking for traps as they always did, before he eased the front door open.

As he stepped inside, the blade hummed so softly only he could hear it.

The moment he stepped into the foyer, he knew the house was empty. *Fuuuck.*

Ace strode down the hallway from the back of the house, and going on his expression, he'd come to the same conclusion.

The scents here were too weak and he couldn't hear *anything* inside.

"We search it anyway," he said to everyone.

He trusted Scott, who he'd assigned to watch this house. He wouldn't have left his post.

"Look for trapdoors," he called out as he strode toward the nearest hallway door. He opened it up and sure enough it led to a cellar. They were incredibly rare in the city since places used to flood—before The Fall—but something told him they were going to find an escape route through this door.

Sword still out, senses on alert, he flipped the switch next to the door. Fluorescent light flooded the stairway and he hurried down. This place had been redone recently, probably a year or two before The Fall. The stairs and floors were covered in luxury vinyl planks and the walls were painted a neutral sage.

Multiple bunkbeds were set up, clearly where the vampires slept during the day. There were no windows and nothing down here for entertainment. Knowing vampires as he did, they would definitely have a bolt hole.

They would have left hours ago, under the cover of night.

He stepped carefully around the room, looking for uneven floor planks or seams in the wall that didn't match up—there! He skated his fingers along an accent wall, which was covered in multicolored wallpaper. The vibrant flora of blues, greens and yellows had clearly been used for a reason that had nothing to do with aesthetics. He wouldn't have been aware of the uneven section of the wall without touch.

Running his hand along the entire seam, he pressed in when he felt a raised bump. Like a button.

A panel popped open with a snick. The door itself was floor-to-ceiling length, he realized, blending in almost perfectly.

A damp draft of air rolled over him as he heard footsteps behind him.

"Son of a bitch," someone muttered.

He turned and started to speak but Ace said, "I've already put out the alert. I doubt he's in the territory anymore but word is spreading to be on the lookout for him."

He nodded. "Where are the females?"

"At Claudine's. She's keeping them safe and I've spoken to them personally. They all say Claudine is taking care of them and they're happy where they are."

"Good." He would expect no less from the vampire. Turning, he stepped into the darkened hallway, breathed in deeply.

The scent of vampire was strong through here. Though he doubted they were still hanging around, he still stayed on alert as he, Zaid and Della hurried through the narrow escape route of paneled wood and dirt.

Sure enough, it emptied out into a garage. He sheathed his sword as they stepped into the dusty workspace. He moved to one of the grime-covered windows and peered out. It was attached to the house next door. "I want to find out who owns this place."

"I'm on it," Della said.

"I've got stuff to take care of," he said as he turned to the others. "Look for anything we can use to track them down." Myles and anyone guilty of rape were going to pay for their crimes.

They all nodded, with Zaid and Della heading toward the door of the house. He trusted his people to handle this. He pressed the garage door and stepped out into the sunlight.

His first stop was going to be talking to Aurora.

* * *

"Are you sure he's not going to care if it's just me?" Phoebe asked Aurora as they reached the gates of King's compound. He had multiple places in the city, but a good majority of his pack lived here in this mansion in the Lower Garden District.

One of the wolves patrolling in human form just waved at her. She'd already talked to King and had agreed to meet him here. Phoebe wasn't ready for her brothers to meet anyone else and they were currently having a ball with Axel and Harlow in the backyard, so leaving them had been easier than Aurora thought Phoebe had expected.

"It's fine, I promise. So you guys didn't have an Alpha or anything before?"

"It was just the six of us. We learned to stay away from most supernaturals," Phoebe murmured quietly, glancing around the huge expanse of yard. The property was walled off, had tons of fruit trees, and other greenery and plants that Aurora couldn't name.

"Six of you?"

"Oh, we had two dads and one mom."

Oh. "My sister and I didn't…reveal ourselves until recently." She kept her voice subvocal, because as of right now they weren't planning on telling anyone but King and her own pack what these kids were. She was going to let Phoebe decide when and if she ever wanted to let people know what she was. And considering how young she was and inexperienced, Aurora was totally fine with that. She didn't want these kids to be targeted when they couldn't yet protect themselves.

"Oh my God," the girl blurted as they walked around the side of the mansion to find Hunter doing little figure eights in the air.

When he spotted Aurora he chirped loudly and flew straight toward them, a tiny little arrow. Or maybe not tiny, though he was small compared to the grown dragons she knew. He was more like a baby elephant with big ears, big wings, and an adorable face.

Phoebe moved behind Aurora as Hunter landed in front of them.

He made a chirping sound, his head tilted slightly to the side as if asking her a question.

"I still can't understand you," she said as she kissed his nose.

He preened under her kisses, then covered his face with his wings. Just as quickly, he popped them open, looking at her expectantly.

Aurora glanced behind her to find Phoebe standing there, eyes wide.

"I'm pretty sure he's talking to you. He's a baby dragon, not a shifter. He's King's pet."

Phoebe blinked. "The Alpha of New Orleans has a pet dragon? That's…I don't know. Unexpected."

"His name is Hunter. And I think he likes you."

Hunter chirped an agreement, covered his face again with his wings then pulled them back and cackled as if he was playing peekaboo.

"He's got the maturity of a toddler," Aurora murmured. Though he was definitely smarter, she was convinced of it.

This made Phoebe smile softly as she took a couple tentative steps forward and reached out a hand toward the dragon.

He slowly stepped toward her too, then nudged her hand, demanding pets. Then he licked her when she didn't pet him.

Phoebe let out a squeal of delight and he did it again before rolling around on the grass, looking a bit like a maniac. "He's a total weirdo," she said on a laugh. Before Aurora could respond, Phoebe continued, "Which is good because I'm a total weirdo too. My brothers are going to love him!"

This made Aurora laugh lightly. "We're all weirdos. Come on, we can wait on the back patio."

Hunter took to the air but he hovered next to them, flying and chirping excitedly as they strode across the grass.

Aurora was aware of other wolves in the vicinity, and a few felines up in the trees, but everyone gave them a fairly large berth. Which surprised her. Normally King's people loved to come and chat—gossip— with her but maybe he'd given them orders. Or maybe they were just giving her and Phoebe privacy.

As they reached the back patio area with its huge, oversized tables and heated pool, Hunter headed straight for the water and dove into the deep end, making a big splash.

"He's so cute, I wish we could keep him," Phoebe said almost wistfully.

"You can totally take him with you when you leave." King's voice was dry, making Aurora nearly jump. She turned to find him standing there.

Shirtless.

She stared for a long moment, her brain completely fritzing. The male had muscles for days. *Holy. Shit.* She knew that, had seen him before of course, but...the sunlight was so bright today, shining down on him as if he was under a spotlight. "I didn't hear you," she blurted, still not able to look up to his face. And why did she have to sound all breathless? And God, why did his chest have to be so muscular, his abs so ripped? Was that...a twelve-pack? It was like he had muscles on top of muscles. As if he'd been carved straight from granite.

Stop staring, weirdo! she ordered herself.

She cleared her throat, met his gaze and found the wolf looking back at her. Immediately she felt her cheeks flush hot and holy shit she *had* to get it together. Her libido had been straight up dead for a year. Apparently it was choosing now to flare to life. "He's kidding about taking Hunter. Phoebe, this is King. King, Phoebe."

They nodded at each other politely and Aurora took a deep breath.

"Phoebe and her brothers are going to be living with us."

King's eyebrows lifted in surprise. "Okay." He stretched the word out ever so slightly.

"She's..." Aurora lowered her voice even more, glancing around. She knew there were plenty of shifters she couldn't see so she needed to speak subvocally. "Like me."

King shot Phoebe a surprised glance and the girl simply nodded.

Then he said, "How old are your brothers?"

"Seven."

He nodded slowly. "And your parents?"

"They died," she said quietly, but that same scent of pain rolled off her.

And King would have scented it even sharper than Aurora. "Do you need anything from me?" he asked as he looked at Aurora.

"No. I think we're going to be figuring things out for a little bit. Eventually we'll get them into one of the schools, but for now they're having a good time back at the house. We'll make this work." That was what shifters did, especially those who lived in packs. By nature, phoenixes were solitary, only living with their own kind, but she'd grown up in a huge artist's compound with her parents, their misfit friends and all of her current friends. She loved being surrounded by other supernaturals. Not to mention there was safety in numbers, in a pack.

Micah, a boy who was maybe fifteen or sixteen, raced out the back door, letting it slam behind him. "King!" he called out.

King turned as Micah skidded to a halt. He was in that gangly stage with his arms and legs a little too long. But he would definitely grow into a strong wolf one day. His gaze landed on Phoebe and his eyes widened. He looked a little moonstruck as he stared at her and a faint flush hit his bronzed cheeks.

He cleared his throat and smiled. "Hi," he said.

"Hi," Phoebe murmured, wrapping her arms tightly around herself.

"Micah," King said with just a hint of impatience in his voice.

Micah blinked and looked back at him. "Right, ah, the healers need to see you about something. They sent me out here." His gaze strayed back to Phoebe and he smiled again.

"I'll be inside in a few minutes," King said.

He turned back to Aurora and Phoebe and the boy still stood there, mostly staring at Phoebe.

King turned and looked at him, eyebrows raised. "Did you need anything else?"

"Ah, no. I'll go tell them you'll be in soon." Then he hurried off, but not before glancing over his shoulder once, smiling at Phoebe.

Hunter had shaken himself off by now and was lying in the grass next to them, chirping at King as he usually did.

Since she was here, she wanted to talk to King about something else. "Listen, I heard Prima found a fairly large group of humans and is looking for people to bring them supplies. I'd like to be included in that group, as I can help."

"I can help too," Phoebe said quickly.

Aurora shot her a quick look. They hadn't really decided whether she was going to reveal what she was yet and Aurora could admit that the thought of her doing so made Aurora feel uneasy. "I'm pretty sure the whole crew wants to help out, unless you've got them on patrols or schedules already."

"I've got a couple dragons on standby right now gearing up. You can definitely go. I'll see about the others, though I need Bella in the city now," King said.

Aurora nodded, having expected that. Bella organized a lot of things for the pack, covens and clans. The woman was a walking genius and managed to keep everything organized in a way that baffled and amazed Aurora.

"Prima said it's the biggest settlement they've found so far. And apparently a lot of them are in pretty bad shape." He sighed, running a hand over his closely cropped hair almost involuntarily.

When he did, her gaze flicked to the ripple of his biceps. *Good God.*

"It's been a cold winter," he murmured more to himself.

She nodded, feeling guilty for checking him out in that moment. "I know. I hate that anyone is stuck out there without supplies, without contact."

Without hope. She knew how that felt, to be trapped, with nowhere to go. And she wanted to help out if she could.

CHAPTER SIXTEEN

Aurora knocked gently on Phoebe's door, not wanting to wake her or her brothers if they'd fallen asleep. She'd heard them moving around ten minutes ago so she figured it was a safe bet they were still up. She and Phoebe had returned to the house hours ago after talking to King. The boys had been in full-on play mode all afternoon until Phoebe had finally told her brothers it was bedtime. And they hadn't argued so she knew they must be exhausted.

Phoebe opened the door a few moments later. Her hair was pulled back in a damp braid and she was wearing pajamas Bella had given her. "Hey, everything okay?"

"Yeah, I was just hoping you had time to talk. Are the boys already asleep?" Her gaze strayed past Aurora to the double bed where the kids were curled up under the covers, eyes closed. They were little copies of Phoebe, with the same copper-colored hair, golden skin and green eyes. Someone, she thought Lola, had strung up a bunch of twinkle lights over the double bed and the daybed. It softened the room, made it more welcoming.

Phoebe snorted softly and nodded. "Yeah, they drop off so fast it's crazy. They'll be chattering away one minute, then asleep the next. Can we talk in here? I don't want to be away from them."

"Of course. We won't wake them?"

She shook her head, snorted again. "No way. They sleep through anything. Which has been pretty awesome, if I'm being honest." She headed to her daybed by the window and sat on one end, so Aurora took the other end.

The room had already been in good shape, they'd just added a couple things to make it more kid-friendly. Though Lola and Bella were already talking about getting books and other things for all three of them. It had been a long time since any of them had been around cubs, pups or younglings in a living situation. Aurora knew their lives were about to change drastically, but she simply couldn't turn away kids in need. But especially not phoenixes. Ones who'd lost their parents. *Nope.*

"So…" Phoebe cleared her throat.

"So. I just really wanted to sit down and talk to you now that it's quiet." They'd had a pretty busy day, with the boys being complete balls of energy. Axel was asleep on the couch in one of the living rooms downstairs already, having passed out from sheer exhaustion after keeping them entertained all day. They'd gravitated to him and hadn't left his side.

"Okay." She sat with her hands folded tightly in her lap, as if she was nervous about what Aurora had to say.

"To start, we're going to want to get you guys into school eventually. Right now it's not like it was in the human world. At least not in King's territory—I can't speak for anywhere else. Education is a bit different and everything is integrated with humans and supernaturals. But I'm guessing you guys want a little time to settle in…"

Phoebe blew out a breath and nodded.

"Okay, good. We'll hold off a couple weeks on school." They'd already been out of it for a year, so really it wasn't that big of a deal. Hell, with the way the world had shifted, it was small potatoes in general. "Also, all of us have various jobs around the territory and sometimes we work odd hours, but there will always be someone here for you."

"I can take care of my brothers and me. I mean, I can cook and stuff."

"That's good, but we're still not leaving you alone for now. You've been through a lot and…you know what you are. I want to make sure you guys aren't targeted for that. Is there anyone you can think of who knows what you are?"

Phoebe shook her head. "No. I mean, we knew of other supernaturals. But we mostly kept to ourselves. My parents had us in a K-12 private school that had a few wolves but they were older than me. I just told them I was a jaguar and they left me alone."

Aurora smiled softly. "Star and I used to say we were snow leopards."

"Oh, like Bella, Lola and Marley. That's smart."

It was survival. "For now…you want to keep what you are a secret?" It came out as a question even though Aurora wanted to order her to do it. The thought of anyone coming after these kids for their phoenix blood made her want to break out in hives.

"Yes. Maybe when we're older..." She looked over at her brothers, whose innocent faces were so relaxed under the twinkle lights. "But not now. I can't protect them now," she whispered. Then she swallowed hard. "When the dragons attacked, my parents got us to the edge of the city. They shed years of secrecy and fled with us because it was the only choice. It was insane, the fire and screams." She swallowed hard, but continued. "Some dragon shifters must have seen us and followed. They waited until we were out of Chicago and attacked. My parents...they killed the dragons but didn't make it. I always thought...they would rise from the ashes. I don't really understand what happened or why they didn't come back." Tears rolled down her cheeks.

Aurora scooted closer and wrapped an arm around her shoulders. "I'm so sorry. I lost my parents to dragons too."

Sniffling, she wiped her tears away and looked up at her. "During The Fall?"

"No. Long before. I was five, and Star ran with me, to keep me safe." She dropped her arm, giving Phoebe some space. "I don't know the whys of all of it. Our fire can kill some dragons but dragon fire can also kill us. Some dragon fire anyway. I think it just boils down to power levels. The fact that your parents killed the dragons says a lot about their strength."

"What happened to the ones who...killed yours?"

"Star hunted them down and killed them."

Phoebe's eyes widened slightly.

"Do you...know how to wield your magic?" She was only fourteen so Aurora wasn't sure what Phoebe knew or didn't.

"A little. My parents had a lake house. We used to spend summers there and we'd get to practice, to be mostly free to be ourselves. I used to live for our summers."

She understood perfectly. "There are places here I can take you to where you can be yourself. Your brothers too. Or any of the others here will take you if you're needing to escape."

"Thank you. And not just for that. But for taking us in. I wasn't sure what I expected when I got here. I just...wanted to find someone like us.

Someone who would understand."

Aurora hugged her again, then stood. This seemed like a good stopping point. "If you get hungry or anything, the kitchen is open for you. We've got mostly fresh stuff that we grow. And...listen, I don't know if you should come on the rescue trip with me tomorrow. Bella can't come and Lola has realized she can't either. So you guys won't be alone. If it was just you, it'd probably be fine, but your brothers are so young." Phoebe was young too, but Aurora wanted to soften the blow.

"Yeah, I get it. I can't leave them again. It's just been the three of us for so long."

When Aurora and Phoebe had returned from King's earlier in the day, the boys had clung to her like moss. They'd had a good time and had loved playing with Axel, but they'd needed to have their sister within their eyesight for the rest of the day. "Bella will put you to work while I'm gone. It'll be fun though. She'll probably let you guys see The Grove—ah, the vertical forest building."

Phoebe's eyes widened slightly, then they both turned at a rustling sound.

One of her brothers had turned over, kicking his comforter off. Thankfully he was still asleep though.

And that was her cue to leave. "If you need me, I'll be downstairs for a while, then heading up to my room," she whispered. She pointed up to the third floor, though Phoebe knew she was only one floor above her.

"Thanks. I'll probably sleep soon though." As if to reiterate, she let out a yawn, then a laugh. "Sooner than later."

Aurora shut the door behind her and found Bella in her pajamas stepping out of her room. "Everything good?" Bella asked.

"Yeah. You feel like getting some tea?"

"That's what I was on my way to do." Smiling, she linked arms with Aurora as they headed for the stairs. "So you're going on that rescue thing tomorrow?"

"Yeah." And she was sort of nervous about it.

"So...how are the kids? Really?" Bella asked as they reached the bottom floor.

"Okay, I think. I also think they're going to be decompressing and processing everything for a while. It's going to take time. They've been on the road for a long time, probably scared most of it. It's why I don't want to put them in school right away. I might have told Phoebe you'd let her come with you to work while I'm gone. So I hope that's okay."

Bella let out a short laugh as they reached the kitchen and made a beeline for the cabinet with their plethora of teas. "I'd planned to do that anyway. No way I'm leaving them all alone. She's a pretty brave kid, making that trip with her brothers."

"I was thinking that too." At seven, her brothers wouldn't be able to fly well or very far. And they would have had to be careful about who to trust for multiple reasons. There were a lot of different types of predators out there. It was a miracle they'd made it here.

"I'm glad they're here." Bella put a teapot on the stovetop.

"Really? Is everyone else okay with this new situation?" There hadn't been any time to discuss it. Aurora had just made the unilateral decision.

"Yeah. Of course. You know how we all grew up. It'll be kind of nice to have kids around."

Aurora's mouth curved up. "Those boys are going to tire us all out, I think."

Bella's grin grew wide at that. "Axel is so exhausted. Lola used a magic potion she got from Thurman to color his hair. He didn't even stir when she did it."

Aurora snickered. "What color is it?"

"Rainbow."

"Lola really loves playing with fire. Clearly she needs more to do with her time." Because that lion had an obsession with his hair.

"I have a feeling he'll love it. I swear nothing looks bad on that male. It's kind of annoying. It wears off in like twenty-four hours though so if he hates it..." She shrugged.

Well, they would see in the morning. Aurora glanced at her cell phone, smiled when she saw King's name flash on the screen.

A text. *I'm actually in early tonight. No fires, metaphorical or literal.*

The night is still young, she texted back. It was only nine.

Don't burst my bubble. How's the kid?

She's settling in. They all are. How are the kayakers? With Phoebe and her brothers showing up, she'd forgotten to ask about them earlier.

Bella slid a mug of tea over to Aurora then rounded the island. "I'm going to go read. Enjoy texting." She gave a knowing smile before she hurried out.

Better than expected. Coping at losing time in their memory. But they should bounce back.

Any news on the hybrid? She didn't really know what else to call him. The asshole? Monster?

None yet. The territory is locked down as much as possible. No one's found anything like the humans. And everyone has been checking in today.

At least that was something.

I did receive a message from another territory...some fae want to talk with me. I'm not sure about what.

Fae? That was interesting. She only knew one half-fae, but that was it. It was her understanding that they mostly lived in a different realm. And that most of them didn't like humans. *Maybe they want to talk allyship?*

He responded with an eye-rolling emoji. He'd come a long way since they'd become friends. He'd never even used emojis before and his texting had been so formal. Sometimes it still was. But she knew she was one of the few people he texted like this. Ace had told her.

Her finger hovered over her cell phone's keyboard. She was so tempted to type back asking if he wanted to come over to her place. Sometimes he'd stop by later in the evenings. She treasured those times with him, where it was just the two of them—because her crew always left them alone. *Can I stop by tomorrow before I head out with the others?* she typed instead.

Of course.

Her fingers hovered over her screen again, but she finally set her phone down. What did she want to say anyway? Want to come over and get naked? Ugh. She rolled her eyes at herself. She wasn't ready for that. Or she didn't think she was. Instead of typing back that, she wrote, *I'll see you then.*

And then she rolled her eyes at herself. She felt like such a coward but couldn't figure out how to make herself take that next step.

To make it clear to King that she wanted more with him. He was the Alpha of the territory. What if things went spectacularly wrong?

Groaning, she shoved her phone in her pocket and picked up her tea.

She needed sleep too.

CHAPTER SEVENTEEN

Lucius slipped through the woods, using the shadows as his friend, making them bend to his will. His power was growing, had been for a year.

All the nocturnal animals around him had ceased their noise the deeper he moved through the woods. They sensed a predator in their midst.

The animals were smarter than the prey he was currently hunting. Though he wanted to make his move on the city tonight, he held off. He still wasn't strong enough. He'd been feeding on settlements of humans as he made his way south over the last few months.

Now…he would feed on something stronger.

Firelight flickered in the distance through the trees, the sound of laughter and voices intermingling.

"We shouldn't have to hide like animals," a male voice grumbled.

Lucius moved closer, his steps silent over the cold forest floor. Considering how obnoxiously loud these vampires were, they weren't exactly hiding. *Fools.*

The woods were thick here, but the fire was a beacon, drawing him closer. Keeping the shadows cloaked around him, he slid up to a moss-covered oak tree, eyed the cluster of four vampires sitting around the fire.

They all looked similar, dressed similar. Dark hair, pale skin, bulky muscles under their sweaters. All their powers and muscles wouldn't save them.

They were young, maybe created a couple decades ago. The scent that filled the air was one of fear, the strong astringent feeding him even now.

Four humans had been tossed onto the ground about twenty feet away from the fire. Three females and one male, from what he could see. None were moving, but they were alive. And he was fairly certain they were awake too. They'd likely tried to escape and found it futile.

The stench of their fear was too strong. An aphrodisiac he wanted to bathe in.

"We'll come back," the one named Myles said. "We just have to regroup. They won't escape from us."

"We shouldn't have left at all," another said. This one was named Jared, Lucius had learned from following these pathetic fools for the last half hour.

All they did was whine, whine, whine. Whoever had turned them should be gutted and decapitated. They were a waste of vampires.

"Stupid bitches," another growled, his fangs dropping as he kicked at the fire. "We could have taken on Claudine's coven."

If this male was referring to Claudine Bonavich, then he was an even bigger fool than Lucius had thought.

And Lucius was quite through with listening to them complain. It was time to play with his food.

He stepped out of the shadows, letting his cloak billow behind him— he had always liked to put on a good show. "If you think you could take on Claudine by yourself, let alone her coven, you four are more stupid than you look. And that, you pitiable excuses for vampires, is quite a lot."

The four males attempted to jump to their feet, fangs out, but he held them in place, flexing his power as he did.

He tilted his head slightly as he looked at the leader, Myles something or other. The male's jaw tightened, clenching furiously, veins popping in his neck as he strained against Lucius's invisible hold.

"It is useless to fight it. To fight me." He stepped closer to the fire, frowned at it. What kind of vampires started a fire in the forest? Or at all? They did not need the heat. Maybe it was a throwback to when they had been human. Lucius held out a hand, ordered the flames higher, brighter.

The vampires all let out shouts of alarm and tried to move back, but could not.

He kicked at one of the logs, laughed when it slammed the one named Jared in the face, landing in his lap.

The male screamed as fire began to consume him, burning away at his flesh like kindling.

Grinning, Lucius stared into the male's terrified brown eyes from across the wild, hot firepit. "That's right, scream for me," he whispered.

"Who are you?" one of the other males shouted.

Myles was still struggling against Lucius's invisible grip.

For a moment, he let his hold on the vampire slip. Then laughed when Myles flew forward, nearly face-planting right into the fire.

But the vampire's reflexes were fast and he bounced back, jumped onto his feet and faced off with Lucius with the grace of a feline.

Lucius froze him again, laughing at the look of horror on the male's face.

He breathed deep, sucking in the life force of the still screaming vampire, letting it invade his veins, feed his soul. The other two were begging now, demanding he let them go with the same entitled sniveling he'd had to listen to for half an hour as they complained about the females of their coven leaving.

It was no wonder they'd left.

Lucius walked around Myles, eyeing him up and down. "Who turned you?"

"What?" he gritted out.

"Was my question not clear?" He grabbed the male by the cock.

Myles's eyes widened with shock then pain as Lucius squeezed. "His name was Arnold. Arnold Young."

Not familiar. "How old was he?"

"Ah...eighty, give or take," he rasped out.

"He's dead?" Because the male had referred to him in the past tense.

"Yeah, for like a decade."

"Good. Saves me the trouble of killing him." He squeezed harder now.

"What's your damage, you psycho?" Myles snarled, then screamed, pink tears rolling down his face from the pain.

Lucius closed his eyes, breathed in the agony and suffering of the male even as he grabbed Myles by the hair, yanked his head to the side and started drinking.

He would take everything from these vampires.

Vaguely aware of the humans crawling away, trying to covertly flee, he ignored them. They were no threat, and not nearly as satisfying as these arrogant vampires. Maybe he'd even let them go.

Or maybe he'd drink them dry too.

As Myles's blood coated his throat, a new sense of strength infused him. *This* was what he'd been missing. Human blood was far too weak, though human fear was strong.

Done with Myles, he tossed his limp body to the side, stalked to one of the remaining vamps. He really shouldn't have set the other one on fire. He could have drunk his blood too.

As he sank his fangs into the sniveling vamp, he could feel another surge of power well up inside him, anchor him more strongly in his magic.

Soon—sooner than he'd hoped—he would cripple this territory.

Then kill King.

CHAPTER EIGHTEEN

Cas knew he should have called first but he'd finally worked up the balls to come talk to Jo. He needed to just be honest with her, tell her that he was a dragon shifter.

Then he would see where they stood, and if she rejected him. If she did, at least he'd know for certain and could stop obsessing.

The door swung open a few seconds later. Jo's auburn hair was damp around her shoulders and she had on that silky robe again. The one where he could see the outline of her nipples. He lost the ability to think for a moment. Why had he come here again?

Mate, his dragon purred.

"Cas," she said, pleasure in her voice as she stepped back to let him in.

He stepped inside with her and glanced around, not hearing anyone. "Where is everyone?"

She blinked in surprise. "You can tell no one's here?"

Normally he didn't point out his extrasensory abilities but he nodded. "Yeah, but I think even a human could notice. It's too quiet and your sisters are anything but."

She snickered softly and locked the door behind them. "My sisters left for work early. Like really early. I think they were meeting friends for coffee first. And Nana is at one of our neighbors until this afternoon. It's quilting day. They're all making quilts for one of the intake centers to give to kids being placed in new homes."

Right, it was Friday morning.

So…they were alone. The first time he could remember being alone with her in months. His gaze fell to her full lower lip. She'd clearly just gotten out of the shower. She smelled sweet and… The faintest hint of arousal rolled off her.

"Jo," he murmured her name, the sound more a groan than anything. He couldn't stop himself. That scent, it was overpowering, making him light-headed.

She stepped forward slightly, her chest rising and falling a bit more sharply. Oh. That was *definite* arousal.

But he'd come here to talk. *Talk.*

Instead of talking about what he'd originally come here to say, he rasped out, "Everyone's gone for hours?"

"All day."

"What time do you have to be at work?" he growled, still staring at her mouth.

"Not for a few hours yet." Her own voice was all raspy and breathy and that was when he realized she was staring at his mouth too. That sweet scent was even stronger...

He wasn't quite sure how it happened, but in the next moment he had her pinned up against the closed front door, his mouth crushed to hers.

She plastered her body to his, wrapping her legs around him, digging her fingernails into his back as he rolled his erection against her. Their mouths clashed in a frenzy, Jo clearly as consumed with need as him.

Now the scent of her arousal was overwhelming, overpowering all sense or thought. He knew he'd come here for a reason—

None of that mattered anymore.

The only thing that mattered was tasting between her legs, to see exactly how turned on she was. He could scent it, but he needed more. She was his mate, something he'd known for far too long. And the need to claim her was overwhelming.

He tore his mouth away from hers for a moment. "Did you touch yourself in the shower this morning?" He desperately needed to know.

Her cheeks flushed pink, her lips swollen from his kisses as she stared at him. "Yes," she whispered. "But I didn't finish."

Good. He wanted to be the only one to give her that pleasure. "I'm going to finish you off right now."

Her mouth fell open, but he crushed his mouth to hers again even as he slid his hand between the folds of her robe. He shuddered at the feel of her bare stomach against his callused palms.

He'd been fantasizing about doing this for a year. *Longer.* Right now as he tasted the coffee on her, teased his tongue against hers, he had no idea how he'd shown so much self-control for so long.

The pheromones rolling off her were so damn potent, making his dragon half wild with hunger. He wasn't sure if she'd been hiding this part of herself, this need for him, but he'd never scented this from her before. If he had, he'd have had her on her back long before now.

He kissed a path along her jaw as he slid his palm even lower. "Tell me if you want me to stop," he growled against the sensitive spot behind her ear. Then he nipped her earlobe.

"Don't stop!" she practically shouted.

He dipped his hand lower under the band of her panties. He wanted to know what color they were, wanted to splay her out on his bed and feast on her for hours. But he was afraid that if he stopped, if either of them had time to think, they would do something stupid.

Like change their minds.

Stopping would be insanity. Because he was damn sure going to make sure she had an orgasm. Multiple orgasms. Ruin her for any other male. So that she would always look at him with hunger in her eyes.

She shoved at his shirt, tugging it upward, making him laugh lightly.

He moved back slightly and finished for her, practically ripping it over his head.

She blinked in surprise, staring at him, the heat in her green eyes flaring bright. He took advantage of that to tug on the tie of her robe, pulled it fully free. He wanted her completely bared to him. Touching her was everything, but he wanted to see her too.

It fell off her shoulders, pooled down around her waist, her body keeping it pinned against the door.

All he could do was stare at her full breasts, her perfectly pink nipples. They were tight little buds, rock-hard and begging for his tongue. His touch. A guttural growl left his throat.

"The bedroom's upstairs. First door on the left." Her words came out in a rush as she held on to him.

On the off chance one of her family members decided to come home early... He scooped her up, her robe falling to the floor, but he didn't bother picking it up. He raced up the stairs like a male possessed.

She let out a laugh, more of a gasping of air as he practically kicked the door shut behind them. "It's not just me, right? We've been building to this for a while?" The question came out breathless, unsteady.

He growled a response that he hoped sounded affirmative as he stretched her out on the bed. Words weren't computing in his head well.

He was vaguely aware of their surroundings, but the scent of her was much more powerful here, making him even harder. This was her room. Her sanctuary. And she'd invited him in.

"Sorry," he rumbled as he accidentally ripped the side of her panties. They were so damn flimsy.

In response, she stretched out on the bed, spreading her thighs wide for him.

He swallowed hard, staring at all of her splayed out for him. Only for him. His very own goddess.

Clinging to his control, he crawled up her body instead of diving straight between her thighs. He had to slow this down just a little. For her.

She arched her chest against his and the skin-to-skin contact had his cock pressing painfully hard against the zipper of his pants.

This was Jo, underneath him, wanting him as much as he wanted her. It stunned him and made him desperate at the same time.

She trailed her fingers down his back, the feel of her soft touch grounding him. Sort of.

"I've wanted you from the moment I met you," he rasped out.

The delicate flush of her cheeks spread down her neck. "Same," she whispered as if it was a secret.

Watching her expression, he reached between her legs, slipped a finger along her slick folds.

Oh goddess, she was so wet.

"Sorry." She whispered again, almost as if she was embarrassed.

Sorry? For what? For being so turned on right now?

He kissed her again, harder this time, swallowing her groan, learning exactly how she liked to be kissed, memorizing her moans before he kissed a path down her entire body. He took his time with each of her breasts, paying homage to them with his mouth. Because they deserved to be worshiped. *She* deserved to be worshipped.

By him only.

The entire time he kissed a path across her body he had two fingers buried inside her.

He loved the way her inner walls rippled around him, how each time he kissed somewhere on her body, whether her nipple or her abdomen, her inner walls tightened.

She seemed to simply like everything he did.

More likely they were both on a razor's edge of wanting each other for so long.

He was so glad he wasn't alone in the hunger. Because he felt obsessed with her, consumed.

Moving lower, lower, he stopped right between her thighs. Wisps of fine hair covered her mound, the same auburn color as her hair.

He pushed his fingers deeper and she rolled her hips, letting out the sweetest moan as he did.

"You're going to come for me." The words came out like a demand.

"Okay," she breathed.

As long as they were clear on that. Lowering his head, he flicked his tongue against her clit, smiling at the reaction.

Her entire body jolted, her hips rolling against his face as he teased her again. Then he sucked her clit into his mouth and earned a cry of surprise as she jolted against him.

Oh, this first orgasm wasn't going to take long at all.

He was vaguely aware of the earth rumbling underneath them, a faint signal of his mating manifestation. When dragons found their mates, when they became intimate with their would-be mate, it manifested in different ways. Some dragons exuded a natural fire, and right now he was glad that his wasn't a visible manifestation. He just hoped she didn't notice.

He started moving his fingers in and out of her in a tight rhythm, wanting to wring her first orgasm out of her now. Then slow down and take his time after.

She dug her fingers into his shoulders, her inner walls clenching even harder around him as he felt her orgasm start to build.

He sucked on her clit again.

"Cas," she cried out, her back arching as her climax rolled through her.

Her scent went wild now, so sharp in the air it was imprinted on him. His cock kicked against his pants again in reaction, desperate to slide into her slick heat.

As she finally fell against her bed, her eyes heavy-lidded with hunger, she reached for him. "We should have found a way to be alone a lot sooner," she said on a laugh. Her damp hair was mussed, the soft waves splaying everywhere.

He crawled up her body, taking her mouth with his, letting her taste her own release.

"We're going to do that again. Soon," he murmured against her mouth.

In response she slid her hand down his stomach and rubbed over his covered erection. "We're not stopping," she murmured, nipping his bottom lip. "We've got hours alone. Later we can talk about why on earth we waited so long to do this."

He found his voice, remembered the reason he'd come here originally. "We need to talk." He spoke softly against her mouth, feeling vulnerable in a way he'd never experienced.

She stopped what she was doing, but kept her palm right where it was, cupping his hard length over his pants.

On instinct he rolled against her hand, unable to stop himself.

"That's never a good thing," she said.

"What isn't?" He could barely think when she was touching him like this. And he didn't even have his pants off yet.

"When someone says 'we need to talk.'"

Hissing, he grasped her wrist gently and pulled it away from him, but settled it on his waist. He still wanted her touching him, just not quite so intimately.

"It's not bad. Or maybe it is, I don't know," he said as he rolled to the side of her, stretching out on her soft covers. His dragon was prowling inside him, demanding he tell her everything. Demanding that she accept him. All of him. "I've got to leave this afternoon. I'm going on a rescue mission. Some of my friends found a community of humans. They're stranded and not doing well in the cold weather."

"Is there anything I can do?" She snuggled up against him, throwing her leg over him as if it was the most natural thing, as if they'd done it a hundred times before.

He settled his palm on her hip, squeezed once. "Maybe. But that's not what I need to tell you." He paused, watching her eyes, hoping against hope he was doing the right thing in telling her. "I know that you've been under the impression that I'm a bear shifter." Because it was what he'd let her believe. "But I'm not."

"Oh...okay." She stretched slightly against him, her breasts rubbing against his chest. "I never wanted to ask, but yeah, I assumed. I mean...you're huge." Her cheeks flushed that delicious shade again. *"Everywhere."*

Goddess, she was going to kill him. And that part of him desperately wanted to be inside her right now. His female.

He didn't know how to say it, knew he simply needed to get the words out. Somehow. It just felt more intimate when they were in bed, her completely naked. "I don't know how to say this."

She must have sensed how serious he was because she sat up, pulled her sheet to her chest. "What's wrong?"

"I'm a dragon," he said as he sat up too, watching her expression closely. Dragons had killed her parents, stolen them away from her and her sisters in fire and violence.

Shock rippled off her as she stared at him. "You're a dragon?" she whispered.

Before he could respond, the front door downstairs slammed open and booted footsteps raced up the stairs. He tensed, but scented Luna. She must have forgotten something.

"Jo—"

Suddenly Jo's bedroom door flew open. "Hey, I forgot my— Oh my God!" Luna pivoted, covering her eyes with her hands before she ran into the doorframe. "Sorry! So sorry!" She raced back into the hallway, cursing as Jo scrambled to find clothes.

He didn't care that Luna had seen them. He only cared what Jo was thinking about what he'd just admitted. "I know I should have told you sooner. I just didn't know how." He looked for his own shirt, remembered he'd left it downstairs.

"Look, Cas," she said, tugging a T-shirt on over her jeans. He noticed that she hadn't bothered with any undergarments as she'd gotten dressed. "I...this is a lot. I—"

Suddenly the door flung open again and it was Grace. "What the hell is taking you—" She looked at the rumpled bed, then them. "Oh, sorry!" She hurried down the hallway. "Luna! We're going to be late!"

"Cas, I...this—"

"It's okay, I get it." He grabbed his shoes and raced out the door.

She cursed behind him, but he ignored her.

As he reached the downstairs, he grabbed his shirt and hurried outside, pulling the front door shut behind him.

His whole chest ached, as if she'd just shoved a spike into it. Jo's *expression* when he'd told her... He wasn't even sure how to read it. She'd looked shocked but also...had she been disgusted? Maybe he was just projecting his insecurities.

His dragon howled in pain, unable to deal with the rejection in human form now.

He reached the middle of the street and let his dragon take over. He couldn't stand being in this form one second longer and he didn't care about his stupid pants shredding. Not when his future mate, the female he loved with everything, didn't want him.

CHAPTER NINETEEN

K ing glanced at Ace, nodded once.
His second moved into action, striding across the open sunlit courtyard. Despite the January weather, there was a wealth of colorful flowers and plants spiraling out from the center fountain with a statue of two naked women holding a jug. Dallas had spelled all the foliage in this particular compound for him so it bloomed year-round. The waterfall was on, spilling out of the jug, the soft flow of water meant to be soothing and rhythmic.

Right now, nothing could soothe him. Almost nothing. But Aurora wasn't here, so yeah, nothing. She would be leaving in a few hours to help retrieve all the displaced humans, and while he adored her for helping, he didn't want her to leave. Didn't want to be far from her. Ever.

He put thoughts of Aurora on hold as Ace strode back into the courtyard, two fae females following him. Four of his wolves were behind them, effectively caging them in.

He swept his gaze over them, looking for weapons, taking in anything that might tell him more about these individuals. He'd already reached out to a couple contacts across the globe about the Latore Kingdom from a nearby fae realm, and everyone had agreed that, according to rumors, they weren't treacherous.

So there was that.

Now he wanted to know what the hell they wanted with him and why they'd shown up in his territory unannounced.

King motioned toward the round mosaic table he'd had set up next to the fountain. "Please, sit."

The taller female, with dark brown skin, ice-blue eyes and faintly pointed ears, looked at the other female with golden skin. She gave a subtle nod. Ah, so the tall one was in charge.

"Please allow me to introduce Cressida of the Latore Kingdom, heir to the Latore throne," the shorter female said, watching him with an unnerving sort of intensity.

King nodded politely at the princess. "I am King. Alpha of this territory, something you already know."

Cressida nodded once, watching him almost...curiously. "I do. Thank you for agreeing to meet with me. This is Lark."

King nodded at her, but did not introduce anyone else here. She didn't need to know his warriors by name. Not now, maybe never. "Let's sit and talk," he said, motioning again.

She seemed surprised by his abruptness, but she sat, while Lark moved off to the side with Ace.

"Can I offer you something to drink or eat?" He was striving for politeness, but wanted to get to the heart of whatever this was. The Alphas he dealt with didn't deal in formalities, and from all accounts he'd heard, the fae did.

"Not right now, but thank you." She sat stiffly, her expression curious as she watched him. Dressed in a rich purple tunic and navy blue palazzo-style pants—though he was sure they weren't from earth as he knew it, but her own realm—everything about her said elegance. But he could see the faint outline of a blade under the left side of her tunic.

"I don't mean to be rude, but I have to ask why you're here. Why a dozen of your people suddenly showed up in my territory, unannounced."

She blinked again. "We showed up and announced ourselves," she said simply. Almost as if he was daft.

"Okay. Why are you here? It is my understanding that the fae don't spend a lot of time in the human realm."

"It's true, we don't." She paused, watching him again in that curious way, her eyes searching for something. Finally she let out a short sigh. "I come here asking for a favor. Or...help." She seemed to push that word out. "Our realm is dealing with weather changes and our mages think it might be because of something going on in this realm. I've heard that some of your witches have essentially raised the earth, among other things."

Ah. That was interesting. "Raised the earth" was pretty spot-on. "Some of the witches in my territory have made some changes, true." It had been at his request, and based on engineering advice from humans and supernaturals alike. New Orleans had always suffered during hurricanes or storms because of its low elevation, so utilizing magic, they'd basically raised the territory so that it was above sea level.

But it was more than that. They'd been rebuilding roads with porous materials, storing and harvesting rainwater, creating more land basins to hold extra water—creating more green spaces in the city and surrounding areas. Essentially using the "sponge city" concept, decreasing erosion, and making the city safer, more stable.

He hadn't even imagined it would affect another realm. Guilt hit him hard to think that it had.

"Our kingdom has been experiencing a shift in…ah, quakes. Not often, but we've never had them before. We don't know if there is a connection to the changes made in your territory, but we're trying to be proactive. The quakes come and go and have unfortunately had dire effects on some of our territory. And our seasons are all off a bit. Right now instead of a biting winter, it's milder with less snow in general. I care about my kingdom as you care about your territory. Since it is clear you prefer that I get to the point, I will bluntly ask if we could speak to one of your witches. Or hopefully, one or more of your witches will visit our realm and see if they can help. Or perhaps figure out what is happening. We will gladly offer many goods in exchange for this. Fabrics, jewels, or perhaps unique flora and fauna. We have many things to offer." She sat back slightly.

King digested her words. "If this is so important to your kingdom, why are you here and not one of your parents?"

"My mother has passed, and my father is currently dealing with some of the fallout from the quakes and rising lakes." Her expression turned almost wry. "And if I'm being blunt, as you seem to prefer, he is not as diplomatic as me. He thought it would be better if I made contact with the new Alpha of New Orleans."

King snorted a laugh at that. "I prefer bluntness. I will speak to my people and let you know what I decide."

It was clear she wanted to say more, but she nodded, the action regal, then stood. Her companion immediately moved to her side. "Thank you for considering."

"Do you have accommodations?" He knew they'd just arrived the night before and had slept in tents on the outskirts of his territory.

From what his people had seen, they weren't pup tents but luxury tents the size of small houses. But he still wanted to offer.

"We do, thank you."

After they'd left, it was just him and Ace. He scrubbed a hand over his face. "So this is new."

Ace just grinned at him. "Days like this, I'm so glad I'm not in charge."

King simply shook his head. This brought up a host of things he hadn't been expecting—and there still wasn't any sign of Lucius anywhere.

And Aurora is leaving, his asshole wolf reminded him. As if he needed the reminder.

* * *

Cas sat against one of the oak trees outside Aurora's mansion, waiting for everyone else to arrive. He felt numb and didn't want to talk to anyone else.

To his surprise, the normally chatty snow leopard shifters hadn't bothered him. Aurora was sitting and talking with the two tiger shifters about twenty feet away at the patio table. He managed to tune out most of their conversation. All he needed to know was where to fly, and someone would tell him soon enough.

Shutting his eyes, he stretched his legs out. Sunlight filtered through the leaves still on the branches, but it didn't do anything to soothe him.

Nothing could do that.

He pushed away from the tree, was on his feet in seconds when he scented *her*.

Jo.

Turning, he spotted her walking around the side of the house with Axel. Whatever the dumb lion said made her laugh.

He bit back a snarl and stalked toward them.

"Cas, I didn't know you knew the doc." Axel's tone was light and warm.

He snarled at the lion.

Axel rolled his eyes and stalked away, muttering under his breath about grumpy dragons.

Cas kept his gaze on Jo, drinking her in. Her hair was down, all around her shoulders in messy waves. He hadn't stopped thinking about her since her rejection. Couldn't make the pain stop. "Why are you here?"

She took a tentative step forward, the scents rolling off her chaotic. "I've been calling around everywhere trying to figure out where you were. I tried calling you too…"

"I turned off my phone." He hadn't wanted to talk to anyone, and his brothers knew he was here so it hadn't mattered. "Why were you calling me?"

She gave him an exasperated look. "Because I love you, you big dumbass!"

He blinked, his lips parting slightly. "What?"

Her cheeks flushed and she glanced over at the table, then back at him. She grabbed his hand and tugged him behind the tree. Not that it would matter, everyone would still be able to hear…that she apparently *loved* him.

"You ran out of the house so fast. I…I was just trying to process what you told me. I'd had this picture of you in my mind, thought you were a bear—which you let me believe, for the record! Also, I was still reeling from the best orgasm I've had in…ever. Then my sisters ran in after you raced down the stairs and wanted to know what was going on. By the time I got downstairs you were flying away. You're gorgeous, by the way. Truly stunning. It was just a lot to take in. Bears are bears, they're not giant-ass flying dragons bigger than my house. *Dragons*, that breathe actual fire. So it's fair that I needed time to mentally process that. I…really wish you'd say something so I can stop rambling."

Shock at her words reverberated through him as he digested them. Actually processed them. He reached for her, unable to contain the need to touch her. "I love you too," he growled, clutching her hips tight as he tugged her close.

She loved him. She *loved* him. That made her his. Forever. His *mate*.

His dragon purred, a deep, contented rumble inside him. "And I will give you much better orgasms than that one."

She let out a startled laugh as she slid her hands up his chest. Which was unfortunately covered. He wanted her touching him skin to skin. "So…what does this mean? You and I…we're like, together, right?" She sounded tentative, something he didn't understand.

He'd just told her he loved her. But he knew from his brother's mate that he couldn't simply blurt out that she was his mate. Still, he needed to make one thing clear. "We are together. You are mine, and I am yours. I don't share."

Jo smiled softly. "Good, because I don't either." She leaned into him, holding him close as she laid her head against his chest. "Why did you run off like that? I didn't even get a chance to really say anything before you…raced out." She looked up at him now, her gaze searching.

"I was expecting your rejection so I took the coward's way out and ran before I could hear you let me down easy." Or harshly. He wasn't sure which would have been worse. "I let you believe I was a bear because of…what happened to your parents. But I should have told you sooner."

The look she gave him was soft, understanding as she cupped his cheek. "I wish you had told me, but I get it. And I hate that you have to leave now."

He did too, but he could not back out. Not when people were depending on him. He leaned into her soft hold. "We won't be gone long. It's a retrieval job. We will bring the humans back to the territory and then I will return to you." He would also need to explain to her about dragon mates, and all the implications involved. Because he wouldn't be able to hold back from claiming her much longer now that he knew her true feelings for him.

"Will you be able to call me?"

"I will try." His cell phone didn't always work and he didn't understand the mechanics of them enough to care why. "Sometimes we don't get service."

"I'll miss you," she murmured, her grip around him tightening.

"I will miss you too. But as soon as I'm back, we will pick up right where we left off."

"Promise?" Her lips curved up and there was a hint of wicked in her green eyes. It was followed with the sweet scent of her arousal wrapping around him.

Ohhhhh, yes please. He growled low in his throat, leaned down to nip her bottom lip. "Most definitely. I will make you come until you beg me to stop. Then I will keep going until you pass out from pleasure. I will not be leaving your bed."

Her cheeks went crimson then, so he kissed her again. He was going to enjoy making her blush—making her come.

Making her his.

CHAPTER TWENTY

"I'll be back in a little bit." Making a split-second decision, Aurora pushed up from the table.

Harlow lifted an eyebrow. "What's up?"

"Just need to do something before we head out." They were still waiting on a few others to join in the human retrieval mission, including a couple dragons, and wouldn't be leaving for likely another forty-five minutes.

Phoebe and her brothers had opted to hang out inside while all these strangers were at their place, and Aurora was more than fine with that.

"Sounds like Cas is officially taken," Lola said, grinning as she bit into her grilled cheese sandwich.

Yeah, it did. And the human female's confession to him, just putting it out there, had struck a chord with Aurora. She glanced over in the direction of the two but they were still behind the big oak tree. She had a feeling the human didn't realize they could all hear them, which was just as well. Aurora took off her sweater, let her wings extend. The racerback tank top underneath accommodated her wings perfectly so she tended to wear them a lot.

Brielle gave her a curious look but didn't say anything as she stole a grape from Lola's plate.

Aurora took to the air, not quite sure what she was doing. Or at least she wasn't sure what she was going to say. But something deep inside her compelled her to go see King again before she left.

She was exhausted with being afraid, with locking down her feelings, with letting "what if" hold her back—letting the past control her. Shape her future.

After clearing the treetops, she headed straight for King's Lower Garden District compound. It was the closest place to their mansion and she had a feeling he'd be there. Her heart thudded wildly in her chest as she angled in his direction, a frantic urgency pushing her faster, faster.

He'd told her more than once she didn't need to bother using the front gates, that she was always welcome, so she flew over them and landed in the middle of the expansive yard.

A second later, Ivy, a wolf shifter with blonde hair and bronze skin, dropped down from one of the trees. "Hey! I thought you were headed out today. Not that I'm not happy to see you!"

Aurora smiled at the bubbly female. "I am, in a bit. I probably should have called ahead." She glanced around, saw there was more security than normal. She waved at a couple wolves who waved at her. "Ah, what's going on?"

"We're gearing up for a meeting with the fae in a couple hours. Well, not we, but King wants security tighter than normal while he's gone."

"I thought he already met up with them?" She'd seen him hours ago and he'd told her about the interesting meeting.

"Oh, yeah, I just meant another one. But we've got pups here, so..." She shrugged.

Aurora nodded, understanding. Before she could respond, she spotted King striding across the yard, looking fit and sexy. As always. Her breath caught in her throat as she stared at him. He was a walking weapon, pure, raw art that sang to her phoenix. Long, lean, muscular *everything*, he moved with the grace of someone who knew he was at the top of the food chain. An apex predator in his prime. She forgot to breathe for a moment, had to order herself to get it together. And by get it together, that meant to *take a breath*.

"See you later." Ivy hurried away.

Aurora's vision more or less tunneled out anyway when she saw King. Tension hummed deep in her chest, an insistent buzzing of uncertainty. She suddenly felt stupid for just showing up like this. What if this was a mistake? *No.* She was doing this.

"Is everything okay?" Concern was etched onto his handsome face as he reached her.

"Yeah. I...I'm going to miss you," she blurted. Oh goddess, she sounded like an idiot. This wasn't anything like how she'd practiced on the way here.

Surprise registered in his face and for one eternal moment she wanted the world to swallow her up. Until raw heat flared in his gaze.

Ooooh. She liked that. So did her phoenix. Soooo very much. Fire danced along her arms, the pale blue a mirror to her wings.

"I'm going to miss you too." His words were a softly spoken growl as he stepped closer.

She erased the rest of the distance and wrapped her arms around him, needing a hug, needing to be held. By him. *Only him.*

He wrapped his strong, capable arms around her on a sigh and held her close. And all those jagged edges of fear and doubts she kept locked up suddenly all disappeared.

She didn't want to let go, didn't want to leave at all. "You mean a lot to me," she said into his chest, a wave of emotion threatening to overwhelm her. But she needed him to know how she felt.

"You mean a lot to me too." His grip tightened ever so slightly as he laid his chin on the top of her head. "You don't have to go."

"Yeah, I do. I promised." It had been her idea. She'd been the one who'd asked everyone to come with her, to rearrange their schedules. She couldn't back out now.

"I know." He stepped back slightly, looked down at her, his gaze all wild heat as he kept his grip around her. "When you get back, I want to make dinner for you."

"Like...a date?" She needed to be certain she was reading this right.

"Wolves don't date, but yes." His wolf was in his eyes as he watched her carefully, closely, almost...cautiously.

"I'd like that." Soooo much. She was still terrified of how she'd react if he touched her intimately. She was terrified she'd freak out, but when she thought of him touching her, desire was the only thing she experienced, not fear. Like right now his hand was gripping her hip in the most possessive, delicious way and she was wondering what that big, callused palm would feel like on her stomach, her breasts—between her legs. Sliding inside her. Heat bloomed in her at the thought.

And the wolf looked back at her. "It's a date, then," he growled. There was a promise in those words and in his eyes.

"King!" someone—Ari, she thought—called out from somewhere behind them.

He closed his eyes, sighed. He let her go then, but picked up her hand, linking his fingers through hers as he turned toward their interloper. Oh, this was a definite signal he was making. As strong as if he'd kissed her in public.

She'd always liked Ari but right now she kind of wanted to punch him.

The big wolf approached, his eyes flicking toward their joined hands once before he met King's gaze. "The fae are at the gate. They're early."

He let out a low growl, nodded at Ari and tugged Aurora with him.

Aurora liked being by his side, being his partner. "I thought Ivy said you were meeting off-site from here," she said low enough for his ears only as they walked across the grass.

"That was the plan. But I asked them here because it's easier. There's a house across the street I'd planned to use as a meeting point."

He'd told her about their original meeting...but he hadn't mentioned how stunning the princess was, Aurora thought as they reached the front gates. They'd been closed when she'd flown over them, but were open now to reveal a dozen fae, an even mix of males and females all dressed similarly in tunics and loose pants. In front of them were two females— and Aurora had no doubt who the female in charge was from her stance and clothing alone.

"I apologize for arriving early. We made better time than we thought." The female with ice-blue eyes and gently pointed ears had a lilting accent, one Aurora had never heard before.

"It's fine." King's words were brusque, his fingers squeezing Aurora's tightly, as if he didn't want to let her go.

A riot of emotions rolled through her. They had a date. King, the male who starred in all her fantasies, one of the best friends she'd ever had, was going to cook for her. And she knew what that meant for shifters. Feeding someone was a big deal. He wanted to officially court her, claim her. And...she hated that she had to leave.

"Cressida, this is Aurora. She's..." He cleared his throat, looked at her with his wolf in his eyes again. She swore the word *mine* hung in the air. Or maybe that was just wishful thinking. "A liaison for my territory," he finished. "Aurora, this is Cressida, heir to the Latore Kingdom."

Aurora smiled politely, not sure of what their customs were. She doubted princesses shook hands. Not that King was letting her hand go anyway. "It's a pleasure to meet you."

"And you as well."

Loud chirping erupted from above them.

The dozen fae behind them straightened, two going for weapons.

Aurora burst into flames, her wings shooting out behind her even as King tensed.

"He's not a threat," King snapped.

Okay so maybe she'd overreacted, but if they were going to pull weapons on Hunter? That was a good way to get burned.

Cressida barked out something in another language that made the two behind her still even as she stared at Aurora.

Hunter hovered down next to them, seemingly unconcerned, and she reached out, blindly petted him, but kept her eyes on the princess.

"Ah, apologies, my lady." She nodded once at Aurora, almost formally. "I did not realize you were a phoenix. That…any phoenixes lived here at all."

She turned to King, who just lifted an eyebrow. What was up with the "my lady" bit? She certainly wasn't going to ask. "It's no big deal." She shot the two males who'd gone for their weapons a glare before she turned to Hunter and kissed him on the nose. "I'll miss you, but I'll be back soon," she murmured against his face.

He chirped sadly.

Then she looked at King, wanted to say so much more to him, but now was not the time and he had his hands full. She wanted to hug him again, to throw herself into his arms, but again, *not* the time.

"Contact me when you reach Prima," he said softly.

"I will." Then she took to the skies, Hunter right behind her. She figured he'd follow her home and want to say goodbye to everyone.

As she reached the treetops, she turned back and waved at King.

He nodded at her, raising one hand in farewell.

Her chest ached as she flew away, but she would be counting down the time until she got to see him again.

Everything between them had changed. And even if she was scared, she was ready for it.

CHAPTER TWENTY-ONE

"How did you come by a dragon?" As they crossed the street, Cressida looked up to the skies, as if she might see Hunter flying back toward them.

King snorted. "He chose me."

She gave him a confused look.

He just shrugged. There was no good way to explain how an Alpha wolf had a pet dragon. He didn't understand it himself.

Behind them, Cressida's people and his wolves kept a fair distance as they headed up the walkway to the house across the street. It was a comfortable meeting place, one meant to put people at ease, and when Everleigh had suggested it, he'd agreed.

"Your phoenix..." She cleared her throat as they neared the front door, slowed her walk a fraction. "She's your mate?"

His wolf clawed to the surface, his instinct to say yes. "She's not your concern." He didn't care if he sounded rude. He wasn't going to talk about Aurora to a stranger. To anyone. But definitely not this fae female who'd come to him asking for help.

"Apologies. I'm just surprised there's a phoenix here in this realm."

He paused as they reached the purple-painted front door. "This realm?"

"I assumed they all preferred fae realms, but obviously I should not make assumptions. I...this realm is confusing to me. There's much I don't know about it." It seemed as if it was hard for her to admit it.

"You have phoenixes living in your realm?"

She nodded. "Of course."

Huh. They were going to go back to that later.

He opened the front door, strode in to find Everleigh in the sitting room to the left with two of her coven members. She immediately stood, smiled at both of them. Everleigh had choppy brown hair, olive-toned skin, wore a loose tunic over leggings and platinum rings on all her fingers. Her earrings were huge, little moons and stars dangling from the big hoops. While she looked to be in her early thirties, he had no idea what her real age was.

He quickly made introductions before Cressida and Lark sat across from Everleigh on a comfortable settee.

"King has explained some things to me, but please tell me exactly what's going on and how we can help," Everleigh said simply as she leaned forward.

There was something about her tone that was always soothing. She truly cared about helping others, he'd found. And she was very, very good at using her truthsense powers. Apparently it was an inborn thing for some witches.

As a wolf he could scent lies, but that wasn't something he could depend on to always know if someone was telling the truth. People were complex and could often convince themselves that lies were truths. Or if their scents were too chaotic, he wouldn't understand the mix of them.

Everleigh...she had a gift for getting right to the heart of things.

Cressida glanced at King, then back at Everleigh. She let out a short breath. "As I've told King, our kingdom, our territory, is experiencing quakes far under the ground and it's affecting some of our water levels, among other things."

As she continued talking, the two witches with Everleigh returned with platters of tea and snacks.

He moved to one of the windows, listening to them converse as he glanced out at the yard, the street beyond. His people and the fae were all standing around almost awkwardly, no one speaking.

The females spoke for over an hour, going back and forth, with Everleigh asking a lot of questions—many of them meant to discern whether these fae were liars.

Finally, there was a lull in the conversation and Everleigh looked at King. She gave him a nod to indicate that the fae were telling the truth, that they did need help.

Hell, it would have been easier if they'd simply been liars. He would have been able to kick them out of his territory and deal with the potential problem of Lucius.

Though he knew it wasn't merely potential. The kayakers they'd found had healed and were back at home, but he'd received a report early that morning of a handful of humans found outside his territory. Dead. Drained of all life force. Same with a few vampires—Myles and the males he'd left with. And they'd been drained of blood.

Lucius was getting stronger, and King had no way to know where the bastard was. He was just glad Aurora was out of the city for now. He didn't want her anywhere near that monster.

"I'd like to go with them, to help," Everleigh said. "If you can spare me right now?"

He didn't like the thought of losing Everleigh. "Your presence is always important." Like Dallas, she was an important member of the witches' covens. "But...what do you think?"

"I think they need our help, and what she's described is something I can work with. I'll need to bring two of my people with me. And I'd like to bring a couple wolves as well."

As backup, he figured she meant without spelling it out. King looked at Cressida. "Will there be an issue with that?" He knew the fae didn't always like other species, though Cressida hadn't given that attitude yet.

"Of course not. We have shifters living in our realm," she added. "We're not like some fae you might have had contact with. We are..." She paused, looking for the right word. "Welcoming."

"Can you two work out the logistics?" He looked at Everleigh, asking her more than Cressida.

"Definitely."

He nodded and pulled out his phone, which had been buzzing in his pocket. "I need to step outside for a moment, then."

The two women continued talking as he made his way to the front door. His people came to attention as he stepped outside, but he waved them off and looked at his phone screen. It was clear Everleigh and Cressida were speaking the same language so he was going to just let them figure things out. He had many other things that required his attention.

Like Aurora.

He smiled when he saw her name on his screen, his heart beating faster. They had a *date*. He'd seen the need in her violet eyes.

Whatever had shifted for her, he just cared that it had. He'd never deviated from wanting to run New Orleans, from wanting to be Alpha, but today...he wished he was just King.

That he was with Aurora right now.

Prima is shockingly good with kids, her text started. *She's currently in dragon form, letting a bunch of human kids literally run all over her. One is rolling a basketball down her tail!*

He snorted at the image. *How are the humans? What do you think of them?*

They're underfed, cold, ready to get to an actual civilization. There are a couple graves, looks like they lost some people in the last month. It's mostly families and a lot of kids. Some of the adults seem more shell-shocked than the kids at the rescue. It's heartbreaking.

Yeah, Prima had said she and Arthur had found them in a sort of connected subdivision. It sounded as if they'd all banded together and had done the best they could, but they'd lost access to power and in some cases, water. And they'd been scavenging for food. *Do you all have enough supplies?*

More than enough. It'll probably take a couple trips to get them back. We're letting them all talk and figure out how they want to travel before we move them. How are things there? With the fae?

Good enough. Do the humans know what you are?

No. I flew in and then shifted before we landed. I rode on Cas so it looked like I was just one of his passengers.

King bit back a growl. He didn't love the idea of her riding any other male. But...until they knew more about who these humans were, if they were a potential threat, he was glad she'd opted not to reveal what she was. *Keep in touch.*

You too. Looking forward to our date.

He paused, words not enough in that moment. *Me too.* Yeah, definitely not enough, but it would have to do until he could show her exactly how much she meant to him. How much he was looking forward to cooking for her.

It was a primal thing—giving her food, feeding her—and he hoped she understood what this meant for him. For them.

"What the hell?"

King looked up at one of his wolves' exclamations. And froze for all of a second before he withdrew his sword.

A gray mist descended all around them, the air thick with dew and...something sparkly. What the hell was this? His sword dripped with fire, residual power from the lightning Aurora had shot into it a year ago.

Suddenly three of the fae dropped right onto the grass. Then two of his wolves. He raced toward them even as Ari did the same, kneeling next to them. Three of his wolves shifted on a growl of pain, not bothering to change clothes.

A chill descended on everything, small icicles forming across the dried grass in the yard.

He turned at the sound of the house door opening, saw Everleigh and the two fae race out. Cressida looked at him in shock, then raced to her fallen people.

"What the hell is this?" Ari growled. "I'm having to fight the shift."

"You are?" King asked.

The big male nodded. "It's like a compulsion, my wolf wanting to take over, to protect me."

King didn't feel it, but he looked at the others. "You all feel it?"

There were murmurs of affirmation even as Ace raced toward them from across the street. "A quarter of our wolves are asleep. Or knocked out really, almost like what we saw with..." He lowered his voice. "With the kayakers."

Lucius. This had to be his work.

Rage surged through him, his wolf slamming to the surface. King pulled out his cell phone, frowned as the screen flickered. *Shit.* He called Aurora, desperate to get through.

"Hey," she said, her voice staticky.

"Stay where you are. Don't return to the city with the humans until you hear from me." He gave her a quick rundown, being as succinct as possible. "I don't know what this is yet, but I'm going to find out. Just don't come back. I need you safe. And the others," he added. "Just stay safe." If anything happened to her... He smothered a snarl.

"We will. Please be careful. I want you safe too." It went staticky, then the call ended.

He cursed and shoved his phone into his pocket as Cressida

approached. "What do you know about this?" he demanded.

She blinked, straightening as she reached him, her gaze straying to his sword for a moment. "I'm not behind this, if that's what you're implying." Her tone was indignant.

"Do you know what this is?"

She paused, nodded as Lark moved up behind her, worry in both their expressions.

The other female stepped forward. "It's a spell. A dark one."

Even as she spoke, the mist seemed to thicken, to almost mute their surroundings. Or dampen them. He couldn't hear any ambient noise coming from even across the street. "From your people?"

"No! Not from our kingdom."

"But there's a hybrid vampire-fae who hates my father," Cressida said. "Lark thinks this might be his work. If we've brought this on your territory...I am truly sorry." Raw emotion flickered in her blue eyes.

King tensed. "This might not be because of you," King said. "What's this hybrid's name?"

"He goes by many names," Lark said. She looked at Cressida, then back at King. "He is before Cressida's time. He's been dormant for so many years, we all thought he was dead. But I can scent him in the air, in this mist. This *is* his magic, I know the signature. I can almost taste it."

King cursed savagely because he recognized this scent too. "Is one of his names Lucius?"

Lark blinked, but nodded slowly. "It is."

"Damn it," he growled. "I didn't realize he was half fae." *Fuuuccck.* King had thought he was a sorcerer or a mage.

"You know him?"

Gritting his teeth, he nodded. "Yeah, thought I killed the bastard a long time ago." But he hadn't used iron. *Fuuuuck.* The fae were damn hard to kill but iron sure would have helped.

"He is very powerful and very old. I don't know of any other vampire-fae in existence than him. Cressida's father, the king, banished him from our kingdom long ago."

"Why?"

The females exchanged a look and something passed between them, something King couldn't begin to read. But his wolf didn't like it. It was as if they were keeping secrets. Then Cressida looked at his sword again. "Lucius did not approve of his choice of mate. Tried to kill her."

"Your father should have killed him then." That was what King would have done. If someone ever came after his mate, they would die. Immediately. Slowly. Painfully.

He sheathed his weapon. Right about now, it certainly wasn't doing him any good.

Lark simply nodded. "He tried. But then Lucius disappeared into this realm so he created a barrier to our kingdom. The hybrid cannot enter."

Guy still should have hunted Lucius down, but King wasn't going to get into that. "How do I break this?" He looked over as Everleigh approached, saw she wavered on her feet once.

"I'm okay," she murmured. "But I can feel his magic crawling on my skin. It's uncomfortable."

He needed to know how far this extended in his territory and he needed to know who was affected.

"I'm not sure," Lark said. "But I know someone who can help. In our realm." When he didn't respond, she continued. "You have three days to release this spell before everyone who has fallen under it dies." Her words were blunt, but he scented the truth in them. "Lucius will then gain all of their essence, their energy."

"She's telling the truth," Everleigh said.

If Lucius gained that surge of power— King knew what he would do. He would raise reapers and attack New Orleans. A chill skittered down his spine.

King didn't like that this had happened right after the fae had shown up. Though...they had found the kayakers before these fae. And he couldn't imagine why they'd do this to his territory. Fae had no interest in anything to do with humans.

"My own people are affected by this." Cressida's tone was heated, as if she'd read his train of thought.

"Can you contact this person from here, the one who can help?"

Cressida shook her head. "We need to return to retrieve her. And you need to come with us."

"I need to be here with my people." There was no way he would abandon his people or territory. He was in full-on triage mode right now. He hated the seconds ticking by that they spoke, that he wasn't helping his people.

"You won't have any people left if you don't come with us," Lark snapped with surprising heat. "And Halcyon won't come with us to this realm. Not under normal circumstances. But she might come if you ask."

Might? What the hell was all this?

"She's telling the truth." Everleigh's voice was calm, but he sensed the urgency in her words.

"Fine. Everyone but Cressida stays," he said, looking at the princess. Lark's mouth pulled into a thin line. "In case we're lying?"

King looked over at her fallen people and the ones standing next to them. "They will be guests here." He nodded at the house behind them. "There is plenty of room. And yes. You would do the same thing."

"It's fine." Cressida spoke before the other woman could. It was clear Lark didn't like it, but she nodded at her princess's order.

"We leave in three hours." He had so much to do before then. He needed to figure out how far this reached, how many people were affected, and start triaging the city.

Unfortunately, he knew most humans would have been affected. There was so little magic in all of them that they would be consumed under something like this.

Turning to Everleigh, he said, "Contact all your people that you can. Including Dallas—I need to know if this reaches as far as the farms and outer territory. And I need to know if anyone here knows how to fight this magic, knows how Lucius created it. Meet at the pack's place in the Quarter in thirty minutes." He assumed it was covered in the fog too, but needed a close central place to regroup.

She nodded and hurried off with her people.

"Ace," he said, turning to his second who'd been busy giving orders of his own. "Further status update?"

He listened as Ace ran through what he knew, watching out of the corner of his eye as the fae loaded up their comatose and carried them into the house. So far it sounded as if the fog had spread out across a few miles, maybe more, of the city proper. As he'd thought, humans were all affected, and younger shifters and vampires were as well. They simply weren't strong enough to fight the spell.

Once he was done, King nodded. "I'll contact the head of every coven, pack or clan, tell them where to meet. You're in charge while I'm gone. I'm not calling anyone back in from missions. I don't want anyone getting trapped in this." He needed the healers in the city to get to work on any human caught in this web.

Ace rolled his shoulders once, as if fighting the invisible magic. The longer King was here, the more he could actually feel it pressing in on him too. Raking against his skin. "Who are you taking with you?" Ace asked.

"No one. I'll travel faster with the princess alone." He wanted Aurora with him but would never risk her safety going into an unknown realm.

Ace gritted his teeth. "At least take Ari."

"No." He wouldn't risk anyone's life. Only his own.

Ace looked as if he would argue, but then he nodded.

King wasn't bringing anyone with him into this other realm. He didn't know enough about them, and if he couldn't handle himself, then he didn't deserve to be an Alpha.

"I at least need to know where the entrance to their realm is," Ace added.

"That, I will make sure you know." The sooner he got to whoever this Halcyon person was who might help, the better. Lucius had taken years from him. The bastard wouldn't take his territory, wouldn't hurt his people.

King was just so damn glad Aurora wasn't here. He could focus on everything that had to be done, knowing she was safe.

CHAPTER TWENTY-TWO

"Be straight with me," King said, looking at Cressida. It was just the two of them now, trekking through the woods of his territory. He'd given his orders and had to trust that his people would triage the city, take care of everyone while he was gone. A territory only lasted so long without an Alpha, however. But if he didn't break this spell, there would be no territory to speak of. "What are my chances of your healer helping us?"

Cressida paused at the tree line of the thick forest, gave him a look he couldn't begin to define. "She'll help you," she finally said. "And Lark is wrong. I think she'll come to your territory."

"Then why did Lark say she wouldn't?"

"Because Lark is ancient." Her tone was dry. "She thinks she knows best more often than not. Never mind that I'm a powerful warrior, the next in line to rule. She treats me like a child more often than not."

In that moment, he felt a small amount of kinship. "I have ancient dragons in my territory who occasionally call me a child. They say it with no insult either. Sometimes I think they would like to pat my head as if I'm an errant pup." He shook his head in exasperation.

She let out a startled laugh, making her look far younger than he guessed her to be. Then she stiffened and turned toward a flapping sound.

He was already turning at the sound. "What the hell?" Hunter was swooping toward him—Aurora not far behind in the air, her wings a bright beacon of flames against the gray sky.

"Your mate follows."

King wouldn't deny Aurora was his mate, couldn't say the words. Instead he growled low in his throat. "She's not alone." He could scent one of the tigers not far behind. And…there was someone else. Someone he couldn't see but had no doubt was in the sky behind Aurora. He sighed.

As Aurora descended, Hunter right next to her, Harlow in tiger form raced across the grassy field he and Cressida had just crossed.

"What are you doing here?" he demanded.

For once, Hunter was silent, landing on all fours next to Harlow, who nuzzled him briefly as Aurora said, "Going with you."

"You can't—"

"She's welcome," Cressida said smoothly. "All of you are." Though she eyed Harlow warily.

Harlow yawned, swatting at a gnat with her big paw, but she watched Cressida as well.

"You're. Not. Coming." He gritted his teeth, his wolf in his eyes as he stared her down. This was too dangerous and his fear for her was making him edgy.

"That Alpha thing doesn't work on me." She stalked toward him, hands on hips, a beautiful phoenix of pure fire. Her violet eyes sparked with temper. "And I'm going. You think to run off to a strange land without backup?"

"I'm Alpha." It was his goddamn duty. "My job is to protect my people." Including her.

"We're going," she said simply.

Hunter chirped in agreement.

Even Harlow nodded, her tail swishing lazily.

He let his head fall back. They didn't have time to argue—and while he didn't think Cressida was lying to him, he couldn't know for sure this place was safe for Aurora. She was a rare phoenix. She would be vulnerable there. "How'd you know to follow us here?" He'd only given the location of this entrance to a few of his people. His money was on Ace telling her.

Aurora shrugged. "Lucky guess."

"Whoever told you will be punished."

She snorted. "Then we better get going so you can come back, save the territory, then mete out a punishment."

He stared at her, a battle of emotions raging through him. "I just want you safe," he finally snarled. If she was with him, his concentration would always be divided. Because she was more important than anything, even his territory.

"And I want you safe. But that's just not in the cards. If you want a chance with me, then we're a team. *Partners.*"

He…couldn't argue with that. Growling again, he grabbed her hand and turned toward Cressida. "If anything happens to any of them—"

"It won't." She gave the tiger another wary look, then nodded toward the trees. "This way."

There was the faintest rustle of noise behind them—likely a dragon shifting to human form, but he ignored the sound and didn't think Cressida heard it.

* * *

Aurora glanced around the forest, immediately struck by the difference in the weather. It was still chilly, with a faint hint of snow covering the forest floor. And the flora and fauna—everything was different. Brighter. Even the winter weather had more of a snap to the air.

"It's normally a couple feet deep with snow this season," Cressida said as she bent to open her pack. She pulled out a long coat with fur lining the collar and offered it to Aurora. "Would you like this?"

"No, but thank you." Her fire wrapped around her, a warm blanket keeping the cold at bay.

King was tense next to her, glancing around the forest, looking for a threat.

Hunter buffeted her other side, on all fours as he looked around curiously.

"It'll be a half hour walk from here," Cressida said, looking at all of them as she slid the coat on. Then she paused. "We'll pass through a village. You will receive curious looks. All of you." Her gaze landed on King, the look she gave him searching, as if expecting something from him.

King stiffened slightly, his grip on Aurora's hand tightening. "As long as no one threatens us, they can look all they want."

Cressida made a very un-princess like snorting sound, as if the concept was ridiculous.

King had been quiet since they'd walked through the "doorway" which had been a seam in the fabric of... Well, Aurora wasn't really sure what it had been. Space? But when she turned back the way they'd come, she could easily see the ripple in the forest. A sort of glow.

"You don't guard the doorway?" King asked, his gaze following Aurora's. The doorway in the human realm was in a thick forest not frequented by people because it was in a wetland conservation area.

Cressida pointed upward to the treetops.

King froze for a fraction of a moment. Two fae, nearly camouflaged, crouched on different tree branches, watching them carefully.

It took a moment for Aurora to realize that he hadn't scented them. She hadn't either, but King scented everything, she'd thought.

"They cover their scents from any would-be predators." Cressida's tone was matter-of-fact, clearly having read his train of thought.

He simply nodded and turned around.

Hunter chirped up at the fae indignantly.

Aurora and Harlow both gave the fae their backs.

Cressida hoisted her pack on and nodded that they follow.

Aurora squeezed his hand once and gave a chin nod, pointing upward.

King paused, then nodded.

She dropped his hand, though she hated to do it, then lifted up, her wings of fire whisper-quiet as she rose toward the treetops.

Hunter wasn't as quiet, following after her, his own wings making furious little flaps.

Cressida glanced up at them but didn't stop her trek, leading them over the well-worn path.

All the snow had been cleared away and there was a lot more foot traffic—boot prints and what looked like hoof prints—once they breached the edge of the forest.

Aurora scanned in all directions. Snowcapped mountains were to the west, and seeing mountains at all was kind of odd. To the east all she saw was more and more forest. But to the north were villages. Or one long village, the small buildings dotted along close to each other, then there was a break from a bridge or two, then more buildings were clustered in the same manner.

No trajectory weapons or dragons in the sky, so that was good. She hadn't actually been expecting them, but still.

Hunter made a chirping sound at her as the others neared the beginning of a softly arching bridge that led to the first row of thatch-roofed cottages. This place was like something out of an English countryside.

She might not speak baby dragon, but she understood the gist of what he wanted and swooped downward. When Ace had called her and told her King was heading off into some fae land without anyone going with him, she'd rounded up Harlow and Cas—who entered this realm behind them with his natural dragon camouflage. Cas was worried about the human female he was apparently intending to mate. So when he'd heard Aurora talking to Harlow about coming here, he'd offered to go as backup. He wanted to fix their territory as well.

Thankfully he'd spoken to one of his brothers and he'd checked on Jo and her family. They weren't conscious, but they were alive and...

They had three days to fix this. Aurora was very aware of that invisible clock ticking away as she landed next to King.

Immediately, he took her hand in his, warming her from the inside out. He might be annoyed with her, but he was still touching her.

And boy, did she need it right now. "This is a beautiful countryside," she said to Cressida, who was walking at a brisk pace a couple feet ahead of them.

"Thank you." Cressida's voice was tense as they crossed the bridge, setting Aurora's teeth on edge.

"Is there something else we need to know?" King must have sensed the same thing Aurora did.

With each step, the tension in Cressida seemed to ratchet up.

The princess turned, slowed, and fell in step with the two of them. "I... This is simply different than what we'd set out to do. I'm worried for my own kingdom and now your territory. For my people who are stuck back there in that coma. I'm worried that Halcyon won't be able to combat the dark magic. And I'm also worried..." She eyed King again in a strange way. "About a lot of things." In that moment the regal female looked exhausted.

King nodded. "I'm sorry your people got caught up in that web."

Cressida simply shook her head. "It's certainly not your fault."

Aurora blinked as a handful of wide-eyed children with pointed ears raced out of one of the cottages. They remained in their snow-covered yard, staring as their group passed.

"Princess Cressida!" One of the younglings waved, revealing two missing front teeth, but all her attention was on Aurora and King. Then her attention drifted to Hunter and Harlow, her mouth falling open now.

"Hello, children! We have friends visiting the palace. They're very welcome guests. Please spread the word," Cressida called out, not slowing her pace. "We probably should have taken a less populated route, but this is the quickest way," she murmured to them. "It's probably better everyone sees you all now." Aurora wasn't sure if Cressida's words were for herself or them.

There was something in her tone, a note Aurora...wasn't sure about. She drew her wings tight against her back at the same time Harlow brushed her head against Aurora's free hand.

The farther they walked, the more fae strode out of their homes or workplaces and stared. It wasn't hostile, definitely more curious than anything but...it was a whole lot of fae. "It's like the quietest, saddest parade ever," she murmured for King's ears only.

He let out a startled snort and looked at her, his expression softening a fraction. "Even though I'm pissed at Ace for telling you, I'm still glad you're here."

"How'd you know it was Ace?"

His smile was pure satisfaction. "I wasn't sure until just now."

"Sneaky wolf." She nudged his shoulder with her own as they reached an arching bridge. Beneath them water babbled gently, not frozen over but icy-looking nonetheless.

King had started to respond when Hunter chirped. They both straightened, stopping completely at the top of the bridge.

Half a dozen horses—or what sort of looked like horses—galloped toward them, complete with armed riders. Behind the riders a giant castle sprouted against the pale blue sky. Sparkling spires glittered with...jewels, perhaps. The place was a fortress, huge and strong.

She kept all her focus on the riders, however.

Cressida, just realizing they'd stopped, turned as she neared the sloping bottom of the bridge. "What's wrong?"

King simply nodded at the oncoming riders. "Get ready to fly," he murmured to Aurora. "Harlow, if shit goes sideways, you jump the bridge and follow Aurora. You too, Hunter. I will follow." His words were almost subvocal, for their ears only.

Cressida frowned, then looked back at them, her expression almost exasperated. "It's the royal guard. They're here to escort us in. Word's definitely spread by now to my father." When they still didn't move, she hurried down the pathway, her coat billowing out behind her. The helmeted guards all came to a smooth halt, the first rider dropping down and stopping to speak to Cressida.

Almost immediately, he jumped back onto his steed and let out a whistle. They all turned back around, but didn't take off.

Cressida then turned back to them and lifted her hands out, Vanna White-style.

"Take to the air," King murmured. "Follow us in that way. See how many archers they have."

"Archers?" Aurora asked.

"They're fae. They've got archers. Trust me. I want a full-scale view of the castle as we enter."

"You're sure we shouldn't stay together?"

"I'm not sure of anything." His jaw was clenched tight.

In that moment she understood how hard it was for him to have them with him. To protect. The male was so damn protective of his territory, his people. Of anyone he deemed under his purview. It would have been easier for him to come here alone, to only be responsible for himself. "I'll follow your lead, then." She extended her wings in a big show of fire behind her, leaned up and kissed his cheek before she shot straight upward. Also in another show of power.

If these fae thought to betray them, she and the others would all go down fighting. She would set this entire place on fire if they hurt King or any one of her friends.

She might have an artist's soul, but if it came down to it, she would always protect those she loved through any means necessary.

A gust of icy wind rolled over her as she flew higher, doing exactly as King had asked—scanning the castle for weapons and archers. And he'd been right. There were a lot of them stationed along the battlements of the palace.

None of them raised a weapon at her, however. Just stared.

This place was a true fortress, built right into the side of a mountain. It would be difficult to attack from any angle.

As they reached the drawbridge, there was a moment when King and the others passed under the portcullis. She flew over, taking in everything she could, memorizing everything she saw.

Only when she saw King and Harlow walk out from the portcullis into the bailey did she breathe out a sigh. Next to her Hunter chirped in what definitely sounded like relief.

King looked up then, searching her out, and though she was far above him she swore she could feel his look searing her straight to her core.

"Come on," she murmured to Hunter, swooping down, flying in a giant lazy circle, definitely showing off for the fae—and a little for King. She liked when King looked at her, and when Ace had told her that he was running off into danger by himself...something had clicked into place.

King meant everything to her and she would never let him run into danger without her.

"My father's been alerted of your presence," Cressida said as Aurora landed. "He's on his way down the mountain to greet us." She paused, then looked at Aurora. "There are other phoenixes living here. They will likely want to meet you."

"Here?" she asked, startled.

"Not in the castle, but in our territory. Our realm has always been a safe haven for your kind. We have many things in common."

Aurora gave a noncommittal nod as a female fae dressed in a luxurious-looking coat similar to Cressida's approached. She nodded respectfully and said something to her in a language Aurora didn't know before her gaze trailed to them. The female stared at King far too long for

Aurora's liking. She felt like going all Harlow on her and baring her teeth. Instead, she took his hand in hers and squeezed.

"There are refreshments waiting for us. And a fire to warm up with," Cressida said as she turned to them. She glanced at Hunter and frowned.

"He comes with us." There was no room for argument in King's tone.

"Very well." Cressida nodded and led the way inside the castle.

Feeling dozens of eyes watching them, Aurora really, really hoped this wasn't a mistake. That they weren't going to end up fighting their way out of here.

CHAPTER TWENTY-THREE

"This place is nice." Harlow, now in human form, wearing her fatigues and a "mess with me and die" expression, stood near the crackling fire where Hunter lounged, barely moving. Her long auburn hair was pulled back in a tight braid and coiled at her neck. Aurora knew she often wore it like that so no one could grab her braid in a hand-to-hand fight. "We need to see about installing a fireplace like this."

"Sure. Once we've saved everyone, I'll look into getting a fireplace installed for you." Aurora's tone was dry as she eyed her friend.

Harlow simply lifted a shoulder. "I was just making an observation."

"Make it in your head." King's tone was just as dry as Aurora's.

He was still wound tight, the power pulsing off him in waves filling up the sitting room they'd been offered to wait in five minutes ago.

Aurora understood his impatience. Every second counted. They needed to speak with the fae healer who would hopefully be able to counteract whatever it was Lucius had done. And she was desperately trying not to think about what might be happening in the city right now. What Lucius might be doing to her friends. At least she knew that Bella, Lola, Phoebe, and Phoebe's little brothers weren't affected by the spell. Right now she was grasping onto that knowledge tightly. If someone attacked them or if the city devolved into chaos, Bella and Lola would make sure they all got to safety.

A gold-plated rolling tray of food had been brought in but no one had touched anything. King had smelled it, so had Harlow. They'd deemed it fine but still hadn't touched it. So she wasn't going to either.

Aurora looked up at the high stone ceiling above them, eyed the stained-glass windows letting in natural light. The room should have felt cold with all the stone, but a huge throw rug took up almost the entirety of the cold floor underneath. An oversized tapestry depicting a peaceful woodland scene covered one of the walls opposite the fireplace. And the long, tufted bench was as soft as the two cushy chairs opposite it.

Everything appeared hand-stitched and of very fine quality. This room was meant to be welcoming, to put whoever was inside it at ease.

Unfortunately, that wasn't working.

"We can escape out those windows if needed," Harlow murmured.

"I know." Aurora kept her tone low as she looked back at her friend, then over at King. She could hold on to Harlow and fly out while King rode Hunter if they needed to make an escape that way. "You hear something?" she whispered to King, who'd gone suddenly still.

He was staring intently at the door as he nodded. "Someone's coming." Moving so swiftly she barely had time to register it, he stood in front of her, angling his body so he was between her and whoever came through the door.

She gently touched his back, wanting to give him comfort even as she took some for herself. She kept having visions of being kidnapped, remembering how helpless she'd been when she'd been shackled in iron. The one thing she knew now: King would protect her with everything he had.

Some of the tension in his back eased and then she heard the footsteps. More than one. She kept telling herself things were going to be fine, that Cressida seemed trustworthy.

Then...

"Holy shit," Harlow blurted.

"Um..." Aurora stepped out from behind King, stared at the tall male with pointed ears who'd just stepped into the room. Then she looked at King, who seemed almost frozen.

Holy shit, indeed.

The male was clearly fae, given his ears, but he was a little broader than the ones they'd seen so far. His skin was the same dark brown as King and he had the same ice-blue eyes as King—and Cressida. Aurora's gaze shot to Cressida, who was behind the male, standing in the shadows. She hadn't seen the similarities between King and Cressida before, but oh...ooooh, she could see them now.

The male stepped into the room, his gaze firmly on King's.

With the exception of the ears, he was an older copy of King. A mirror image almost.

Cressida was right behind him, tension in every line of her expression. "King, this is ah...King Sorgin, of the Latore realm. My father. Father, this is King of the New Orleans territory."

The male strode forward in long, even strides. "Who was your mother?"

King bristled slightly. "Why don't you tell me?" he finally growled.

Aurora slid up next to him, unsure what the hell was going on. Could this be...King's father? And Cressida would be his half-sister. The male was graying at the temples, but the similarities were striking. They had the same skin tone and eyes. And now she realized how much Cressida looked like King. Not as much as this male, but it was in their noses. They had the exact same noses. All the intense staring at King made a lot more sense now.

Sorgin cleared his throat. "Was your mother Zahara?"

King's tightened jaw was answer enough. "So you're the bastard who abandoned us?"

The king's eyes flared bright. "I thought you were dead! I thought you were... Goddess, where is Zahara?" His eyes shone with a raw hope.

King stared hard at the male, and Aurora could practically see his wolf beneath the surface, ready to strike. "She died."

Pain extinguished the brightness in the male's icy eyes before his expression went carefully opaque. "How? When?" His voice wavered.

King ignored him, looked past him to Cressida. "Is this why you came to me?"

She stepped forward, her expression distraught. "No...I'm telling the truth about the weather anomalies. The quakes. The warmer winters. But when I saw you, I... You look just like him. I didn't really understand but then I figured you had to be the boy he had before me. Before..." She cleared her throat, looking to her father for guidance.

But Sorgin was just staring at King.

"You should have said something." King's tone was slightly softer when he spoke to her.

"Would you have believed me? And would it have changed anything? I didn't lie about Halcyon. She can help you and she's racing back here. But we need to... There is a lot to discuss." She spread her hands out in a helpless gesture and Aurora could almost feel her worry.

Gone was the regal, elegant female from before. She was just as out of sorts as Aurora imagined King and his father were. Because this was a whooooole lot. King had a father. And a half-sister. And…she wanted to wrap him up in a hug and just hold him close. "Why don't we all sit?" she murmured, placing her hand gently on King's forearm, needing to give him comfort at a time when his world had turned on its side. She hadn't even known he was half fae—and she didn't think he'd known either.

He covered her hand with his other one, held it in place before he nodded. Moving with Aurora to the long bench, he sat next to her stiffly as Cressida and Sorgin sat across from them in the purple chairs.

Hunter and Harlow remained where they were, basically statues by the fireplace.

"Where have you…" The king cleared his throat. "I never abandoned either of you. Your mother and you disappeared one day. We thought you were stolen from us by the Benz vampire coven. We'd been at war and they hated shifters in general, but they especially hated that I'd mated with your mother instead of allying myself with one of them." He paused. "Is any of this familiar?"

"No." There was a lot of heat in that one word. A lot of anger.

Aurora squeezed his arm once in comfort, reminding him that she was here for him.

"I was told you were both dead, murdered," the king rasped out, clearly unable to stem his emotions. "I scented your blood. Zahara's blood… We slaughtered the Benz coven. They do not exist anymore. If I'd known you were alive, I'd have never stopped looking for you. Where have you been all these years? Why did your mother not return to me?"

"I've never heard of the Benz coven. We were kidnapped by a male named Lucius."

Cressida sucked in a sharp breath.

King looked at his half-sister before he focused on his father again. "I was five."

"That's how old you were when you disappeared," the king said, his expression stricken. "One day, the two of you were just…gone."

"We were taken to what is now Alaska and held captive for two years until we escaped."

"He hurt you." A low growl.

King simply nodded.

The king stood, his hands balled into fists as he paced in a circle. He abruptly sat again. Tension vibrated off his big body as if he wanted to strike something. Anything. "Where did you go from there?"

"All over. Until we found a pack that took us in. Took care of us. Eventually Lucius hunted us down. I thought I killed him." His tone was dry. "Clearly I was wrong."

"Who told you King and his mother were killed?" Aurora asked quietly.

Sorgin almost jolted, as if he'd forgotten she was there. He looked at her with eyes eerily similar to King's. "His name is Orson. He's been summoned."

"Only one witness?" Aurora asked.

"There were others who witnessed your kidnapping. Who said they did," he added, looking back at King. "Three others total. They're all dead. But not recently. They all died years ago, of various things. I don't know why Orson lied, but I will get answers."

In blood, Aurora had no doubt. This king could be lying, but the rage and pain rolling off him was real. If he was lying, he deserved an Oscar.

"How did you end up in New Orleans?" the king asked his son.

"It's my home."

He didn't exactly answer what Sorgin had asked him.

"You were born there, you know. Zahara wanted to have you in the human realm, not here."

King simply nodded. "Why did Lucius take us?"

Sorgin glanced at Cressida and they had a sort of silent conversation with their eyes until the male turned back to King. "He hated me—hates me. He thought he should rule, and when he tried to kill your mother, when she was pregnant with you, I fought with him. He escaped and was banished from this realm. He's unable to get in here. When you first disappeared, I thought it had to be him who took you both, but..." His expression hardened. "Orson has a lot to answer for."

"Dragon!" A voice echoed from somewhere outside the sitting room.

All four of them jumped to their feet. Before the others could race off, Aurora blurted, "He's my friend! He followed us as backup."

"His name is Casimir," King added.

"You knew he followed us?" Aurora asked.

King raised his eyebrows slightly as he looked at her, as if to say *of course.*

"Wolfy senses," she murmured.

"Let's go greet your friend, then." The king looked between them before turning away and hurrying out.

Aurora held on to King's hand as they followed. She wanted to ask him how he was doing but obviously now was not the time. And she already knew the answer anyway. This was a lot for anyone to handle. He'd come here for help and found a father he thought had abandoned him. And a half-sister.

Maybe the king had actually let his son and the mother of his child go. Maybe he was a giant liar who'd given up his kid and mate to a monster. If he was lying, Aurora would set the guy on fire.

But...she didn't think he was.

CHAPTER TWENTY-FOUR

King felt as if he could crawl out of his skin. Today...had not gone like he'd thought it would. He'd been preparing to be betrayed. To be attacked. With fire or blades. From a dragon or the fae.

Not to meet his sperm donor. He couldn't quite think of him as his father. Not yet. Maybe never. His mother had never spoken of him. Even when King had gotten older and asked more questions, she'd simply shut down, the pain on her face gut-wrenching. So he'd simply stopped asking. She'd always told him he was magical, however.

"How long is this Halcyon person supposed to take?" Casimir asked, energy buzzing off him. He'd dressed after shifting to human, but the male was huge, as most dragon shifters were, and the fae had given him a wide berth.

They were all back in the waiting room, but it was just his own people, not Sorgin or Cressida. They'd left to speak to their own people—who were still reeling after seeing a dragon swooping down from the skies. The fae and dragons did *not* get along.

"She'll get here when she gets here." King kept his voice even. He knew Cas was worried about his human, Jo, and her family. King was worried about the whole damn territory. All his people. His family.

Aurora.

She stepped toward him, then tugged him over to a little alcove tucked behind the fireplace. It wasn't completely private, but it gave the illusion that it was.

She wrapped her arms tight around him. Breathing in deeply, he hugged her back, buried his face against the top of her head. Her dark hair was coming out of its braid and he resisted the urge to tug it completely free, to run his hands through it. He wasn't sure if he had the right to do that. Sure, they were moving toward something more, but they didn't have a defined relationship. He wasn't sure what the hell they were at this point, but he was damn glad she was here with him. No matter what he'd said before.

She leaned back to look at him, her violet eyes bright with warmth and—he kissed her, crushed his mouth to hers with an all-consuming hunger.

He felt possessed with the need to claim her, to reassure himself that this was real. She was here in his arms, and even with all the shit going on she was here. His. For now anyway. And forever if he had any say in it.

She let out a soft moan as she melted against him, tangling her tongue with his. This wasn't the time or place. But he didn't care. He needed this, needed her more than his next breath. He savored the feel of her fingers digging into his shoulders, the bite of her nails, the scent of her arousal.

The urge to pin her up against the stone wall was overwhelming, threatening to short-circuit every brain cell he had, but somehow he pulled back, sanity taking hold. He was very aware of the others in the room even if he and Aurora were out of sight.

Aurora's lips were swollen, her violet eyes bright. She opened her mouth to say something, then stopped, buried her face against his chest and sighed.

Yeah, that about summed it up.

At a slight shuffling sound nearby, he straightened, moved Aurora behind him and stepped out of the alcove just as Cressida entered the room. The band around his chest eased. She wasn't a threat. And even though he was working hard to bury a shit ton of emotions after discovering he had family, he found he wanted to get to know her.

She smiled tentatively at him and hurried over even as she glanced at the others. "Please eat, I know you all must be hungry." She motioned to the food absently, even as she came to stand next to King. "I'm sorry about...everything."

"It's not your fault."

"I probably could have said *something*." She clutched something small in her hands.

King was aware of Aurora easing away from him, knew she was likely trying to give him space, but he wanted her right next to him. He needed it; his *wolf* needed it. Because his wolf was prowling right under the surface, ready to fight anything that stood between them. "It's...fine. You were in an impossible situation."

Her shoulders relaxed and she held something out to him. "My father keeps this in his nightstand. It's..." She swallowed hard. "It's a picture of him and your mother. An artist's rendering—a picture of the two of them imprinted through magic onto this. I know you have a lot of questions and probably don't trust him. Or me either," she said, her voice taking on a sad quality. "But he never stopped loving her or you. *That* I do know," she rushed out, glancing over her shoulder as if she was afraid of being overheard. "He never loved my mother... And she didn't love him. They were friends and they respected each other, but it was a relationship born out of duty. It was different with your mother. I know now isn't the right time but I wanted to show you this. I hope you and I can get to know each other. I have no siblings, but, well, now I do. I guess I'm saying that I hope we can be friends. And I hope you give him a chance. This is a lot for him to process. He mourned both of you for a long time and I think he's mourning your mother all over again now."

Chest tight with emotions, he said, "I hope we can be friends too." He looked down at the cloth and the band around his chest grew smaller. His mother looked happy in the image, younger, her smile wide and carefree.

He looked away, handed it back to Cressida. It hurt too much to see, and right now he needed a clear head. Not one clouded by pain and memories of the past.

He would find out who this Orson was, find out why he'd lied about him and his mother being kidnapped by some other vampire coven.

But first, he had to save his territory.

Cressida turned at a commotion behind them. Three guards dressed fully in breast-plated armor and helmets strode in.

Cas growled low in his throat as he stalked forward to stand next to King. Harlow hissed even as King heard her shift to tiger. Hunter let out a chirp of surprise, jumping into the air and knocking down one of the fire pokers as Aurora let her wings and fire free.

King tensed, preparing to fight, but wasn't too worried, considering none of them had drawn weapons.

One of the males stepped forward. "Presenting Halcyon of—"

"That's enough of that. Introductions aren't necessary." A petite woman with pale brown skin many shades lighter than his own, gray hair, amber eyes and a long, heavy coat similar to Cressida's hurried forward. Her ears were more pointed than anyone he'd seen so far and she was a solid foot shorter than the other fae as well. And...she had to be ancient, given her graying hair. Fae aged in the same way shifters did so he could only imagine how old she must be.

She strode right up to him, staring with a hint of wonder. "Zahara's little king. That's what she used to call you," she murmured. "So it seems fitting that's your name now. Do you remember me?"

He started to say no but...her eyes. "Maybe." He didn't remember much before he and his mother had been taken. Trauma had affected his memories, his mother had told him. He'd suffered nightmares for years even after they'd escaped, pain and agony his only memories for a long time. Until he'd created new ones.

She reached out and patted his hand gently, tentatively. "I was there for your birth. Your mother was my best friend."

"I remember your eyes." He forced the words past his tight throat.

He wasn't ready for all these stupid emotions threatening to overtake him. Smother him. Choke him. He'd buried them over a hundred years ago. Completely written off dreams of meeting his father, his family. Of knowing his heritage. He and his mother had created a whole new life for themselves. First they'd survived. Then they'd flourished.

He didn't need these people. Didn't want to need them or know them.

But it was hard to ignore the woman with the kind eyes telling him she'd known his mother. He believed her and had a hundred questions. None he would ask right now. But if he survived, he wanted to know...everything.

"Later, we'll talk," she said, maybe reading his expression. "For now, I need to know anything important about your territory and what that bastard has done to it. My assistant is currently packing up supplies and I believe I know how to null the spell. But I need to know anything you think is important."

"You know Lucius?"

Her lips curled back slightly, and if she'd been a wolf, she'd have been baring her canines at him. "Yes. He tried to kill Zahara once."

"Can you track him down?"

The grin she gave him then was feral. "Once we're in the human realm, I will try. Then you will kill him."

"I thought I did before. I ripped his heart out and set him on fire, watched him burn to ash."

She shook her head slightly. "The male is old and powerful so it's a testament to your strength that you managed to do that. But he would have reformed, his ashes drifting to his birthplace as he recovered over decades. Or—"

"Over a century ago."

She continued. "You'll have to use iron to kill him—injecting it into his blood is the best way. And you'll have to decapitate him—then set him on fire. He won't come back from that."

Okay, then. He'd killed the bastard once, he'd do it again.

Only this time he would make sure it stuck.

CHAPTER TWENTY-FIVE

Lucius crept along the fence line of the farm, inhaling the animal and shifter scents. Shifters had an earthy smell to them but it was still different than regular animals. And there were at least five shifters out patrolling this farm.

This area was far enough from the main territory that he wouldn't have to deal with a wealth of shifters attacking at once.

Soon enough they would try, but by then he would be strong and ready for them. The city was already on lockdown, in a state of chaos. Not as chaotic as he'd predicted—the fucking vampires, shifters and witches were all working together.

But their communication was limited and that was working for him as he picked off lone shifters one by one. He'd managed to spell the city, to sink his figurative claws into the life force of all the humans in a five-mile radius. Soon, in barely two days, he would be able to drain them completely.

Then he would be unstoppable. He could call upon his reapers and finally destroy King.

Until then, he would keep going, keep feeding.

Covered in hay and dirt, he crouched low by a thick wooden fence post as he peered across a pen of goats. He could scent the shifters but not see them, so he took a chance and unlocked the gate, opened it up slightly.

Then he quickly jumped over the wire fence, creeping toward the sleeping goats in a flash of muted movement.

He startled them and their prey instinct kicked in. Instead of attacking him, they began running around wildly, bleating like they were possessed. He herded them to the gate, then slipped through it, once again bending the shadows to his will.

The sound of footfalls greeted his ears even as he climbed a nearby oak tree.

"What the hell?" A female shifter of some kind hurried after the goats. "Oh, come on!" She started muttering about irresponsible cubs leaving the gate open as she raced after a cluster of the small beasts enjoying their newfound freedom as they ran in four different directions.

As she neared the tree, making calming sounds to the goats, trying to coax them toward her, he slipped down from the branch nearly soundless.

But he must have given himself away somehow.

The slender female with dark curls pulled into a bun on her head turned. Her eyes widened slightly and he thought she would speak to him.

But she shifted into a deer and sprinted away so fast he could barely track her movements.

No!

He sprinted after her, the wind blowing off the hay he'd rolled around in to cover his scent.

She ran past a long rope, and when she slowed his fangs descended. She was losing steam— *No!* She pulled on the rope and a bell sounded out, echoing loudly in the still night air even as she continued sprinting across a field.

She'd signaled an alarm.

He heard a door open from somewhere behind him. The house, maybe. He was so far ahead of anyone that he ignored them. He zeroed in on his prey as she darted through an ice-covered field.

And that was when he heard the flap of wings. The deer shifter forgotten, he slowed, looked to the sky.

A giant wingspan covered the faintly winking stars and half-moon. And it was arrowing straight for him.

Rage punched through him at the interruption.

He turned, looked in all directions. He was fast, could maybe outrun the dragon. Could possibly take it on. But he wasn't willing to risk it. Wasn't willing to expend energy and power in a fight with a dragon. Not when he wasn't at full capacity.

The dragon dove down at him, fire extending from his big maw, the orange ball curling through the air.

Lucius clutched the talisman around his neck, chanted an old spell he rarely used because of the aftereffects—and transported away, letting the fire consume the spot where he'd just been.

* * *

Rhys glided over his and Dallas's farm one more time, their pet dragon Willow in tow. She'd grown stronger over the last year, her flying skills massively improved. But her wings were still a little big for her body.

No more peoples. No more death. Her stilted words sounded in his head. Her communication came in fits and wasn't always easy to understand, but she could mostly get her point across when she wanted to.

I know. Let's land. He slowed himself as he gently landed fifty yards from Dallas and the other farmers who'd gathered at their farm. He quickly dressed, then patted Willow's head. "You flew great tonight. I'm proud of you."

She chirped in response and fell in step with him as he hurried across his massive yard. A vampire had nearly attacked Hazel, and unfortunately, he'd found four bodies at nearby farms. It looked as if whoever that bastard was, he had just gone farm to farm, targeting anyone he saw, killing innocent shifters and draining them of their blood. Rhys had been doing aerial security flyovers but he couldn't be everywhere at once. Still, guilt punched through him hard. These were his people out here. His neighbors. He should have protected them better.

The male had disappeared as he'd blasted fire at him, so Rhys couldn't even track him.

Dallas hurried toward him, her gray eyes wide with worry as she reached him. "Anything else?" she murmured.

"Not that I could find. No one else in our territory." For now they'd left the bodies where they were, but would soon give them a proper burial.

She shoved out a breath. "There's that at least. Naomi and Deacon have made contact with everyone else on the fringes. Everyone's responded and not under duress."

They had codes to use in case they were ever attacked. "Good." He pulled her into his arms, savoring the feel of her against him for a long moment before they turned and hurried over to the others. "There's no sign of him and I didn't find anyone else," he said, looking out at a dozen of his neighbors.

Their shifter and human neighbors all sighed in relief even as they grieved for the friends they'd lost. Before Rhys had met Dallas, his brilliant witch had moved to the outskirts of King's territory and worked a farm. She and a bunch of others had created a co-op of sorts, growing vegetables and other things they provided for the whole territory. They were more like family than friends.

"I'll need to report this to King," he said to the group. And unfortunately he knew that King was still out of the territory. So he'd more likely need to contact Ace.

"I already tried to call Ace while you were doing recon." Dallas shook her head slightly. "Call won't go through."

"I can't get in touch with my sister either," Alice said. "And she's in the city."

There were a few more murmurs of the same.

"I was afraid of that," he muttered.

King had explained what was going on directly around the city—a spell had been cast and was keeping a vast amount of humans in a five-mile radius basically in a coma. If the spell wasn't broken, those humans would die and the treacherous bastard who'd cast it would steal all of their energy. Dallas was beyond worried and unable to break the spell—something that had Rhys worried. Because Dallas was powerful.

Rhys was pretty damn sure that the male he'd almost incinerated was the vampire hybrid King was after. And Rhys would have ended him if the bastard hadn't transported away. Another sign of his power level.

"We'll go to the outskirts of town, try and get a message to Ace or someone," Dallas said, looking at him for confirmation.

He didn't like the thought of bringing Dallas with him since King had already warned them all to stay as far away from the epicenter as possible, but he couldn't leave her behind. Hell, he *wouldn't*. His mate was strong so he knew she could take care of herself, but he didn't know anything about this enemy other than the male was ancient and dangerous.

And that the bastard didn't care who he killed to get what he wanted.

"I want everyone to gather at Alice's farm. For the next few hours everyone stays there while Dallas and I head to New Orleans. Willow will stay with you." She wasn't nearly as strong as him, but she was a dragon and could breathe fire. Most of the shifters here on the outskirts weren't Alphas. They were mostly peaceful vegetarians—or hippies, as Hazel liked to call herself.

Everyone nodded in agreement. Except Willow, who glared at the two of them, her blue eyes narrowed.

Dallas cupped Willow's face in her hands and murmured sweet platitudes to her about why they couldn't take her.

No fair, Willow grumbled, the sound of her frustration echoing in his head.

Dallas kissed her nose. "We know it's not fair, but you've got to stay here and protect everyone."

Willow sighed, then made a sad-sounding chirp before she butted her head against Rhys's hip. Hard. Oh, she was pissed. Without another sound or word she took to the skies, following after the group who was trekking across their yard.

He turned to Dallas, held her close again. "Ready?"

"As I'll ever be."

They would do what they had to in order to protect the territory while King was away.

CHAPTER TWENTY-SIX

Aurora tried to quell her nerves as she stood in the giant courtyard next to a horse that wasn't really a horse. Its ears were longer, wider, almost like a rabbit's but not quite. And its legs were stouter, more muscular. But it looked close enough to one that she was just going to think of it as a horse.

Harlow was still in tiger form, having decided to just stay that way after she'd shifted in alarm an hour ago. Cas hadn't shifted yet because he "didn't want to scare the fae again," and Hunter was standing next to her, his head nudging her hand every so often for reassurance.

The big steeds made soft whinnying sounds occasionally, but didn't seem nervous around Harlow or Cas, which surprised Aurora. But she was glad for it because as soon as King came back from speaking to his father they were leaving.

"It's lovely to have another phoenix here in our realm," Halcyon said as she approached, her expression warm and welcoming. She was definitely a healer all right. The energy that rolled off her was kind and made Aurora want to give away all her secrets. "In case you haven't been told, we have many phoenixes who make their homes here. Most are up in the mountains."

That was…interesting. Aurora nodded politely. "I would say it's nice to be here, but…"

The older female laughed lightly. "I hate the reason that's brought you here, but I'm thrilled to have King back. Shocked too. Thinking of him as King instead of…" She sighed. "Well, that doesn't matter now." Her accent was heavier than the others, but her English was still impeccable.

"Thank you for helping us."

Halcyon nodded. "Of course. I just hope we're not too late."

"Cressida said we'd have three days."

The female nodded, her expression pinched, though it was clear she was trying to smooth it out. "She is correct. I just fear what Lucius might be doing now. Him coming back from what King did to him is a testament to his power."

Aurora was afraid too, but bit back the words.

Harlow strolled over then and plopped down next to Aurora in what was likely supposed to be a casual manner. But Aurora wasn't fooled. Harlow didn't trust anyone and was sticking close.

"So you and King are..." The older female looked at her expectantly.

She blinked. "Ah..." Aurora wasn't sure what they were, and was surprised by the bold inquiry from a total stranger. She cleared her throat, then let out a breath as King strode out of the castle, his sister and father behind him. She hurried across the cobblestones to meet him. "What's wrong?" she asked as they reached each other.

"They're coming with us." He ground the words out.

"Who?"

"My... Cressida and Sorgin."

"Oh, good." Right now they could use all the backup they could get. Lucius wouldn't stand a chance against their combined power. At least that was what she was telling herself. "Or not good?" she whispered. Because King's expression wasn't exactly murderous. More like frustrated with a side of annoyance.

He sighed. "It's..."

"A lot?"

His hard mouth curved up at the corners a fraction. "If possible, I'd prefer you to ride the horse while I'm in wolf form. I want you close to me."

"You're shifting?"

"We'll make better time. And those things are fast." He nodded at the not-horses.

"How do you know?"

He paused. "I just do."

The king and Cressida approached then, apparently done giving them space. "We need to get moving," Sorgin said. "It will be dark soon and I want to get through the forest before then. We need to stop Lucius."

King bristled but nodded. "We're taking a different route to leave, but the place we'll exit on the other side is the same place we came in," he said to Aurora and the others. "I'm told that this will just be a slightly longer route to leave."

"Why?" Cas demanded as he approached.

The fae all gave Cas a wide berth, but Sorgin didn't flinch as he met the dragon's gaze. "Because we can move faster without fear of terrifying my people again. They are not used to seeing *dragons*. This way there is no worry of being slowed down by any of my citizens, no curious gazes." And an unspoken *because I say so* was clear as Sorgin eyed Cas.

Cas simply grunted, but he nodded.

"Any news on the male, Orson?" Aurora asked, watching Sorgin. The more she thought about the male who'd lied, who'd let a five-year-old boy and his mother be kidnapped by Lucius—or at least lied about it—the more she wanted to incinerate him into nothingness. King had been imprisoned just like her, but unlike her, he'd been a child. And who was she kidding, she loved the male. She wanted to destroy anyone who hurt him.

"He's gone on the run." Sorgin's words were simple enough, but Aurora saw the anger in his blue eyes, the way his jaw hardened. "We will find him."

Hunter chirped impatiently behind them. Apparently he was ready to get the hell out of here too.

She stepped back, placed a comforting hand on his head. He nuzzled her before he took to the air, hovering next to the not-horse Aurora planned to ride.

King brushed his mouth over Aurora's, just a quick kiss, a bare meeting of their lips before he stepped behind the cluster of riding beasts while Sorgin and the others packed up a couple of the not-horses with what seemed like a lot of supplies.

It was weird how *not* weird it was for King to kiss her, to claim her in a subtle but very public way.

Moments later he stepped out from behind the animals in wolf form and she sucked in a breath. She sometimes forgot how gorgeous he was as a wolf. And how huge. He was almost as tall as the not-horses—who now whinnied nervously. His shimmering black coat would blend into the shadows well, and his blue eyes... Well, they were all King looking back at her now.

He dropped his loaded pack in front of her and she scooped it up. It fit perfectly on the steed.

Once everyone was ready, she jumped onto the animal, using her wings to lift her up high enough to get onto the saddle. It wasn't the same as the ones she'd seen before. There was no strap underneath the animal securing it in place. But the thing didn't move at all, almost as if it was secured by magic.

King remained right next to her on her left and Hunter on her right. Harlow was on the other side of King, and Cas had opted to ride one of the animals.

Sorgin gave a command in his own language and everyone fell into line. The not-horses lined up two by two, all carrying packs, with Sorgin and Cressida at the lead. Halcyon was right behind them and a handful of soldiers were behind her, while Aurora and the others pulled up the rear.

She wondered if King had told them he would be at the rear, because no one had said anything or acted surprised. She definitely wasn't surprised that he wouldn't want anyone at his back. Right about now, she felt the same way.

The animals' hooves made clomping sounds against the cobblestones as they exited over the huge drawbridge. Instead of heading east back toward the town, they went down a different path that curved northeast.

And King had been right, the animals picked up speed almost immediately. Wind rolled against her face faster than when she flew. She kept her wings curled up tight against her back, but allowed her fire to spread all over her. It warmed her and the animal beneath her without burning it.

Ahead of them thick trees stood in the distance, lining the beckoning forest. Snow covered either side of the unpaved path, stretching out in what were likely fields for some kind of food in warmer months. Someone had done a good job of clearing it of snow so they weren't kicking up slush everywhere.

Hunter's fascination with the place had worn off and he was flying right next to her, with only enough space so his wings had free movement.

"I'm glad you came with us," she murmured to him, the wind eating up her words.

But he heard her. He gave a happy chirp as he continued his flight.

A distant rumbling rolled above them, making Aurora shudder as the sky darkened, and not just from the falling sun. She wondered if it was the same sun as theirs or... Wow. She was going to have an existential crisis if she started wondering how all this worked.

Nope. Now was not the time.

As they neared the line of trees, she looked over at King.

The glorious wolf looked back at her, and she didn't think it was possible but she swore he smiled at her.

Her breath caught in her throat and she knew that she was going to spend the rest of her life peeling back all of King's layers. And never get tired.

As they blew past the curtain of trees into the forest, darkness enveloped them. Her fire and a few lights from the others ahead lit the way, but suddenly she was glad King had asked her to ride instead of fly.

Above them a triple canopy rose, the whistling wind from before muted. All she heard now was the clomp of the horses and the animals' heavy breathing.

And she was very aware of the dark forest stretching out on either side of them. Rows and rows of trees. And darkness.

Even before they reached it, she could see the shimmer of energy in the distance, lighting up the dark forest. It was a long, wavy...door of sorts. Not a typical one, but she knew what it was. And it would lead them back to New Orleans.

Home.

Her fire flared at that as she internally readied for battle. They would be facing Lucius soon, facing...whatever had happened in the last few hours.

As her not-horse raced along, something zinged past her face. She blinked at the blur. *What the hell?*

King snarled and suddenly jumped at her. She held out her hands on instinct even as he shifted to human, tackling her off the animal with shocking speed and force.

A short scream escaped as he held her tight, absorbing the blow as they hit the ground. It did a little to ease the impact as they slammed into the cold snow.

He kept his body over hers, protecting her—and that was when she saw a hooded figure with a bow and arrow in the trees.

She screamed as he lifted the bow, and acted on instinct, releasing a stream of fire at him as he drew the arrow back.

At an odd angle, she shot lightning fast, hitting the branch he was on instead of his chest. A crack rent the air as he started to fall.

She heard a whoosh of air as one of the arrows flew free, but King was already dragging her behind a tree.

Before she could blink, King jumped off her, shifted back to wolf and raced after the shooter with a growl.

Aurora was aware of shouts of alarm and the others moving into action. But she ignored them, jumping up as well, letting her wings unfurl. Taking to the air, she flew after King, zinging through the trees, ducking and twisting to avoid low-lying branches.

She was fast, but he was faster, his paws pounding against the cold earth as he sprinted toward the hooded male racing away.

The male tried to jump onto a waiting steed, but King sprung through the air, slamming his paws into his back before pinning the male to the ground. King rolled the male over with his huge paw, manhandling him as if he weighed nothing.

The male's hood fell back, his black hair spilling around his face, his green eyes glittering with rage as King thumped his paw against the male's chest.

He grunted underneath King, trying to move, his left hand creeping down toward his pants. Probably had a weapon.

"He'll rip your throat out before you get to it," Aurora snapped as she hovered over them. "And if he doesn't, I'll incinerate you." Fire dripped at her fingertips, ready to be unleashed.

The male paused, turning that rage on her, but his gaze drifted to her hands and he lifted his own as the others raced up behind them.

Harlow circled around to the other side, growling low in her throat as Sorgin stepped forward.

"Orson," the king snarled. He withdrew a blade, held it to the supine man's throat. "Why did you do this?"

The man rasped out an angry word, a curse in his language she had no doubt.

King pressed on his chest and Aurora heard a definite crack. Orson let out a short scream of agony before he gritted his teeth. Oh, King had definitely broken a rib or two. *Good.*

"What did you do?" Halcyon strode up, slightly out of breath, holding out a long, slender dart tipped with a lavender liquid.

The male simply grinned, the sight nothing short of pure evil. "You're dead," he rasped at King in English, glee rolling off him. "A dead abomination walking."

King slapped him across the face with his paw, knocking him out before he jumped back and shifted to his human form.

When he did, Aurora saw the puncture mark on his back left shoulder. A sort of purple color was spreading out in a circle against his dark skin, the size of a dime. "King!" She pressed her hand to his shoulder, above the wound, as she inspected it. "He shot you."

"Yeah." King winced, rolled his shoulders once. "Kinda aches."

Halcyon moved up behind her and Aurora motioned for the others to stay back even as Sorgin ordered one of his people to shackle Orson. She was aware of a fae soldier hauling up Orson's limp body and tossing it over one of the not-horses, but she kept most of her focus on King and Halcyon.

"This is bad," Cas said in his slightly accented voice as he ignored Aurora and peered at the wound. "I can smell it."

"I can too." King's voice was neutral. Too neutral.

Panic flared inside Aurora. "What are you smelling?" She looked at King, whose expression was carefully blank. Cas looked at her with pity, and Halcyon...she winced.

"I know what this is," King said bluntly. "It's called acontibane. It's deadly for shifters."

Her vision went white for a moment. "Deadly?" God, she sounded like a parrot. *No. No, no, no.* She reached into one of the side pockets of her pants, pulled out a switchblade that had been a gift from Bella. Whipping it open, she sliced her palm open and pressed it onto his wound. She was a *phoenix*. Her blood would heal him.

She stared as the purple circle started to fade, felt a sharp pop of relief—until the color spread again, right back to the dime size. "Why isn't my blood working?"

Halcyon gave Aurora a pained look and said, "There's an antidote for it, from a flower, but it's high in the mountains. And it's very hard to find because of the way it blooms. I wouldn't even know where to look."

"But my blood—"

"This is a very specific type of poison, created from something natural and something fae-made. It is not of this realm or any other realm. Not naturally. Your blood won't help against it."

Panic punched through her, stealing her breath. "I've never heard of it."

"Thousands of years ago it was created by fae mages, to battle shifters." Sorgin paused, his expression tortured as he looked at King. "The use of it is outlawed here and I've all but eradicated it from our territory, but..." He trailed off, the pain in his expression sending another wave of panic through Aurora.

They were all just accepting this, giving up.

"It's fine." King nodded at Cas. "Get me some clothes."

"It's not fine!" Aurora grabbed his face, angry bees buzzing through her. "We need to go search for the antidote."

"There's no time." He took the pants from Cas, tugged them on and couldn't hide a wince as he stood and pulled his shirt on over his head.

"What are the effects? How... I need details," she said, looking between King and Halcyon. Panic bubbled up inside her, making it difficult to draw breath.

"Without the antidote, there's a one hundred percent fatality rate. He has four days," Sorgin answered, his voice rippling with unconcealed pain. And rage.

So much of it reverberated in his words. Orson was going to die soon—that much Aurora knew.

"King—"

He cupped her face then. "No. I can't go look for it. I have to get back to my territory. My people are depending on me."

"Halcyon can break the spell." Or she thought the female could.

"Then what?" King's expression was soft as he stroked his thumb across Aurora's cheek. "I have to kill Lucius. This is what being an Alpha is. New Orleans is my territory to protect. Period. I can't abandon it. I will not."

She could feel tears pricking her eyes, but she blinked them away. She didn't want to cry, she wanted to scream. "This is insane! You've been poisoned."

"I'll be fine for a few days." He did that neutral thing again with his expression as he pulled away from her.

"Fuck that," she snapped.

"I'll go hunt for it." Cressida stepped forward, her pack still on. "I don't know exactly where it blooms, but I'm familiar with the cave system in the Lablanc Mountains. That's where it is, right?"

Halcyon nodded, her face pinched.

"I'll go with you." Harlow had shifted to human form, grabbed a coat and wrapped it around herself. "I'm fast and I'm a good tracker. If you tell me what it smells like, I can help."

"Make sure Jo and her family are safe." Cas looked between Aurora and King. "I'm going to fly them. We'll get there a hell of a lot faster with me. Just *swear* you'll protect them."

"I swear on my honor," King said. "And thank you. All of you." He looked at the three of them, his expression stoic, but she heard the raw emotion in his voice even as he tried to keep everything locked down.

Aurora was torn between going with them or staying with King. But...she couldn't leave him. Not now.

"We'll find it." Harlow grasped her shoulder once, pulled Aurora into a tight hug. "Go with him."

A sense of surreality wrapped around her as they gathered their supplies to leave and Harlow dressed fully, readying to ride on Cas into the mountains.

King pulled her close. "It's going to be okay."

"Don't comfort me when you're the one who's been poisoned." How was he not freaking the hell out? He could die. *Would* die, if they didn't find the antidote. She couldn't accept it. Could not face a future without him in it.

"I could die at any moment. Could die when I go up against Lucius. I can't operate in fear mode right now."

She clenched her jaw, stared up into his ice-blue eyes. This was why he was the Alpha of New Orleans. "Okay. Tell me what you need." She wasn't brave like him, but she would be what he needed right now.

"You. By my side."

There was no other place she would rather be.

CHAPTER TWENTY-SEVEN

"**W**hat are you doing here?" King growled at Prima and Arthur, who were waiting outside the door to the fae realm. The Louisiana night sky above them was dark, with clouds muting everything. "You're supposed to be with the stranded humans."

Prima shrugged. "We're going back to the territory to help. Besides, I haven't killed anything in months," she added, as if that explained everything.

King took a breath and had the fleeting thought that ancients were actually worse than toddlers. And far more dangerous. But this gave him a distraction from his poisoning, regardless.

"The humans we found are fine. They are well fed now, with warmth and clothes," Arthur said. "A healer has seen to all the sick. All their immediate needs are met. If we lose New Orleans, they'll have no home to go to. It is better we help." Arthur leaned against an oak tree wearing a kilt, his face completely painted as if he was going to war.

Which he was, King supposed. He ignored the two of them, looked back at Sorgin, Halcyon and Aurora. Sorgin was eyeing Prima with wariness.

"How the hell did you know we'd be here?" King asked, turning back to them.

"We didn't. But Ace told us where the door was and we'd planned to go in after you." Her gaze trailed to Sorgin. Then back to King. She lifted her eyebrows. "I always wondered what your other half was."

King rubbed a hand over his face even as Aurora moved up next to him. He'd made her and the others promise not to tell anyone about his poisoning. And he wasn't going to get into his heritage right now with Prima or anyone.

"Have you been in contact with your niece Victoria lately?" Aurora blurted to Prima.

The dragon shifter blinked. "We spoke a week ago."

"I need her contact information."

Prima raised her eyebrows slightly, but nodded. "Okay. Though the phones aren't working well now."

"Your human electronics will be affected by Lucius's spell," Halcyon said, her first words since they'd crossed over. She looked up at the dark, early morning sky. Her jaw tightened. "We need to hurry."

He wasn't sure what she saw other than a gray blanket of clouds, but he nodded, anxious to get on the move.

"There's a Jeep by the road. About half a mile from here," Arthur said.

King nodded. Ace had told him he would leave a vehicle should they need it when they returned.

"Unless you would prefer we transport you?" Arthur's tone was polite as he looked at the fae, but Sorgin shook his head, still watching the dragons with a wary eye.

"We will ride in the motor vehicle," his father said. It still felt so strange to think of him as that.

Tense, his wound a pulsing ache in his shoulder, King motioned that everyone should follow. Hunter and Aurora took to the air as they hurried through the thick underbrush. Prima and Arthur didn't shift yet, thankfully. This patch of forest was too dense for their huge forms and he didn't want them too near Sorgin or Halcyon when they shifted.

"His spell is growing stronger." Halcyon's words were tight as they reached the desolate two-lane highway, essentially in the middle of nowhere.

Aurora's fire was the only thing lighting their way, illuminating the old dirt road and the overgrown field across from the forest.

"How can you tell?" King asked.

"I can feel it," she said simply. "It's scraping against my skin."

"I can feel it too," Sorgin said tightly as they reached the Jeep.

The keys were in the ignition so King motioned for them to get in as he turned to the dragons. "Stay behind us a ways, but be prepared for anything. I don't know what to expect as we reach the city." And he hadn't been able to contact anyone when he'd turned his phone on. His phone was as useful as a brick right now.

They both nodded and remained where they were in the grass as he turned to Aurora. He wanted to ask what her interest in Victoria was, but had a feeling he knew. The wolf shifter who lived in Montana now was an expert at research and held more knowledge in her head than almost anyone he'd ever known. King might have an eidetic memory, but Victoria was a sponge. If anyone would know more about the poison invading his blood, it would be her.

"I'll fly behind you with Hunter," Aurora said as she landed lightly by the driver's side door. "We'll stay close."

He nodded, settled his hands on her hips for a long moment and brought his forehead to hers. There was so much he wanted to say. Hell, he wanted to rail at whatever higher power there was right now. He'd just found Aurora; now he might lose her. Lose *everything*. Lose the future he desperately wanted with her. And he'd never wanted anything as much as he wanted to be her mate. Not even to be Alpha.

The silver lining was that he'd been hit with the poison and not her.

"Stay alert," he murmured, brushing his lips over hers, not trusting himself to deepen it. He couldn't say more, couldn't let Prima or Arthur know he'd been poisoned.

No one else could know yet. They either found the antidote or they didn't.

But no matter what, he was going to kill Lucius and protect New Orleans. And keep Aurora safe.

* * *

"Do you want tea or anything?" Aurora murmured. Her house was unnaturally quiet with just the two of them here and it felt odd.

"No. And you don't need to be here." King's words were tight as they waited in her living room. He sat on the couch next to her, a tight ball of contained energy.

They'd come back here to meet with Greer and Dallas while Halcyon worked with Everleigh and a handful of other witches to break the spell. Hunter was back at the pack's mansion and was not happy with King for leaving him there. But King needed to stay focused right now. Aurora had asked Bella to head to the mansion with the others for the time being so it was just the two of them—he didn't want to risk any of his pack overhearing about his poisoning.

She gave him an exasperated look as she shifted against the couch. "Are you trying to push me away intentionally? Because you can't really think I'd leave you now."

He simply watched her, his wolf in his eyes.

She narrowed her own. "Will it make you feel better to push me out? Will it make it better if you..." She couldn't say the word *die*. She didn't even like thinking it. The world was so damn unfair and made her want to scream, made her want to set everything on fire right now. Or more specifically, Lucius.

King stood, paced away from her toward their ancient fireplace before he turned back. "Maybe it will make it easier! I'm tearing up inside right now." Raw emotion rippled off him, filling up the room until it nearly suffocated her. "We haven't even had a chance—" He broke off, jaw clenched hard.

She jumped up and closed the distance between them. Throat tight with emotion, she flung herself into his arms. "Say we only have a few days together... I don't want to spend one second apart from you. Please don't push me away," she whispered. "If it comes down to it, we'll fight Lucius to the death, together. I'm not walking away from you, from us."

He swallowed hard as he stared down into her eyes. "I won't push you away. I shouldn't have even tried."

Her own emotions were spilling out, her fire completely engulfing her as he held her close. She started to respond but there was a sharp knock on the door.

She wanted to ignore it, but it had to be Greer and Dallas. King had called them to Aurora's house. They wanted to keep the circle of who knew about the poisoning small, and if they'd met them anywhere else— his compound or even Greer's place—the chance of someone overhearing grew wider. Greer was a powerful healer and Dallas a powerful witch— and they would keep this secret, Aurora knew.

Aurora was hoping against hope that they could do something. *Save him*, her internal voice screamed.

Though it was clear by King's expression that it pained him to let her go, he hurried to get the front door, stepped back as the two females entered, their expressions tight.

Aurora knew Greer had been dealing with all the comatose humans, helping to triage the city, and attempting to awaken anyone she could. She'd been successful with almost a hundred humans, and looking at her now Aurora worried the healer was expending too much energy. She also knew that Dallas had lost friends to that bastard Lucius in the last few hours. He'd preyed on farmers out near where she lived.

"I mean this in the nicest way possible, but you need food or other sustenance," Aurora said, eyeing Greer. She looked as if she'd lost fifteen pounds in the last couple days. "We've got a whole fridge full of food right now. I can get you anything you'd like."

"You sound like my mate—who is currently in the front yard waiting." She looked at King as she said it. "I know you said this was a private meeting, but he won't be separated from me right now. And I'm fine on the food, promise." She gave Aurora a quick smile. "I'll rebound eventually. This is just a side effect of all the healing."

"Rhys is with him too," Dallas murmured. "Sorry."

King simply motioned for them to step into the sitting room. "It's fine. What I say stays between us. And your mates," he tacked on. "I'm going to make this as succinct as possible. I was poisoned in the fae realm."

The females both gasped.

He continued, his tone neutral. "There is only one known antidote." He quickly explained everything Halcyon had told him about the poison itself and the flower that counteracted the drug.

Aurora dug her fingernails into her thighs as she sat there listening, trying to keep her emotions in check. Having a freak-out wouldn't do anyone any good right now.

"I'd like to see the wounded area," Greer said as he finished.

King nodded and stripped off his shirt, turning so they could both look.

Both females stepped forward, Greer taking the lead. She leaned closer, inhaled deeply with a frown. "I want a sample of your blood. More than one sample. I can work with it and various antidotes and see if I can find something that will work or at least stave it off until the others find the antidote. But the fae healer was right, this is dark poison." She inhaled again, then shuddered as if the scent made her queasy. "I've never scented anything like this. But I might be able to isolate the poison once I draw your blood."

"I'll work with her," Dallas said. "If what the fae says is correct and this was created, I might be able to figure something out. A spell that might counteract it."

"Are there other healers you can contact? Maybe a database to check or something?" Aurora asked Greer. She wasn't sure how healers communicated all their information but she guessed they might have something of a database to keep records. Cas, Cressida and Harlow might be looking for the antidote but she wanted to contact everyone possible who could help. They had to cover every angle.

"I'll reach out to everyone I know. We have a network I can tap into. I'll have to leave the territory to get cell phone service but I'll do it. Your blood might help for a while," Greer continued, looking at Aurora. "I know you said phoenix blood didn't work but...it has a healing agent unlike anything I've ever seen. I think we should at least try to give him more for now and maybe stave off the clock. If we can't find the antidote, I want to fight this off as long as possible."

"Yes," Aurora said before King could respond. "You can take as much as you want. For him, for samples, whatever you need." She'd been held captive and used for her blood before, had killed the male who'd stolen her. For King, she would give all of it to save him.

Greer nodded and opened her healer's bag, started pulling out supplies. She'd clearly come prepared.

Even though Aurora was still screaming inside at the unfairness of it all, at least she was doing something. It wasn't enough but it was still something.

"Would it be possible for you to do another finding spell for Lucius?" King asked Dallas.

"I actually tried again," Dallas said. "It's different than the time I did the spell for..." She cleared her throat, trailing off for a moment. "For my mother. I tried doing one from the place Rhys tried to blast him, but I couldn't get anything."

"What do you need for it to work?" King held out his arm for Greer, who was preparing to draw his blood.

"I need something of his, something he's touched."

"The clothing the kayakers were wearing," King said, looking at Greer. "He would have touched their clothes."

"I've still got them...they left in the scrubs I provided. And I haven't washed anything yet. We've been too busy."

King closed his eyes as Dallas said, "That might work."

Aurora allowed that spark of hope to grow inside her. "Can I send one of your mates to go get the clothing?" She looked between the women. As the hope grew, so did fear. What if someone decided to wash those clothes in the time they were here? Would it destroy their chance of tracking Lucius? She didn't know enough about magic to even guess. And Lucius was very clearly fine living in the shadows until... She clenched her jaw, tried not to think about what would happen if Halcyon and the witches couldn't break the sleeping spell on the city. Lucius would gain all the energy from the humans, would be damn near unstoppable, per King.

Greer nodded and looked at Dallas. "You can go straight to the house if you want. Do you need anything specific for the finding spell?"

"I've got everything I need," Dallas said.

Greer told her where to find everything and King handed her a radio. "This should work, even with the spell. A few of my wolves and other leaders around the city have them. I'll keep my line open."

Aurora scooted closer to King on the couch and waited until Greer took her blood. The world funneled out as she watched the vials fill up.

Her whole life she'd had to hide what she was because of her blood's healing properties. And now, when she needed it most, it was useless, failing the male she loved. It might stave off the effects of the poison but it wasn't permanent, couldn't heal him.

And she couldn't fathom a world which King wasn't a part of.

CHAPTER TWENTY-EIGHT

King shut the door behind Greer, leaned against it for a long moment. Part of him wanted to give in to hope that Cressida, Cas, and Harlow would find an antidote but he was operating on the assumption they wouldn't. Hope was too dangerous now. And regardless, it wouldn't change what he needed to do.

He frowned when he realized that Aurora wasn't in the kitchen or out back. She'd ducked out of the sitting room as he'd been wrapping up with Greer, but he knew she wouldn't have just left. When he heard a slight sound from somewhere above him, he realized she must be upstairs.

He jogged up the two flights of stairs to her room, feeling rejuvenated from the shot of Aurora's phoenix blood even with the poison coursing through his veins. He knew he was dying but it didn't feel like it.

And he couldn't feel sorry for himself. He'd lived a long damn time, had seen and done things people only dreamed of. And...he'd met his mate. Even if he wouldn't be able to mate her. Not if they couldn't find the antidote.

Her bedroom door was open so he peeked his head in. "Aurora?"

She stepped out of her bathroom and gave him a smile that didn't reach her eyes. They were glossy with tears as she moved toward him.

"What's—" King started.

"What's wrong?" Her tone was...defeated.

Hell. Of course she was upset.

"I didn't want to cry in front of you," she said. "I'm just having a hard time processing everything and I don't want to lose my shit in front of you."

He gathered her into his arms, inhaling her sweet scent as she melted against him, her head hitting right in the middle of his chest. Holding her like this grounded him, made him feel sane.

Clearing her throat, she still clutched him close but leaned her head back to look at him. "King, I need to say something. I should have said this before. I've been fighting this for so many reasons that seem stupid now. I lo—"

"No." That was the one thing he couldn't handle. He could see in her eyes what she was going to say and he shook his head. "Please don't say it," he rasped out.

Because he loved her too, had known it for longer than he was pretty sure she had. But if she said the words, he was afraid it would break him. He didn't want her telling him because he was dying. Just. No. And he didn't want her to live her life grieving for him once he was gone. She was beautiful and strong and extraordinary. She deserved every bit of happiness she could find, including another male who loved her.

She gritted her teeth, her expression defiant as she opened her mouth again.

He silenced her with a crushing kiss.

She kissed him back, almost savage as she clutched at him, her fingers digging into his shoulders with a brutal intensity.

Her fire was everywhere, though she didn't let her wings out. But pale blue flames danced along her entire body, her skin glowing the same color. It cast wild shadows across the dim room.

He knew there were things he needed to do in the city, but for a brief time he was going to be selfish. He was going to take this time with her. Because he didn't know if he would get it again.

Still…guilt slashed at him. He tore his mouth from hers, looked out the window. Everything beyond the pane of glass was a milky gray. The city was still under a spell as the fae and his witches worked to break it. And that was something he couldn't help with.

Aurora grabbed the front of his T-shirt and yanked him back to her. "Give us just a little bit of time," she rasped out. "You can't help Halcyon or the witches. Just give me this. Please."

The desperation in that one word slid the knife of regret deep. He should have made a move on her sooner, should tell her right now that he loved her. But if he did, he would absolutely break and mate with her. And he *knew* she would mate with him. He wasn't going to do that to her. She might want him, might even love him, but he wouldn't ask her to mate with him when he was dying. No. She would make the decision based on his short life span. That would just leave her with an even bigger ache in her heart if—when—he died.

Still, he couldn't resist the powerful tide of desire tying them together.

He reached for the bottom of her tank top, slid his hands underneath, his fingers skating over her bare skin, and he shuddered. Before he could ask if this was what she wanted, her flames flashed against her body once and...she incinerated her clothes without burning him.

He stared; he hadn't even realized she could do that.

His brain short-circuited, however, as he stared at her gloriously naked body. He wasn't some untrained pup; he was the Alpha of New Orleans but...he still *stared*, unable to do anything else as he drank her in. Her dark hair flowed around her, shifting with the flames but not burning. The tight little buds of her nipples tipped her full breasts, begging for his touch, his tongue. Hell, he had to taste her. She'd stripped herself bare, literally, in seconds. She was telling him exactly what she wanted with no words.

There was no way he could deny her. Or himself.

He clutched onto her hips, tugged her close as he dipped his head to her breast.

She arched into him, gasping as he sucked a nipple into his mouth. Goddess, he wished he had more hands. Another mouth. He wanted to touch, tease her everywhere all at once.

She clutched at his head with one hand, holding him close as she wrapped one of her legs around him, melding to him completely, as if she couldn't get close enough.

He felt exactly the same.

His erection was heavy against his pants, his wolf prowling beneath the surface. Demanding that he mate with her. But that wasn't a decision he could make now. Not with so much uncertainty. Even so, he was going to enjoy every stolen moment with her.

In this position, with her leg wrapped around him, she was open for him, the scent of her arousal slamming into him.

With shaking hands, she shoved at the hem of his shirt even as he sucked her other nipple into his mouth, flicking his tongue against the hard bud.

She shuddered and then suddenly incinerated his shirt instead of taking it off.

He smiled against her breast at her impatience. Pleasure punched through him at the feel of her lightly callused fingertips roaming over his chest and arms. She stroked all over him, as if she couldn't stop.

The skin-to-skin sensation of her touching him wasn't enough.

Definitely not enough. He needed to taste her pleasure, to be inside her. To mark her.

He gripped her hips and backed her up against the nearest wall. Then he went down on his knees and that spike of arousal from before now saturated the whole room.

Her chest rose and fell as she stared down at him, the scent of her arousal the sweetest aphrodisiac. It was nearly impossible for shifters to get high, but right now he felt like he was.

"That thing I'm not supposed to say, I'm thinking it right now," Aurora whispered as she looked down the length of her body at him.

He stared up at her for a long moment and his chest tightened with too many emotions as he looked into her violet eyes. They were just as bright as her glowing blue fire. He knew she loved him, he simply couldn't hear the words. Couldn't bear it.

He also didn't trust his voice, knew he wouldn't sound coherent, so he grasped one of her calves, slid it over his shoulder and did what he'd been fantasizing about for far too long.

When he flicked his tongue against her slick folds, she jerked against him, pushing at his face.

Her fire spread then, covering him entirely. Each time he flicked his tongue over her clit, she groaned.

"King," she rasped out.

Hearing her call out his name had his cock kicking against his pants.

He was glad she hadn't incinerated those. He needed to show some control, at least until she came.

He gripped her inner thighs, squeezed as he focused solely on her clit, adding more pressure with each groan she made.

And that was what set her off.

She jerked against his face, her body slick and open for him as she started climaxing.

Surprise ricocheted through him that she was coming so fast, but maybe he shouldn't be shocked. They'd been building to this, heading down this path for a year. He kept going, stroking her until finally she squeezed his head once.

"That was...not enough," she rasped out, her chest rising and falling. "Need more."

Fuuuck. He needed more too. Needed all of her. He stood, dipped his head to hers again to let her taste her own pleasure. They didn't have enough time together so they would fill every second they had.

In response, she hoisted herself up, jumping him as she groaned into his mouth.

Gripping her ass, he managed to order his legs to move. He was going to be inside her soon and he wanted her on a soft bed. Or a soft surface at least.

At the edge of her fluffy bed he tried to stretch her out on it but she didn't let go, just held on to him, her breasts rubbing against his chest as they kissed. The scent of her pleasure, her desire, was so damn overwhelming, he could barely think. The urge to mate rode him hard, demanded he sink his teeth into her neck when they came, but he forced himself to hold back.

Reaching between her thighs, he cupped her mound and slid two fingers inside her. She was so damn slick. "Is this what you want?" Somehow his voice worked.

Her eyes bright with hunger, she nodded. "I want all of you."

He had an idea of what she'd been through, even if he didn't know everything about her time in captivity. "If at any time you want to stop—"

"I know." She pushed at his pants in a frenzy, her arousal drowning him.

In that moment, he knew he had to trust her. If she wanted to slow down or stop, she'd tell him.

Quickly taking over, he shoved his pants off, tossing them onto the floor.

Before he could cover her body with his, she reached between their bodies and wrapped her fingers around his erection, stroked once.

Oh, fuuuuck.

Caging her in, his hands planted on either side of her head, he closed his eyes and savored the sensation of her gently touching him, stroking him.

She did it again, even as she cupped his balls with her other hand.

Her touch was light, barely there, the slight calluses from her artist's fingers perfect and... He unclenched his jaw, managed to force the words out. "Slow down," he growled. Because he wasn't coming in her hands.

The smile she gave him was just a little bit mischievous as she squeezed again, stroked again.

In that moment he wanted to rage against the poison in his body, rage against all the years he'd lose with Aurora. He wanted forever with her, a hundred years, a thousand, to explore every inch of her over and over, to peel back all the layers of the unique phoenix who'd stolen his heart.

Shoving that thought aside, he took over and wrapped his own fingers around his cock and guided himself to her entrance. No more waiting for them.

Slowly, he dipped the head of his erection between her folds.

She let out a shudder, her flames flaring across the bed as she rolled her hips against him, as she opened wider for him.

Slowly, using control he didn't know he had, he eased inside her when all he wanted to do was thrust, to give and take pleasure.

But he was going to do this right. This time might be all they had.

She rolled her hips up to meet him and he slid deeper. Sucking in a breath at how tight she was, he cupped one of her breasts, lazily teased her still hard nipple as he slid home another inch. Then another. Goddess, she was absolute perfection.

She moved suddenly, forcing him deeper, and he gasped at how tight her body clenched around him.

She slid her fingers around his body, stroking over his back, then his ass as he thrust inside her.

Her dark hair splayed around her face, flames covering it, the pillow, the entire bed. He pulled back again, thrust again until she met him stroke for stroke. Their bodies joined together in a wild rhythm until he couldn't stand it anymore. His balls pulled up tight, the need to release overwhelming. This was Aurora with him, the taste of her climax still on his tongue as he pushed deep inside her. And she was close, her inner walls tightening around him harder and harder.

He reached between their bodies, rolled his thumb over her clit—and was rewarded when he felt the small contractions around his cock increase. She was so damn close—with a gasp, she suddenly surged into orgasm, her fire everywhere now.

He let go, his control snapping as he thrust hard and climaxed, completely losing himself in her, *drowning* in her.

In that moment nothing existed but the two of them. Mated in their hearts if not in reality.

* * *

Aurora curled up against King, knowing their time was limited. She was surprised he'd taken this time with her, but she was grasping on tight.

Before they left, went to see Halcyon, his pack, all the others, she wanted to say something. Needed to get the words out. She wanted to explain why she'd been holding back with him. "When I was held captive, I started to lose hope near the end. Before Star rescued me."

He stiffened slightly under her, but wrapped an arm around her, trailed his fingers up and down her spine in a lazy rhythm.

They were entangled with each other, and she loved the skin-to-skin contact. She couldn't believe she'd been so afraid to let him touch her, had been afraid she wouldn't be able to be intimate with him. Maybe she would have moments of panic in the future—and she was determined that they would have a future together—but everything had been so natural between them. As if they'd been made for each other. She knew, at her basest level, that he would never hurt her. He was incapable of it.

"I knew my sister would never stop looking for me but...I was in this sort of dungeon. A very luxurious padded cell, but it was a prison nonetheless. I told you it was lined with iron," she said.

"Yes." His body was taut now, all his muscles rigid.

"I thought maybe he..." She swallowed once. She couldn't say her kidnapper's name, didn't want to right now when she was naked in bed with King. "Might get lax with security if I put, ah, the moves on him." Her words were stilted as she forced them out. She wasn't sure if she'd ever get a chance to tell King this again and she wanted him to know everything about her. This was the fear that had held her back with him as she'd emotionally healed this year.

King didn't stop stroking her bare skin, just kept her pulled tight against him.

She shifted slightly so she was splayed on his chest more and could fully see his expression. "You understand what I'm telling you?" *Of course he understands.* She inwardly cursed herself.

He nodded. "You did what you had to in order to survive. Trust me, I get that. And it makes me admire you even more. Absolutely *nothing* could ever change the way I feel about you."

He said the words so simply that she suddenly felt foolish for ever doubting him. She'd been so caught up in her head, so worried about something she had no control over. "I slept with him. Intellectually, I know that it wasn't consensual because I was in prison and had absolutely no power but still... I faked it. He wasn't violent or anything." She closed her eyes for a long moment as that familiar sweep of shame threatened to take over.

King pulled her fully on top of him. "I'm so sorry you had to live through that. That you had to make that choice."

Of course King wasn't pushing her away, wasn't shaming her. She should have told him this months ago. "I lived with that shame for a while. Then he lost it when he realized I'd been faking—because I tried to escape," she said, her voice dry. That male really had been full of himself, so *shocked* that she hadn't wanted or enjoyed him. "I gave up hope after that." She knew she shouldn't have, but it had been so damn hard, so lonely in that room. She'd been isolated, drained of her power for almost a year at that point.

"I hope you never feel any shame ever again." His words were whiplash sharp. "He is the only one who should have ever felt shame.

You're more than a survivor. You're a brilliant fighter. You literally slayed your dragon." His grip around her tightened, his wolf in his eyes now.

She laid her forehead against his. "Now we're going to slay yours." She would make that happen. No matter what it took.

He held her even tighter, brushed his lips over hers. "Yes, we are."

CHAPTER TWENTY-NINE

King looked out at males and females, supernaturals and humans alike that he'd asked to meet at the warehouse where they normally met for any city issues. Though this was different than anything they'd met about before. "Thank you for coming here."

Everyone nodded, their expressions grim as they faced King and Aurora. None of them knew he'd been poisoned. That he was dying.

"So far everyone has worked in the best interests of the territory." And for that, he was grateful. He'd been able to go to the fae realm and not worry whether everyone would do what was right—and not make a stupid power play. Right now they couldn't afford to deal with petty shit or interpersonal fights. "That needs to continue, especially since Dallas has located Lucius." He glanced once at her and her mate, Rhys.

There were slight murmurs and he knew the questions would start so he held out a hand and first looked at Logan and Sergei, two bear shifters. Logan led most of the bears in the territory but Sergei worked closely with him. "I need you and your clans to take up protecting all the hospitals and healing centers. This will keep you away from the immediate action, but you're best suited to protect humans. If we fail on the front line, I need to know that the humans and anyone else will be safe."

To his surprise, the bears didn't argue, simply nodded.

Next he looked at the cluster of dragons, all from different clans who'd made New Orleans their home. "Prima, Arthur, Ivyn, Cale and Reaper. You'll work with the bears. If needed, evacuate as many people as you can."

With the vampires, he focused on Claudine and Ingrid. There were other covens in the city and vampires without covens, but these two powers would make sure all the vampires fell into line while he and his wolves were fighting Lucius. He also gave orders to Thurman and a couple other human leaders, as well as the few feline packs, that they would be under the orders of Justus and Cynara, who he'd already tasked with keeping the core of the Quarter protected.

The city was covered in the fog, the same five-mile radius submerged in the grayness. Anyone who was feeling the oppression of the spell grow had left the epicenter, and for now, the healers were working hard to bring back anyone who was still under the spell. Everyone else still in the city were strong supernaturals only, looking out for the humans in comas and trying to help the healers as best they could. The only positive was that it wasn't spreading. Unfortunately, King knew that would change if they didn't kill Lucius and break this spell. If Lucius managed to get the surge of life force from thousands of people at once, he'd be unstoppable.

"Most of my pack and Everleigh's coven will be with me, so everyone needs to work as a unit." Fighting together with witches was new, but he trusted all the ones who would be working with him today.

King looked at Dallas and Rhys, knowing they weren't going to like this. Dallas was ready to jump straight into the fight with Lucius, and Rhys was right with her.

"I need you two protecting the outer territory. Pick two dragons, I don't care who, to go with you." It was all he could spare. Because if he failed, he needed dragons, witches and his own wolves to descend on Lucius. And if they failed... *No.* They wouldn't.

Couldn't.

To his surprise, they both nodded without argument.

He looked back at the group, took Aurora's hand in his as he did. He loved her so damn much and having her by his side was making all of this bearable. "I've also let the Moana dragon clan to the east of us know what's going on, as well as the Stavros pack." Finn Stavros, a wolf shifter, ran most of the southeast region of Mississippi with his vampire mate Lyra. "But we're not going to need them. This is our territory and we'll protect it. Everyone needs to work as a unit or we could lose everything."

"Who are the fae in the territory? And why are they here?" Logan asked quietly, his tone neutral.

"They originally came to talk to me about creating an alliance." That was more or less the truth and he didn't want to get into specifics. Not now. The minutia wouldn't change anything. "They got caught up in

Lucius's spell. One of their healers is working with our witches to break it. They're very close." But even if they didn't break it, he knew that once he killed Lucius it would dissolve.

"Can we trust them?" This from Ingrid.

"Yes," Aurora answered before King could. "They're going to help protect the territory."

A sore spot for King. He didn't want Sorgin involved at all, didn't know enough about the male, but Sorgin had insisted he would be helping whether King liked it or not. His exact words had been, "I've missed your whole life. I will not remain in my realm when you need help!" King could kick the male out of his territory but…he wasn't going to. He needed all the help and power he could get.

King looked at Aurora then, his breath catching in his throat as he stared at her, his female. Her wings were tight against her back, her body awash in pale, flickering blue. And she was dressed for battle in thick boots and tactical-style pants. Her skintight tank top molded to her, revealing toned, strong arms. She also had a couple knives strapped to her pants, but she wouldn't need them. Not with her firepower. She nodded at him, giving him the answer to his unspoken question. He hadn't been sure if he would tell the others about Sorgin, but knew he needed to be transparent. Especially now. If anyone had seen Sorgin, they'd know anyway.

He faced the group once more, scanned all their faces as he spoke. "King Sorgin of the Latore realm is my father—a father I didn't know I had until recently." As he looked at Claudine, he saw no surprise in her expression. Everyone else had a reaction, however slight, but not her. "I believe his intentions are good. Either way, his presence doesn't affect what we have to do."

There were a handful of questions, but they were short and everyone took his answers at face value. There was no pushback like he'd expected. Which was good, because he wasn't in the mood for it. They simply didn't have time.

Energy buzzed under his skin, the need to track down Lucius whipping through him. He'd sent four scouts ahead and they'd all radioed back that they had him in their sights. He knew exactly where his enemy was.

Now he had to go meet him and end him. He squeezed Aurora's hand once. "You ready?" No matter what, he would sacrifice himself if it came down to it. For her, for his territory. And if he was going to die, he was damn sure going to take Lucius with him. Unfortunately, he knew exactly how to do that now. She wouldn't like his plan—so he wasn't going to reveal all of it to her.

She nodded, her jaw tight. "Let's go kill this bastard."

CHAPTER THIRTY

King crouched down low, using the thick bushes and trees as cover as he eyed the decrepit two-story house in the middle of a snow-covered field. Aurora was next to him, her glow completely dimmed, her wings hidden. She was dressed in the darkest charcoal from head to toe, the color of her tank top and pants helping her blend with their surroundings.

All his wolves were here, plus a handful of felines and other shifters, almost everyone in their shifted forms and sticking to the shadows. Two dragons were in the air, camouflaged, and he'd just confirmed with Dallas again that the location hadn't changed.

Lucius was in that house. Hiding or waiting. Maybe both. But King's instinct told him that he wasn't hiding. Not truly. From everything Halcyon had filled him in on, and from King's past experience with the hybrid, Lucius was aiming to be at maximum power. And that would only happen once all the humans under his spell died.

King had to stop him before that happened. He'd seen firsthand what Lucius could do at full capacity—the male could control the elements. Could make the earth rise up and swallow people. Could rip trees out of the ground and pummel enemies. Could call forth reapers to rape and destroy everything in their path.

He rolled his shoulders once, looked at Aurora, then Ace on his other side in wolf form. They both nodded. Then he let out a low whistle to the others.

The witches released a combination spell that created a barrier behind him as he moved forward, but was also a mirror of sorts. Lucius wouldn't see the wolves or anyone else moving in behind him. He would only see the reflection of the woods. It wasn't a physical barrier, but a mirage. He wanted all of Lucius's focus on him. King's time to bring the male down would be limited.

He had to draw him out, trap him, then destroy him.

Easy peasy lemon squeezy, as one of his young packmates liked to say. *Yeah, fucking easy.*

Withdrawing his sword, he crept from the shadows, his focus on the house a hundred yards away. The dragons above had already swooped down while still camouflaged and couldn't find any invisible traps. Neither could the witches stationed at various intervals.

He couldn't sense anything with his own pulsing magic. But that didn't mean traps weren't there.

Striding forward, aware of his wolves doing the same, he stilled as he reached about twenty-five yards from the house. Everything around them was covered in a thick layer of snow—not from the weather, but Lucius himself. He wasn't going to cross that boundary.

It had taken King months to realize that when he'd been captive with his mother—something about Lucius created ice and death all around him. It was likely why he'd moved them so far up north, to help conceal his presence.

King was better prepared for Lucius this time around. Knew the male's weakness.

Unfortunately, poison still pulsed through King's blood. "Come out and face me," he snarled into the growing darkness. "Unless you're too afraid to face the male who ripped out your heart before." King played on Lucius's other weakness—hubris. "I, a mere wolf, managed to kill you." His voice was taunting.

The ground rumbled slightly, the ice around him rippling, and King knew he'd hit his mark. He'd wondered why Lucius hadn't come at the city with all his elemental power, and since this was only a rumble it confirmed that Lucius definitely wasn't at full power.

It also confirmed that King had to kill him *now*, before that happened. Sword at his side, he readied to make his final move. One he'd only told Ace about.

If he'd told Aurora, she would have fought him on it. Argued. Maybe even tried to intervene. It was why he was playing this close to his heart. While Ace had told Aurora about the entrance to the fae realm, he knew his second wouldn't tell her about this.

Too much was riding on what he did next.

The front door blasted open, wood splintering everywhere before Lucius strode out, a thick cloak billowing around him. He released the clasp around his neck, let the cloak fall to the ground as he reached the snow-packed earth.

He wore all black with the exception of jewels in his ears and around his wrists. His entire being glowed with power so that King could have seen him even without his extrasensory night vision. His hair was the same bluish, midnight black, a mirror of his black, soulless eyes.

Tensed and ready, King remained where he was, his sword humming with magic. All the bolts of firepower Aurora had ever slammed into it over the last year sang deep inside it. The power contained within would allow him to do what he needed to.

To make sure Lucius never drew breath again.

"You should have stayed away," King growled. "I never would have known you were alive." *Keep him talking, get him closer.*

Lucius took another step toward him, menace vibrating around him in pulsing icy waves. "I've never had a choice in killing you."

Internally King frowned at his words. What the hell did that mean? *Come closer,* he silently ordered. Just a few more steps. "You never had a choice in kidnapping a helpless pup and his mother?" He knew the others would hear on the other side of the spelled barrier and didn't care. Everyone should know the depths of this male's depravity. "That you enjoyed breaking my bones when I was only five?"

Lucius growled, the sound inhuman as he took yet another step. "You deserved it! I knew one day you would kill me if allowed to grow up. Saw the vision. Your whore mother never should have mated with Sorgin," he snarled.

King clenched his jaw at the slur against his mother even as he digested the word *vision.* "You saw a vision that I would kill you?"

"Yes. And it came to pass. But I'm stronger than you and now you will die."

"Oh, blah, blah, blah." Instead of reacting with fear or anger, King took a page out of his young pack members' playbook. Apathy would piss this male off more than anything and he needed him only a few feet closer. "You loved to whine back then and you still whine now. You're not even worth my time." Turning, he gave Lucius his back and stalked in the other direction. When he heard the swift, surprised intake of breath and the quiet pounding of feet following, he knew Lucius had given in to his primal impulses and run after him.

If Lucius had thought for two moments, really thought, he would have realized King wouldn't have come all the way out here close to the swamps to hunt him down, only to run away. But this was what King needed.

Goddamn hubris was going to kill this male.

King slammed his sword into the earth as he called out the three-word spell and swiveled back to face Lucius. King's own magic was strong, but the magic contained within the sword was unbreakable. And it was how King was going to trap him. This was the only chance he had.

A ball of blue fire burst into the air in a conflagration of flames, lighting up everything around them, creating a bubble of fire—a prison keeping them both trapped until King won. And if he died, Lucius was still trapped. So King won either way.

The snow beneath their feet evaporated as a dome of impenetrable fire formed completely around them, over them.

He could see his wolves beyond the dome now as the magic from his sword finished weaving the spell into place. Aurora's blue wings flashed wild behind the dome, but he ignored her. He had to.

This fight was between him and Lucius. With no distractions.

"What have you done?" Lucius screamed, the sound echoing off the impenetrable walls of fire. They were as solid as titanium—more so.

"You're dead no matter what happens." King's wolf was in his eyes and his voice now. "If you kill me, you still won't get out of here." He'd created a prison with his sword, his magic, Aurora's magic. One he was willing to die in.

Because either he walked out of here alone or not at all. He wouldn't risk Lucius killing him and being allowed free upon the earth.

Lucius screamed again and threw out his hands. Blasts of ice slammed into the walls of fire, only to melt immediately, falling harmlessly to the dead grass below.

King withdrew two short blades he had strapped to his back. It was time to end this.

"I'm going to kill everyone you've ever loved." Lucius screamed again, and behind him, directly outside the fire prison, the decrepit house burst into flames—and shadows flew into the air.

King heard the sounds of shrieking as the shadows dove for his wolves and dragons.

For Aurora.

It was almost impossible to see behind the dome, but Lucius grinned widely. "Reapers," he breathed out in glee before he raised his hands and blasted King with magic.

King dove out of the way and forced himself to focus on the fight at hand even as he heard the screams of nightmare creatures Lucius must have summoned from a Hell realm.

CHAPTER THIRTY-ONE

"King!" Aurora screamed as fire descended all around him and Lucius, trapping them behind a giant bubble of flames. She stared, feeling her own magic pulsing from the...bubble. Her wings unfurled even as panic pulsed through her. "What the hell is this?"

Ace shifted to human, his expression opaque. "King's plan. He didn't tell you because he knew you'd want to join him inside. He had to get Lucius close enough so the magic of his sword could trap them. He needs Lucius's powers contained. If he doesn't kill Lucius, the dome is designed to remain in place, to trap Lucius until he dies. Or until the others have enough time to kill him."

Horror lanced through her as she turned back to the dome. She could see the shadows of King and Lucius behind it, but they were only shapes moving, facing off with each other. "We have to get in there, to—"

The house Lucius had come from exploded suddenly, rotted wood and plaster a geyser raining down everywhere, bouncing off the bubble.

Aurora tensed, rolled to miss a sharp piece of plywood flying at her face. Then froze at what followed. "Reapers," she breathed even as she took to the skies, her wings flapping hard to greet the shrieking creatures. Lucius had been luring them into a trap—he'd been ready for them.

There were at least a hundred emerging, flying out like bats from a cave.

They weren't human, had never been. From a Hell realm, the flying creatures with humanoid-ish bodies had sharp razor teeth and hollow sockets where their eyes should be. Their entire bodies were a flowing gray marble that glowed, with no body hair, no clothing, no discernible gender. They were what nightmares were made of; part of the horror stories Axel had told her when she was a kid had been all about reapers.

And they were real and terrifying.

But they weren't going to survive.

Aurora took to the air, her wings flapping hard as she arrowed higher. Three followed after her, the screams filling the air scraping against all of her senses.

Angling her wings like weapons, she released pure bolts of fire at two of them. Their screams were cut off as they burst into dust, their ashes shimmering as they fell.

Above her, two dragons dropped their camouflage as wild streams of fire shot through the air, right at a cluster of seven reapers.

The third reaper who'd been about to attack flew to the left, letting out a sharp whooping sound.

Below her she was aware of other shifters battling, saw one reaper diving for Ari's back as he tore into the neck of another.

She shot fire directly at it, watched its head explode into dust. The rest of the body fell with a thud to the ground.

As she turned, she saw six reapers flying right toward her. They wanted to attack en masse.

Going on instinct, she shot upward, avoiding dragon fire before she turned sharply and arrowed down toward the dome of flames. She risked a quick glance behind her and yep, they were still following after her, screaming, their mouths elongated with rage and fangs.

She released two quick streams of fire upward, hit one, missed the others completely. Heart racing, she continued diving toward the flaming dome—and hoped she was right about this.

Going almost full speed, she curved her wings at the last second to slow her pace fractionally as she slammed into it. Her own magic pulsed around her, through her, instead of burning her. Turning on her back, she arched her wings and shot fire upward as the reapers descended on her.

Two burst into ash as the others opened their mouths, kept flying at her.

The fire from the dome itself shot up all around her and…incinerated them.

She blinked, momentarily stunned. The dome couldn't be sentient, but it was built from her magic and would do anything to protect her.

Rebounding quickly, she shoved off and spread her wings out before diving toward another cluster of reapers attacking two wolves.

She hated that King had enclosed himself with a monster, but she knew he was strong. He would win. He had to. But he was poisoned and she couldn't stop the fear pulsing through her that it would weaken him.

No. She couldn't think like that. She had to fight for him. For their territory. Their friends. All the innocents.

No matter what, no way in hell was she going to let him come out only to find his people dead.

CHAPTER THIRTY-TWO

L ucius threw out a bolt of magic that slammed into King's stomach.
       King flew back against the dome, felt the flames lap around him,
imbue him with energy. He wiped sweat off his brow as he shoved up
from the cold earth. Still in human form, he bared his canines at Lucius.

Who bared his bloody teeth at King.

King wasn't sure how long they'd been fighting; probably less time
than it felt like. He felt stronger than ever, while his prey was weakening.

Time seemed to slow as he battled the vampire-fae hybrid—because
King knew Aurora was on the other side, fighting for her life against
monstrous creatures. She was capable, but it didn't stop the protectiveness
punching through him.

He had to get to her. Had to keep her safe.

Had to keep *everyone* safe.

King raced at Lucius, iron blades in his hand. He hauled back as if
he'd throw the one in his right hand.

Lucius dodged to the left.

King held back on that blade and launched the one from his left hand
lightning fast. It slammed into Lucius's upper shoulder.

The male screamed as the iron embedded deeper. He fell to one knee,
blood dripping down his chin from an earlier blow.

King tossed the blades to the ground as his wolf took over, fur
replacing skin as his beast soared through the air. He slammed into
Lucius, his heavy paws breaking ribs as they hit the ground with a thud.

Lucius blasted him with magic as he bared his fangs.

The pulse of the blast sent King flying back a few feet but it was
nothing like before. Lucius was getting weaker.

It had to be the iron.

Unfortunately King was starting to feel the effects of the acontibane
poison.

King had been slicing away at Lucius, cutting at him with the iron blades every chance he got. It wasn't enough. He needed to inject directly into his bloodstream with liquid iron. And he needed to be in his human form to use the syringe he'd brought.

But his wolf wouldn't relinquish this fight yet, was desperate with the need to tear off Lucius's head.

Because his wolf still remembered the savage vampire-fae who'd broken his bones as a child. And he wanted blood.

King sprang back up, crouching as he slowly circled Lucius.

The male stumbled once as he shot a blast of magic at King again.

The blow went wild. King dodged easily, gained a few feet.

Lucius shot again.

King dodged again and rammed right into Lucius's middle, tearing his bowels out with his canines.

Lucius howled in pain and grabbed his middle, shoving magic into his body to stop the disembowelment. But he stumbled, fell to his knees.

King shifted to human, dove for his discarded clothes, grabbed the syringe. When he killed Lucius this time, he was going to make sure he stayed dead.

His prey was still down. Summoning the strength for another blow he would never have the chance to release.

With a snarl, King stalked to Lucius and jumped onto him, keeping him pinned in place beneath his own body. He slammed the syringe right into his neck, depressed it directly into a vein.

Lucius's eyes widened, a sharp glow of light emanating from his eyes as the veins in his neck popped up, turning black.

"Enjoy Hell." King bared his canines at him, started to shove up when pain pricked his upper thigh.

He looked down... Nausea swept through him.

"I'll see you there," Lucius rasped out as blood started pouring out of his mouth, his body going limp.

King blinked as he stood. The scent of the acontibane poison permeated the air, flowed through his veins, weakening him.

The lavender liquid rolled down his leg as he yanked the syringe out. Lucius had apparently had the same idea as King.

Crafty bastard.

Sucking in a sharp breath, fighting against the pain biting away at him, he stayed on his feet, stumbled toward his sword.

He had to finish this, had to end this for good. The moment he tore his sword out of the ground, the dome vanished, the spell broken.

As the bubble of fire disappeared, a rush of noise rolled over him. Voices, groans—he ignored everything as he stalked back to Lucius, lifted the sword and sliced through his neck.

The male's head rolled slightly as everything went wavy.

King started to fall, but felt strong, fire-covered arms around him, easing him to the ground.

Aurora.

"King! You did it! He's dead and so are his reapers."

He swallowed hard, tried to lift a hand to cup her cheek but his body wouldn't obey. He could only stare at her glowing, dirt-streaked face. *I love you,* he wanted to say. Tried to say. But nothing came out.

"He's been poisoned." Ace was suddenly there too, and then Ari, both kneeling next to him.

"No!" Ari snarled.

"No, no, no." Aurora grabbed his sword, sliced her palm on it, and he felt the cool press of her blood on his thigh.

But he knew it was too late. There was too much poison. Lucius had given him a full vial and he could feel it eating away at him. And now he could see a soft glow around the edges of his vision. This was it. "Don't. Too late," he rasped out. Or he thought he did.

"Run!" she suddenly screamed, tearing her gaze from him. "Everyone run now! Or you'll all die!"

Die? He couldn't sense another threat, couldn't sense anything. He couldn't move, the pain rushing through him keeping him immobile as she turned back to him and cupped his cheeks.

He heard Ace shouting, people running, but he tuned it all out as he stared up at Aurora. Her dark hair was coming out of its braid and she was brighter than he'd ever seen before. An angel.

His angel.

"I love you. I should have said it before, shouldn't have been so stupid." A sob racked her as she laid her forehead against his. "I was so cowardly. But I do love you. More than anything. And I'm so mad at you for not telling me what you planned." She sobbed, tears rolling down her face as she leaned back slightly, still cupping his cheeks. Her face grew brighter until he had to shut his eyes against the illumination.

But it didn't matter. Pure light blasted all around him, her heat infusing him, enveloping him as she wrapped her arms and wings around him.

I love you too, he thought as heat seared through him, tearing him apart.

CHAPTER THIRTY-THREE

"It has been a week. We have to make a decision. Or at least start talking about the next step." Claudine's words were muted, her expression grim as she sat across from Ace under the starlit sky.

They'd decided to meet at a local, mostly unused marina. He'd brought Ari with him and he knew she'd brought some of her own people, but it was just the two of them at the end of this long dock.

He scrubbed a hand over his face. "I know." He heard both what she said and what she didn't say. They needed to figure out who the next Alpha would be. But that was going to be a monumental task for such a diverse territory. He and King had talked theoretically about what would happen if he ever died, but Ace had never truly considered it a possibility. Had never considered his Alpha, one of his best friends, might actually die.

They had contingencies in place to make sure things kept running smoothly for a while but...now that King was actually gone, he didn't know what to do. Or maybe he simply didn't want to acknowledge that King was gone. Aurora too. If there was an afterlife, he hoped they were finally together. "We could split the territory up into part vampire, part—"

"No." Her voice was whiplash sharp, her eyes sparking. "King was building something beautiful here. We need to honor it. We need..." Her jaw clenched tight and she looked away, out over the water for a moment. "He made me feel hope for a different type of society. A kind of hope I haven't felt since I was a child."

Ace couldn't even begin to guess how long ago that was. "Agreed." He paused before he said, "You're one of the strongest in the territory." And King had respected her.

With a faint smile, she shook her head. "We will not even entertain that idea."

"You need to at least consider it."

"I'm too old, too stubborn. I run my coven well, and if it was a matter of simply governing vampires, it would be no question." She sniffed haughtily before she sighed and shook her head. "There are far too many species and personalities to rule in this territory. We need someone well liked by all species. Someone old enough, powerful enough to hold on to it. But also someone young enough to adapt, to change with the needs of their people. Someone who has a vision for the future in a way I can admit I do not always see clearly. Someone..."

"Willing to put their territory before their own self. Someone who cares about New Orleans, loves it. Not a power-hungry tyrant," he finished. King had been the epitome of what an Alpha should be. He'd only told Ace at the very last moment about his poisoning, right before the battle against Lucius. Instead of racing to find an antidote for himself, he'd come back to his home to fight for it. And Cressida, Cas and Harlow had returned with the antidote only hours after King had killed Lucius.

Sighing, she nodded. "The dragons are too obnoxious. Though there are some strong enough to rule. They simply don't have the personality for it."

Ace let his head roll back, stared up at the brightly lit sky. "There's no one like King." New Orleans had been in his blood. He'd loved the territory as if it had been a part of him.

Since his and Lucius's deaths, most of the humans had woken from their comas. Some had succumbed to the spell that had broken when King had killed him, but the majority were now awake and still recovering. Every day since then had been bright and sunny with cloudless skies. And it was the same at night, with stars blanketing the sky, everything seeming brighter than ever before. It pissed him off.

"I know." Sadness crept into Claudine's voice. "I will miss both him and Aurora. I...had high hopes for them."

Yeah, Ace had too. And he'd never forget what he'd seen on that battlefield, the way Aurora had gone supernova, screaming at all of them to run.

They'd all just barely made it out of the blast zone before she'd blown a huge crater into the earth. He'd never witnessed anything like that. She'd been...a nuclear weapon.

There'd been nothing left of her and King. They were just *gone*.

Aurora's pack…they were not dealing with it well. From what he'd heard, they hadn't been able to reach her sister to tell her either. That was going to be a brutal conversation and he had a feeling the Alpha female would be headed here soon after, if just to comfort her former pack.

He straightened. He'd been King's second for a reason. King had trusted him to make hard decisions and he needed to step up and do just that. "Let's call a meeting for tomorrow night. We'll start talking serious names of potential leaders. It won't be an easy process, but we'll do it."

"I've already heard whispers from some younger vampire covens who want to make plays for power. I think this could get bloody before it gets better."

He stood, nodded. "I know. But the strongest of us, as long as we act as a unit, we'll be okay until we decide on an Alpha. We just have to make it clear that we won't tolerate violence or bullshit." They'd gone through so much to get to where they were. Ace refused to let it topple. King had died for them. He was damn sure going to do his best to make sure his legacy lived on.

She stood with him, all liquid grace. "I know you'll just say no again, but you should consider yourself," she said. "You're strong enough. And my coven and Ingrid's will stand with you."

He lifted a shoulder. Being an Alpha, the kind of Alpha King had been, was different than simply being strong enough to hold on to a territory. King had been all about the big picture. All about unity and building a better future. "I'm strong enough to run the pack but…" He shook his head. "Let's just table this until tomorrow." Because his brain hurt and he couldn't fathom the level of responsibility of taking on a territory this size, let alone while he was numb and reeling from their loss.

"We'll need to invite the fae. King's father," Claudine added.

Ace nodded as they started down the dock toward the empty parking lot of the marina. "I'll take care of that." King's half-sister and King Sorgin were distraught. That being an understatement. They hadn't left, even a week after his and Aurora's death. "They want an alliance with our territory at least."

"That's something." Claudine gave him a brisk nod as they reached the end of the dock, then fell in step with two of her vampires who bled out of the shadows.

Ace turned to Ari, who stepped away from one of the railings overlooking the quiet water. "Let's go— What is it?"

Ari's frown deepened as he shoved his phone into his pants pocket. Now that the spell on the city had been broken, most electronics were working again. "Darius called in a sighting of a phoenix in the outer territory. Blue flames just like Aurora's. Said he saw them flash in the sky, then disappear."

Ace's heart skipped a beat, but then… "Cliona. King had her off on a mission. She's likely just returning."

"Right." Disappointment flickered across Ari's normally stoic face. "Right," he sighed.

"Let's go check it out anyway." Because he wasn't sleeping tonight, that was for damn sure. Or likely the next few nights.

A small hope slid its way inside him, but…he'd seen that blast, had felt the raw heat of it. No being could have survived that.

CHAPTER THIRTY-FOUR

Arms over her chest, Harlow stood next to Ace and Cressida as they all watched Hunter chirping wildly. He was flying in unsteady circles between a cluster of cypress trees along the lonely stretch of beach.

Ace had called her an hour ago, had asked her out to this overgrown area of one of the bayou reserves. The gators had all scattered, likely at the overwhelming scent of predators gathered here. Apparently Ace and Ari and a few others had been here all night after someone had reported seeing a flash of blue phoenix wings. Ace told her that he thought he'd seen a flash of blue right at sunrise, but hadn't been sure the light hadn't been playing tricks on his eyes.

"He clearly senses something," Harlow murmured, giving in to the sliver of hope that had wedged its way into her rib cage. She wouldn't say aloud what she hoped Hunter sensed. That King and Aurora were still alive. *Somehow.* Aurora was a *phoenix.* They could rise from the ashes. She'd gone supernova for a reason, of that Harlow had no doubt. She'd wanted to save King. But King wasn't a phoenix so Harlow wasn't sure how he could have survived, regardless. And Harlow didn't know enough about phoenix deaths and rebirths to even guess how that would work. Still…

Screw it, Harlow was holding on to that hope hard.

Sorgin, who'd also come with them, strode toward the anxiety-ridden dragonling, his boots kicking up wet sand as he looked up at Hunter. "Do you scent King?" he murmured to the dragonling.

The dragonling made distressed crying sounds, trying to communicate so hard.

"What if it's them?" Cressida asked, voicing the words no one else had wanted to say.

"Like…maybe they're trapped in another realm or something?" Bella had her arm wrapped around Phoebe, the young phoenix now living with them.

"Maybe. I don't know." The fae princess shook her head.

Harlow liked the female, had gotten to know her when they'd been hunting for the antidote. Only to come back too late for King. And by extension, Aurora. She swallowed down the wave of emotion shoving up into her throat. She hadn't even been able to tell Star. Hadn't been able to mourn because she simply couldn't believe Aurora was gone. She hadn't seen it with her own eyes and her brain was fighting against reality.

"There!" Cressida stepped forward, blinking against the bright glare of the sun.

"What?"

"I thought... I don't know." Her shoulders slumped slightly. "I saw blue. Or maybe I just wanted to."

Harlow squinted, but all she saw was a bunch of cypress trees along the stretch of sand.

Hunter hovered in the air, his back to them as he stared into the distance down the beach.

So she took a step forward, hoping she saw what he did.

Suddenly Ace and Ari shifted, along with the other wolves. Harlow tensed, her tiger prowling under the surface.

Light flashed in the air by one of the trees about thirty yards ahead, rippling out in a wave of energy. A tree cracked up the middle and—

"Sweet Goddess!" Harlow raced after the wolves, aware of Bella, Lola and the others all behind them.

Aurora and King were crouched in a crater of sand and mud, both naked and staring at everyone running at them. A sob built in Harlow's throat and she cursed the stupid sand slowing her down.

Aurora was alive. So was King.

For the first time in as long as she could remember, tears stung her eyes as they all skidded to a halt.

Aurora extended her wings as she and King jumped up out of the hole that blast had created.

"What...where are we? And why are you crying?" Aurora stared at Harlow in shock, her pale violet eyes wide.

"I know where we are," King murmured as he looked at Aurora with all the love of a mate. "This is where I was born. My mother took me here more than once. So long ago." His voice was low as he looked out at them and then the quiet water lapping against the shore.

"We thought you were dead!" Bella shoved past all of them, a streak of jet-black hair before she launched herself at Aurora.

Then Ace shifted and tackled King in a hug. Ari followed suit.

Harlow ignored the wolves now piling on King and did the same to Aurora, wrapping her arms around her friend. A woman she'd once viewed as a little sister and watched grow into a full-grown, powerful Alpha. "You've been gone for a week." The words came out as a sob as she stepped back to let Lola into the pile.

Both Aurora and King looked at each other, their eyes wide. "A week?" King asked.

Ace nodded, his expression miserable. "Longest week of my life."

Sorgin stepped forward then, all awkward as he faced his son, but Cressida just pushed past him and threw herself at King.

King stumbled back in surprise but wrapped his arms around her and patted her gently on the back, the gesture a little stilted.

Suddenly Hunter shoved into them, tired of being left out, and flapped his wings around both Aurora and King in what looked like his attempt at a hug as he chirped excitedly at them. Laughing, Aurora kissed the top of his head as King rubbed behind one of his ears affectionately.

Harlow wiped at her cheeks, unable to stop the flow of tears as she dragged in a breath. And then another. She had a whole lot of questions. They all did.

But the answers didn't really matter.

Aurora and King were back.

CHAPTER THIRTY-FIVE

"I can't believe we were gone for a week." Aurora stepped out of her walk-in closet, a rich plum-colored sweater in her hand.

"Me neither," King murmured, his gaze falling to her bare breasts, staying there as he drank her in. The last thing he remembered was a bright light filling his vision. After that, he only had the sense of being surrounded by warmth and love. Then they'd woken up in the place of his birth.

"I still have so many questions," she said as she held up the sweater. "Yes or no?"

"Yes."

"You've said that about the last four things I've shown you." Her mouth pulled into a thin line, but there was only love in her expression. And maybe a little exasperation.

"It's because you look good in everything. Or nothing at all." He wished they were both naked right now and that they didn't have anything else to do but stay that way.

She snorted and turned away from him, giving him a perfect view of her unfortunately covered ass as she stepped back into the closet.

After meeting with his wolves, and hugging almost everyone in his pack in reassurance that he was real and back, then meeting with the other leaders of New Orleans to go over what he'd missed, and spending time with Cressida and Sorgin while Aurora spent time with her pack, six hours had passed. And they only had an hour before sunset. The vampires would be arriving then at Aurora's house, along with all the other leaders, for what would essentially be a giant party. A celebration—something the territory deserved.

Everyone had questions about how they were here, but the truth was King and Aurora didn't really know.

Aurora had said she'd let her phoenix take over, had given in to a primal instinct that told her to save him. She didn't even remember telling everyone to run, but she must have known on a molecular level what was happening. In her grief, she'd turned to pure phoenix fire and...now here they were. He'd thought phoenixes could only rise from the ashes alone, but she loved him and he'd had her blood inside him. Maybe that had been a factor. Or maybe a greater power had decided to give them back their lives. King wasn't going to think about the details too much. He was just grateful he had a chance at a life with Aurora.

She stepped back out with a black sweater dress now and held it up, but there was a mischievous glint in her eyes.

And he realized she'd stripped her panties off.

Stepping forward, he tugged her dress out of her hand, tossed it to the floor as he pushed her back into her closet. "Your pack will hear us." They were all downstairs getting ready for the party.

"They can go outside if they don't like it." Her gaze fell to his mouth and heat flared.

His cock kicked against his pants, even harder when he caught the scent of her arousal.

She reached between their bodies, grasped the button of his jeans and started shoving them off even as he cupped her breasts.

He loved touching her, couldn't get enough. Didn't think he ever would.

Growling low, he dipped his head to her neck as he kicked his jeans away. "I love you." He'd already told her a dozen times since they'd "gotten back" this morning. And he'd keep telling her over and over.

"I love you too," she groaned, taking his erection in her hand, stroking him hard.

"I want to mate with you." He nipped her ear once, biting down with enough pressure that the scent of her arousal spiked even more.

She squeezed him closer as she arched into him, her hard nipples brushing against his chest. "How about right now?"

His hips jerked forward of their own accord, the need to be inside her, to thrust into her, overwhelming him. He nipped at her neck in response, pressing his teeth against the soft arch where her neck and shoulder met. Right now sounded perfect.

Leaning back so he could look at her, he reached between her legs, cupped her mound. Her fire flared, lighting up the entire closet in a brilliant blue as she met his gaze.

He dragged a finger through her slick folds, shuddered at how wet she was. Then he slid another one inside her.

She arched her back again, rubbing her breasts against him deliberately as he thrust his fingers into her, then pulled out. "Take me right here," she demanded.

He growled low in his throat as they tumbled to the floor. The thick throw rug in the middle of her closet was soft enough that he didn't worry about abrading her back. And his control was razor-thin, had been since they'd returned.

They'd been surrounded by people every second since they'd woken up on that stretch of beach and he needed her desperately. Needed to mark her.

Claim her.

Needed everyone to know that she was taken by him. And that he was hers. He wanted to be claimed—she already owned his heart. But he wanted it official—and his wolf was primal enough to want the whole world to see his mark on her.

He crushed his mouth to hers as she guided his cock to her entrance. There would be time—years—to take things slow. Now wasn't that time. For either of them.

The energy rolling off her, the wild fire illuminating the closet, her sweet scent, told him what she wanted.

As he slid inside her all his muscles pulled taut. She was so slick, but so damn tight, clamping around him as he thrust forward.

"King." She cried out as he slid home, all the way to the hilt. Wrapping her legs around him, she held him tight to her.

Breathing hard, he stared down at her, savored the feel of her inner walls pulsing around him as they joined with each other. This was everything. She was everything to him.

His whole world.

She rolled her hips once, slowly, and his dick throbbed, pulsed with the need for release.

But he had a hell of a lot more restraint than that. He hoped.

"You are the greatest male I've ever known," she whispered. "I'm lucky to have you as my mate."

Oh, hell. Maybe he didn't have restraint. "I'm the lucky one." He pulled back then and she rolled her hips up to meet him.

Time lost all meaning as he thrust inside her, as she stroked her fingers all over him, as if she couldn't get enough of him. The feel of her stroking him, digging her fingernails into him, was too much.

Reaching between their bodies, he started teasing her clit, applying the right amount of pressure as he buried his face against her neck. His canines descended the second he did, the instinct to claim his mate taking over.

She grabbed onto him hard, her fingers digging into his lower back as he scraped his canines over her sensitive skin.

Simultaneously, he increased the pressure on her clit—and she surged into orgasm. As her climax took over he bit down, piercing her skin with a sharp bite.

Her inner walls convulsed around him as her climax hit even harder. As she came, crying out his name again, he let go of his own control. He came inside her in long, hard strokes, finding release as he claimed her mouth again.

She kissed him back hard and wild as they both found release in each other.

For the first time...ever, he felt complete in a way he'd never known possible. He was linked to her, could feel the tug as if it was a physical tie. And right now, he sensed his mate's utter happiness and contentment.

All was right in their world.

Though he didn't want to, he slowly eased out of her and stretched out next to her on the rug.

She sidled even closer to him, threw her leg over his waist with a satisfied sigh. "Want to skip the party?"

He let out a short laugh. "Pretty sure no one will let that happen."

"We're the Alpha couple. We can do what we want."

He laughed again. Which made her grumble slightly. He was proud to have such an incredible female at his side as Alpha.

A thump sounded from somewhere close. He froze, listening. It happened again. What the hell?

"What the heck is that banging sound?" she murmured, still curled up against him, her voice slightly drowsy. "Is that...coming from the window?"

"We're three stories up."

Then it happened again.

Groaning in annoyance, he eased up and poked his head out of the closet—and froze. Then he snorted out a laugh. "Hunter is at the window." And he was flapping wildly as he butted his head against the pane, making it shake ominously. King hurried to the window and threw it open, only for Hunter to chirp animatedly at him. Oh, he was *annoyed*. King recognized that tone.

King looked down at the backyard to see at least fifty people there already. Extra lights had been strung up and...hell. "We'll be down in five minutes."

"Ten," Aurora called out.

"Ten," he told the dragon.

Hunter simply shook his head, then dragged his tongue over King's face before swooping back down to the gathering.

"So I guess we can't just hide out up here," he grumbled, wiping his face as he shut the window behind him.

"Nope." Aurora stepped out of the closet in the formfitting sweater dress she'd been holding up before. It hung off one shoulder, and even though they'd just been naked together—he had just been inside her— seeing that flash of skin had his body reacting all over again.

"We'll get out of there as soon as possible," he said as he grabbed his own pants from the floor. He figured everyone would understand—they were newly mated.

And if they didn't understand, King didn't give a fuck. He and Aurora had been granted the miracle of another chance together. He wasn't going to waste a moment of it.

CHAPTER THIRTY-SIX

"This is wild," Jo murmured, staring out at the huge backyard.

Cas kissed the top of her head, grateful to have her in his arms as he scanned the place full of all shifter species, vampires and witches alike. Running after that antidote instead of returning to New Orleans had been one of the hardest things he'd ever done. But Ivyn had been watching out for Jo, her sisters and their grandmother. And Jo didn't remember any of it—the only silver lining. "It is quite festive," he agreed. Aurora's packmates had gone all out for the party at their place.

"Just wait until the wolves and jaguars start playing soccer in animal form," Avery murmured, shaking her head at a bunch of dancing bears. Avery and Mikael had just returned from Scotland that morning, stunned at all they'd missed, but caught up by now.

"Wait...what?" Jo looked at Avery, wide-eyed.

The two females had quickly become friends and Cas felt like a fool for keeping his shifter side a secret from Jo for so long. She accepted all of him, loved him for exactly who he was.

"Oh yeah." Avery nodded and took the drink Mikael handed her with a smile. "And it's not just soccer. I've seen them play volleyball too."

"I don't even know how that would work."

"Oh, it works. And it's crazy entertaining." Avery shook her head and Jo slipped out from his hold, kissing him quickly before she stepped up to Avery and they started talking about something.

"I heard from Zephyr," Mikael murmured, moving in close to Cas. "Said he's returning today with a new job or something. He'll be stopping by the party soon enough."

Cas glanced around, hoping he'd see his oldest brother. "I hate that he's been gone so much recently."

"Me too. I think...perhaps, he is still not adjusted to our new living situation."

Cas nodded in agreement. "Yes, I've thought the same thing.

Speaking of, I'll be moving in with Jo and her family."

At that, Jo turned around and gave Cas a sweet smile before turning back to whisper with Avery, asking questions about dragons and mating—clearly she had forgotten about his extrasensory hearing.

"I figured." Mikael clapped him once on the shoulder. "And I'm so happy for you. We'll help you move your stuff over there as soon as you'd like."

Tomorrow wasn't soon enough. Cas started to respond, then elbowed Mikael gently. "Look."

It was one of their brothers, Ivyn, slowly making his way toward them. And he wasn't alone. He had his arm wrapped protectively around a petite, curvy female who Cas guessed was human given her wide-eyed looks at the melee around them.

There were a couple designated dance areas in the yard, strings of festive, colorful lights strung up in all of the oak trees and around the lanai, and enough food to feed a small dragon army. And the shifters— wolves in particular—were acting foolish as wolves were wont to do. But they'd all earned it.

Cas grinned as he watched his brother. "Finally." Ivyn had been pining after a human female for…as long as Cas had been pining after Jo.

"He was as slow as you at claiming your female, I see." Mikael shook his head slightly, but was grinning.

"You're one to talk."

"True enough."

Cas wished he'd been quicker to claim Jo, to be open with her, but now that they were together he never wanted to let her go.

* * *

"So we all agree that no one is telling Star about what happened to me and King?" Aurora had her hands on her hips as she stared down Harlow, Marley, Axel, and her whole pack. She had so much to deal with—adjusting to now being the Alpha female in a huge territory. And that was after she'd risen from the literal ashes with her mate—*mate*. "I'll tell her later, but I don't want her to go all big sister on me."

Around them, the party was in full swing with a jaguar shifter acting as DJ—and doing a damn good job. Both their back and front yards were filled to the brim with various supernaturals, the party spilling out into the street and down the whole block. After what the city had been through—and for King's wolves in particular, thinking they'd lost their Alpha—everyone was letting loose. She swore she'd heard someone say there was a brass band setting up to play a block or two away so she might go check that out later.

King was a whole four feet from her right now, talking to Claudine and Claudine's mate—and he was a big surprise. A sweet artist who loved gardening. Aurora had a feeling that she was going to be good friends with the gentle male even if he was like five hundred years old.

"Uh, she's going to find out." Axel lifted an eyebrow. "We all stalked her, calling her over and over and—"

"I already told her!" Lola blurted. "An hour ago," she added, wincing. She'd changed her hair yet again so that it was now red- and pink-striped. Maybe because it was Valentine's Day next month? "I can't lie to her. Or you. I think she's planning a trip here in like a week."

Aurora started to groan, but smothered it as Phoebe hurried over, her eyes bright with excitement. Her brothers were right behind her and they jumped on Axel and Brielle, climbing them like trees until they sat on their shoulders, perfectly content as they bounced up and down, chattering away about something they'd just seen.

"Hey, some of the wolves asked if I could go hang with them down the street." Phoebe looked at Aurora hopefully. "A witch is doing a magic show. Like a *real* one."

Aurora's instinct was to tell her that she didn't have to ask her for permission, but she loved that Phoebe was checking in. This whole guardian situation was new to her but they were off to a great start. "That's great. You want the boys to go with you or..."

"No!" the twins shouted in unison. "We wanna play with Axel and Brielle," Legend added, one small hand covering Brielle's eye.

Phoebe simply snorted. "Clearly they're fine without me." She looked over her shoulder and waved at two teens Aurora recognized from the wolf pack, one boy and one girl. They waved back.

"Have fun but be smart." As far as Aurora was concerned, Phoebe was a smart, resourceful kid who could take care of herself. But she'd been through a hell of a lot and shouldn't have to be alone. Aurora was so happy that Phoebe and her brothers had found them.

"I will, promise." There was no rolling of her eyes, just a serious nod before she ran off.

"She's such a good kid," Bella murmured. "When you were gone, in the fae realm and…after, she helped out around here like a boss. And she was ready to run with us in an instant if things had gone south. She's impressive."

"She's the best big sister," Enzo said as he covered Axel's eyes. "Shift!" he shouted, commanding Axel as if he was a pony.

Aurora let out a laugh when Axel did just that, sending Enzo into a fit of giggles as he tumbled into the air. Aurora also noticed that Christian was at this party and not doing a good job of ignoring Axel. She figured those two would either finally get together or kill each other soon enough.

King slid up to her soundlessly, wrapping his arm around her shoulders and stealing her away before heading toward Sorgin and Cressida, who were on the fringes of the party, both standing sort of awkwardly as they sipped sparkly drinks. He kissed the top of Aurora's head before they reached them and warmth spread throughout her.

She hadn't realized how different she'd feel after mating, but *wow* was all she could think. There was like this almost physical connection between them, letting her sense his emotions. Right now, all she sensed was contentment and a bright, burning love for her. A feeling she returned.

"Thank you for staying," Aurora said as they reached the two fae. Halcyon had needed to return to her own realm after expending so much energy trying to break Lucius's spell.

"Of course." Sorgin watched King with a mix of emotions. "I would like to extend the offer of an alliance with my kingdom. Officially."

"I would like that too." King was all formal and stiff, but she figured once these two got to know one another better that would change. Hopefully.

"There are phoenixes in our realm who would like to meet you as well," he said, turning to Aurora. "Many of them have never left our realm at all and will be curious to talk to someone who's lived in the human realm."

"That sounds interesting." Meeting other phoenixes was something she'd never really thought about. Now to have Phoebe and her brothers living with them, and to know that there were others out there like them? Yeah, interesting to say the least. She couldn't help but wonder how many just like her and Star had been living in hiding all over the world.

"And I would like to invite you to visit. Just because," Cressida said with a smile, clearly more at ease with King than her father. "I want to get to know my brother and his mate."

"We would love for you to visit as well. Any time you'd like," Aurora added. "Under much calmer circumstances."

"Absolutely. And thank you for allowing your witches to travel to our kingdom," she added with a soft smile. "We will actually be leaving within the hour. Everleigh and her people are packed and ready."

"I've been away from my kingdom for too long," Sorgin said. "And I wanted to let you know that Orson has been executed for his part in...helping cover up what Lucius did all those years ago."

King's jaw went tight, but he nodded. "Thank you. Was there anyone else involved?"

"Just the others I mentioned before. The ones who died of various causes over the years. We used a truth serum on Orson and he confessed everything under its influence. They did it for a mix of reasons. Financial gain and because..." He cleared his throat.

"Because my mother was a shifter," King said simply.

"Yes. For the record, if any of them were alive, I would execute them as well." His blue eyes were hard as he spoke.

"Thank you." King started to hold out his hand, but Aurora nudged him slightly. He stepped forward, and to Aurora's surprise Sorgin moved first and the two embraced. It was definitely awkward but it was a start.

Aurora had no problem hugging Cressida, pulling her in tight. From what Aurora could tell, she was a kind female who simply wanted to get to know her brother. Aurora hugged Sorgin too, taking him by surprise, but he gently patted her back and cleared his throat as if he didn't know what to say.

As she stepped back, his gaze strayed past her and his head tilted slightly as he stared at something.

Aurora turned and saw Zephyr moving through a cluster of dancing bears—in shifted form—with a woman she'd never seen at his side. It wasn't like she knew everyone in the territory, but *that* was a female you'd remember.

"You know them?" King asked, turning back to Sorgin.

"Ah…no. The female just looks like someone…" He shook his head, as if shaking away cobwebs, before he turned back to King. "We will take our leave now but I would like to see you soon. With or without an official alliance."

"I'd like that too."

A few minutes later they left and Aurora turned into King's arms, ready to suggest they sneak away for a bit—but King nodded behind her. "Your mentee seems to have admirers."

Aurora turned, following his line of sight, and raised her eyebrows. A vampire and dragon were both talking to Mia, the human artist with a load of talent Aurora couldn't wait for her to grow into. "She seems to be holding her own at least."

The two males were talking in earnest, shooting glares at one another every few moments.

King simply snorted. "Claudine wasn't surprised about my heritage for a reason," he said quietly, not loud enough for anyone around them to overhear.

Not that anyone was listening. So many conversations were going on, so much laughter and music, it made her heart happy. "Really?"

"She knew my mother, it seems. Long ago. My mother had always been a bit of a rebel, leaving her pack at a young age to explore the world when it simply wasn't done. She says my mother stole the heart of a king, then settled into the fae realm. Claudine thought all was fine with her until…she showed up in New Orleans decades ago. After we escaped Lucius, she simply couldn't go back to Sorgin."

"Why not?"

"Fear, she thinks. Claudine didn't know for certain, says she only saw her a couple times over the years, before we settled in Wyoming. The captivity, me being hurt by that monster... Claudine says it scarred her on a deep level. That she thinks my mother didn't want to take me back into a world where I might be hunted again, hated for my wolf heritage." He let out a sigh. "I would have been next in line to rule the Latore realm, so I would have always been in danger by a certain sect of fae if we'd gone back. Claudine thinks that's why she stayed away, let Sorgin think we were dead."

"I'm sorry," Aurora whispered.

"She did what she thought was right. And I can't say I would have done anything differently had I been in her shoes. She was a mother protecting her pup, putting aside everything to keep me safe." His voice grew thick before he cleared his throat. "It is in the past."

Maybe, but the past had a way of shaping who they were. She squeezed his hand in her own, laid her head on his shoulder in a show of comfort, but straightened as Zephyr suddenly strode up.

The ancient dragon had been off on a mission for King and only arrived back today. He'd missed most of the chaos, it seemed, but from his grim expression she thought he might have news of something.

Aurora wasn't sure what he'd been doing, but King had already told her he would be catching her up on everything going on. He wanted her fully immersed in everything inside their territory and it only made her love him more. He truly wanted a partner—not that she'd ever doubted it.

"I'm glad you're back," King said, holding out his arm.

He and Zephyr did that warrior thing where they gripped each other's arms in greeting. "Glad to be back," Zephyr said as he stepped back and motioned to the tall, stunning female. "This is Juniper." Then he introduced King and Aurora.

Juniper's hair was covered in a sort of thick wrap and she was tall in the way of dragons, maybe six feet or just an inch shy of it. Her cheekbones would make models weep in jealousy and her eyes...one gray, one the color of the Mediterranean on a clear day. Stunning didn't really cover her.

"It's a pleasure to meet you both. Thank you for allowing me into your territory," she said, looking between the two of them. Then she looked at Zephyr, eyebrows raised.

He nodded once, then glanced around before focusing on King. "I took care of that thing you asked me to and…that's how Juniper and I met. She works for August McGuire. He's—"

"I know who he is," King murmured, flicking a glance at Juniper, his expression opaque before he turned back to Zephyr. "Is he in my territory?"

"No," Juniper answered. "He's up in Montana. His base is with the Petronilla clan. But…I think you know that?"

King simply nodded.

She continued. "I worked for him before The Fall and I still do. We're still doing what we did before. Right now I'm hunting down traffickers and it's led me here, to your territory. I would like permission for me and my crew to stay here until we've found them."

King looked at Zephyr, clearly to see what he thought.

Zephyr answered immediately. "They saved my ass from some rogue demons and they're good people. I vouch for all of them. And I'd like permission to work with them while hunting down these monsters."

"I'll need more details, but that's acceptable. Just let me know where you're staying," he added. "And I'll want to speak to all of your crew. They will obey all my laws while in my territory."

"Of course," Juniper said.

Once they wrapped up and hurried off, Aurora turned to King and cupped his face with her hands, smiling up at him before she brushed her lips over his. "I think it's going to be impossible to sneak off now."

He softly groaned in defeat. "You're definitely right."

"So who's August McGuire anyway?" she asked as she snagged a drink from a nearby table. She couldn't believe how quickly her pack had set up this whole spread, but she shouldn't be surprised. Not when Bella was in charge. That female could always make anything happen if she put her mind to it.

"He ran black ops for the United States government before The Fall— a paranormal division. But his loyalty was always to supernaturals. And, if my intel is correct, he's ah, with, Mira, Prima's twin."

"*With*, as in, mated?"

"As far as I know, not mated, but they're together nonetheless. And now that I think about it, he and Arthur kind of look alike. They're both giant, loud redheads anyway."

"So the scary dragon twins have a type?"

"Yeah, big and crazy, from what I've heard," he said dryly.

Aurora let out a laugh. "There's so much for me to learn. How do you keep all of it organized?" All the territories, and relationships and all those other interpersonal things.

"I've got an eidetic memory."

She blinked up at him. "Seriously?"

"Yep. But I also have actual binders on all this shit—who's mated to whom. The various powers in all territories. And I'm not kidding. You're in for some serious reading."

"This sounds a whole lot like homework."

Grinning, the sight taking her breath away, he leaned down again and kissed her. "Yep. That's what happens when you mate with me. Extra reading and memorization that you will be quizzed on. Let the good times roll, my mate."

She laughed and wrapped her arms around him tight, pulling him close. "I still wouldn't change a thing."

"Good. I wouldn't let you." He buried his face against her neck as he held her and, in that moment, she felt like the luckiest female on the planet.

Aurora had no doubt that becoming an Alpha's mate was going to have pitfalls and a sharp learning curve, but she got to do it with King by her side.

She wouldn't have it any other way.

—THE END—

ACKNOWLEDGMENTS

As always, I owe a huge thank you to Kaylea Cross. I'm lucky to have such a wonderful critique partner (and best friend). For my readers, who wanted more from this series, thank you for all your support of not only the Ancients Rising series, but the one that came before it (Darkness). I'm also grateful to Julia for her valuable edits! And of course, thank you to Sarah for all the things! Jaycee, I never get tired of saying thank you for the gorgeous covers you create, this one included. For the best pups a writer could have, thank you to Jack and Piper for the constant companionship.

BOOKLIST

Ancients Rising Series
Ancient Protector
Ancient Enemy
Ancient Enforcer
Ancient Vendetta
Ancient Retribution

Darkness Series
Darkness Awakened
Taste of Darkness
Beyond the Darkness
Hunted by Darkness
Into the Darkness
Saved by Darkness
Guardian of Darkness
Sentinel of Darkness
A Very Dragon Christmas
Darkness Rising

Deadly Ops Series
Targeted
Bound to Danger
Chasing Danger
Shattered Duty
Edge of Danger
A Covert Affair

Endgame Trilogy
Bishop's Knight
Bishop's Queen
Bishop's Endgame

MacArthur Family Series
Falling for Irish
Unintended Target
Saving Sienna

ABOUT THE AUTHOR

Katie Reus is the *New York Times* and *USA Today* bestselling author of the Red Stone Security series, the Redemption Harbor series and the Ancients Rising series. She fell in love with romance at a young age thanks to books she pilfered from her mom's stash. Years later she loves reading romance almost as much as she loves writing it.

However, she didn't always know she wanted to be a writer. After changing majors many times, she finally graduated summa cum laude with a degree in psychology. Not long after that she discovered a new love. Writing. She now spends her days writing paranormal romance and sexy romantic suspense. For more information on Katie please visit her website: https://katiereus.com

Made in United States
North Haven, CT
14 June 2023

37716997R00161